THE DEMON
MISTRESS

By Jordan K. Rose

Lyn —
Thanks for coming
to RomFest 2014. You
& Belinda were a loved
of fun!
Jordan K Rose

Jordan K. Rose, Publisher
PO Box 714
West Kingston, RI 02892

The Demon Mistress
Jordan K. Rose

ISBN: 978-0-9894175-0-1
Ebook ISBN: 978-0-9894175-1-8

Cover Art:
Cris Ortega

Editors:
Judith Roth
Jane Haertel

Jordan K. Rose Publishing October 2013

for Ken,
if Eva were real, I'd have to beat her off you with a stick
and some holy water, and probably some dark chocolate, and maybe a glass of
Chianti, a new cell phone, a car, some jewelry and a solemn promise to be her
Friend For Eternity

.

PROLOGUE

October 3rd

Exeter, Rhode Island

My Flower,

I wish I were with you, but maintaining the sovereignty of our region calls me away from home, from you, the one I love above all others. Tonight being your birthday brings me added pain. Not being with you to celebrate the anniversary of the most glorious day in all my existence breaks my heart.

Each morning, when I lie down to rest, my memory is flooded with thoughts of you. Your brown eyes sparkle as your hot, demanding gaze wanders over me. That hungry smile sets my blood aflame. Your long, auburn hair tickles my skin while you trail soft, urgent kisses over my chest to my neck. I can barely contain myself as I enjoy the memory of your body against mine, the scent of your skin, the taste of your blood.

I shall do my best to deal with this situation in Maine and swiftly return to you, to your arms, to your love.

I've sent your gift with the messenger, a laptop computer to keep you connected to the world around us, to me. I look forward to your first vmail.

Your faithful and loving husband, Stefan

P.S.—Remember, Chrysanthemum, I am still your master so don't try anything in my absence. This includes but is not limited to: creating a fledgling, scaring humans who refuse to see things from your perspective, fighting with the wolves (who by the way told me about the incident at the Tasty-Freeze), attempting to force any of the remaining captains to answer to you, excessive use of the credit cards (This includes online shopping. The computer is not to be used as a portal into every store in existence.), and spending time in my personal library. REMEMBER, YOU ARE FORBIDDEN FROM READING THOSE BOOKS!

CHAPTER ONE

-Eva Prim Writes-

A Blog of Vampire Thoughts.

October 24th

Friendship¬

I consider you all my friends, well, not all of you. Not you, Studmufflicker69. You are definitely not my friend. In fact, you're banned from this blog. Do not ever comment again. Yesterday's comment about bondage was completely inappropriate. No one wants to hear about your deviant sex life.

Everyone else, you are all my friends. I don't know where you are or what you look like, but over the past three weeks I feel like we've come to know each other. And I like you. Especially you, PenPro58. You've been very kind and have truly made my blogging experience a pleasure. Without friends, life can be so lonely. You've all made me feel loved.

Good friends are so hard to find. Thank you all.

"Chryssie?"

Ooh! Time to go. I await your comments. Eva.

"Chryssie, darling, what are you doing?"

I close my laptop and shove it into the drawer just as the door opens and Stefan steps in, looking utterly dashing.

"Blogging." I pause to enjoy the sight of him as he walks toward me. The muscles in broad shoulders fill out his suit jacket quite nicely. "Why are you dressed like that?" I drag his desktop back into place, returning the keyboard to its rightful spot.

He pulls me up from the chair and presses a soft kiss to my lips. "I'll never understand what you find so entertaining about those foolish conversations."

"It's just fun to talk with people who…" I glance toward the computer.

"They don't know who you are. They're not your real friends, my flower." His fingers skim along my chin.

"I know. But I like them anyway." I sit on the desk as he takes the seat I just vacated. "What's with the suit?"

"You don't like it? I thought for sure you'd like this suit," he answers, clicking away at the keyboard.

"It's nice." It's very nice. Navy blue, cashmere blend with a crisp white shirt accented by gold cuff links and a periwinkle blue silk tie. The ensemble plays up his deep ebony eyes. His long black hair is tied back at the nape of his neck, and his face is shaved, baby-smooth, revealing the cleft centered in his perfectly chiseled chin.

"It's unusual for you to dress so formally when you're simply going to the office." I run my hand down his ponytail allowing the thick hair to slide through my fingers, fanning his cologne into the air.

He smells heavenly. Eternity cologne, my favorite, blends with his scent, a manly, woodsy, sort of campfire-ish aroma with a sweet tang. It makes my mouth water.

"I have a meeting that requires more formal attire."

The V Mail System opens on the screen. The nightly news flash features a very angry looking Cletus Shiftbottom snarling as he's dragged away in chains.

"They finally caught him. I knew it wouldn't take long," I say.

"That is a picture from three days ago. He's escaped again," Stefan comments as he navigates to his personal vmail.

"They should have known he'd escape. Why didn't they just kill him when they caught him?"

As he stares at the picture on the screen his left nostril twitches, and I know he's thinking about his honor. "I will deal with Cletus myself."

I purse my lips. A good master is honor-bound, which is just a nice way of saying, *you made it, you deal with it.* I've seen Stefan deal with the whole honor-bound issue a lot. It's never pretty.

"Well, let me know if you want some help. I'll be happy to stake him myself after what he's done. You know he's making you look like an idiot, right? Everyone is talking about how he's gone bonkers, terrorizing other vampires, scaring humans, even giving shit to the wolves." A chip in the nail polish on my pinky finger stands out in stark contrast to sparkly dark pink paint. "Damn it. I just painted these."

"I am well aware of what's being discussed and why, darling. I do not need you to remind me." His tone is less than grateful.

"You don't have to get snippy."

"Cletus overpowered the four guards assigned him. He's much more powerful than anyone realized." He opens a message titled Blue Moon.

"Like I said, let me know if I can—"

"No. You can't help." He clicks on the attachment in the email, and the financials for one of his subsidiary companies opens. As he stares at the information in front of him his cheek pulses.

My shoulders sag. "It's always the same answer." I glance at the screen. "Is there supposed to be so much red?"

He inhales sharply as he clicks the keys on his computer. "No." The pages scroll down moving like a slot machine reel. He nods and closes the application.

"I will be very late tonight, possibly not returning until just about dawn." He stands and kisses my forehead. "I would appreciate you staying home."

"That's fine. I have some…" I smile. "Some reading to catch up on."

His gaze wanders over me, a heated brush of his presence.

I feel my cheeks flush.

His left eyebrow rises. "What are you reading?"

I squeeze his hands and avoid his eyes. "Oh, a little something."

I turn away to lead him toward the door.

"Chryssie, what book?" He's right behind me, close enough that it's not his presence I feel, but his body molded to mine. His arms clamp around my waist and he pulls me back against him. "What book?"

"Nothing to worry about." I try to wiggle loose, but he only holds me tighter.

"You haven't been down in my personal library again, have you?" He breathes the words against my hair, and my legs go all rubbery.

I giggle, sliding my hand between his lips and my ear. "Stop that. You told me not to read any of those books, so I'm not."

"You're sure?"

"Positive. The last time I read one I didn't really enjoy the ending." How was I supposed to know? When you read some book of odd scripture and end up releasing forty demons, you don't enjoy the ending. Trust me. I learned my lesson.

"The story hasn't quite ended. Cheng and Martin are still working on apprehending the fugitives," he says, sweeping my hair back from my neck and kissing me.

Cheng and Martin work for Stefan. They're wonderful. Two of the most talented, strongest, fastest, deadliest—but in a nice way—vampires I've ever met.

"How many more?" I rest my head back against his chest.

"They've managed to send twenty-eight back. They'll be busy for a while." He kisses my cheek. "I love you, darling. Promise me you will stay home tonight." He steps in front of me, straightening his jacket and reaching for the doorknob. "The wolves are on duty this evening. You shouldn't have any problems."

"I promise." I spin around and head back toward the desk.

Before I've taken a full step, he appears in front of me. "You're up to something."

"What do you mean?" My voice is perfectly even, not a single note raised.

I have perfected Poker Face. Most vampires are good at it. I am not good at it. I am exceptional.

There's just one little problem.

"Look at me, Chryssie." And there it is.

You see, to look at him gives him an opportunity to study me, my emotions, my thoughts. I've been working on blocking him and on occasion I am able to do it. That is, I am able to do it if he's not completely focused on me and if there's a lot of distance between us. But when he's standing two inches from me, it's a whole other story.

I blink up at him, slowly, my brown eyes widening. Poker Face melts away and is replaced by another very familiar face. Her name is Crybaby.

My lips pucker to a very slight pout. Then, I glance down, just for a second to allow my hair to fall forward, hoping to gain some composure. A blanket of copper waves falls over my face. I push the left side behind my ear and look up, blinking slowly, the pout making my lips tremble. Tears form in my eyes.

"You don't trust me," I croak, and my bottom lip quivers as I fight to hold back the rush of tears. "I've been so good for so long. The demon thing was an accident. I didn't know. I thought you were hiding dirty books. How was I to know you had that down there? And what are you doing with them anyway? You still haven't explained." I can't stop the waterworks and tears rush down my cheeks.

"I'm sorry, my flower. You have to understand, it's awfully odd how you simply agreed to stay home tonight. You never just agree. It's always an argument or a fight to get you to do what's best for you. I wasn't prepared."

He hugs me against his chest, and I cry all over his beautiful new suit.

"I just like my new computer." I hiccup. "And I'm learning how to use it." I sniffle. "And I like talking to my new blog friends." I wipe my nose on his lapel. "That's all."

"I'm glad you like it. I wasn't sure if it was the best birthday gift, but you seem quite happy." He rubs my back. "I do need to leave, Chryssie. I'm sorry I upset you."

He pushes me away from him and stoops to look at me.

I glance up, absolutely certain my mascara is running down my face and my lipstick is smudged along my cheek. The evidence is smeared across his chest.

He pulls out a handkerchief and wipes my cheeks. "I'll make this up to you. I promise."

"Your suit is ruined." I use his handkerchief to dab at the red stain on his shirt.

"Don't fuss about it. I'll change. You know I have others." He kisses my cheek before heading for the door.

I nod. "I won't leave the house. There won't be any trouble tonight. I swear."

CHAPTER TWO

~Eva Prim Writes~

22 Comments

Margaritaman says…

Hi Eva. You're great. I luv you babe. Thanx for the post on cologne. I tried the Vetiver. My girl luved it.

PS—Luv the website. Here's the link for anyone who hasn't visited: www.evaprim.com.

Eva says…

You're welcome Margaritaman. Vetiver is very manly and clean. Glad it's working for you. Like I've said, I'm an expert on men's cologne. There's nothing better than a good smelling man.

Thanks for the props on the site. It's just the two pages, but I'm working on adding more.

Studmufflicker69 says…

BANNED! YOU CANT BAN ME! YOURE JEALOUS. YOU WISH SOMEONE WOULD BIND YOU.

Eva says…

Listen you, Fucknut, either you stay the hell off my blog or I'm going to find you and redefine the word bind with my foot—right up your ass.

PenPro58 says…

Good evening, Eva. Thank you for the compliment. I feel the same about you. I find your blogs both entertaining and informative. The tip on how to remove bloodstains from linen is a lifesaver. I was making a Bloody Vlad and the lemon slicing got out of hand.

You should consider a tip page for vampires on the site. It would be helpful.

Mac says…

Hi Eva. I enjoy your posts and I like PenPro58's idea of the vampire tip page. With Halloween right around the corner and costume parties looming I'm thinking of dressing as a vampire. Any tips to make me more realistic will help.

A shout out to Fangman333—thanks for the Bleeding Vlad recipe. I got the joke about substituting tomato juice for blood. That was pretty funny man. I tried the Vlad. It was a bit strong, knocked me on my ass for two days.

Fangman333 says…

Not a Bleeding Vlad. It is a Bloody Vlad.

PenPro58 says…

You mean Bloody Vlad.

Studmufflicker69 says…

WHAT IS WRONG WITH YOU? YOURE AN IDIOT. ITS A BLOODY VLAD.

Moongirl2nite says…

Bloody Vlad. Bloody Vlad. Bloody Vlad.

Sleepslikethedead says…

Man, it's a Bloody Vlad. Not the other.

Goldenrae says…

Yes, Fangman333 did say bloody and not bleeding. Cyber conversations lead to everyone correcting one little error. Bloody Vlad. Bleeding Vlad—it's all the same.

Fangman333 says…

Not same. Bloody and bleeding—2 different things. It's a Bloody Vlad.

Moongirl2nite says…

Bloody. Bloody. Bloody.

PenPro58 says…

The two words are not interchangeable and mean completely different things. If one is bleeding, one could potentially become bloody. But, just because one is bloody does not mean one is bleeding. Do you understand? In this case the word bloody is very important. There is a very clear distinction.

Also in my last comment about the vampire tip page I meant fun, not helpful. Fun. It would be fun. Not helpful. Why would it be helpful? I definitely meant fun.

Goldenrae says…

It's a drink, people!!!!!!!

Studmufflicker69 says…

YOU FUCKING IDIOTS. BLOODY! HES BLOODY. NOT BLEEDING. IF YOU USE BLEEDING ONE MORE TIME IM GOING TO FIND YOU AND BLEED YOU. ILL BE DRINKING BLOODY VLADS ALL NIGHT.

Mac says…

Hey man, there's no need for that. Fine, a Bloody Vlad. Happy?

Moongirl2nite says…

Yes. Thank you Mac.

PenPro58 says…

Thank you Mac.

Fangman333 says…

Good.

Studmufflicker69 says…

ASSHOLE.

Eva says…

Oh, my. Thank you, Mac, for making the correction. It is a Bloody Vlad, not the other. Let's try to calm down. Does anyone know how to work the blocker on a blog? Studmufflicker69—you're out of here! I told you to stay the hell off my blog and I meant it. I'm blocking you. Can someone email me at mistress@evaprim.com *with the directions?*

I'll get working on the vampire tip page. PenPro58, you're right. It would be fun. See you tomorrow. Eva.

"A vampire tip page. A vampire blog. A vampire information site."

I log off the blog and wander the house, visions of my new venture swirling in my mind. I could do posts on all sorts of vampire issues—how to go unnoticed, how to track, hunt, feed without killing. How to fit in! How to deal with the challenges of vampirism— breath issues, skin color, heartbeat, remembering to breathe.

Who better than me? I mean, I *am* a vampire. I've been one since 1831. My experience certainly qualifies me.

I'm not a master or anything like that, but I have a master. I can talk about the master-fledgling relationship. I can discuss the challenges of being a vampire. I can advise on vampire culture and community and relations between territories. I could even dispel all the vampire myths that are total bullshit.

This is brilliant!

I already have seven friends on my blog. I could go viral! I could touch millions. My advice could help the world. Everyone would love me.

I jump onto the red velvet sofa in the parlor and bounce up and down.

"Everyone would love me!" I close my eyes and shout the words, letting them echo up to the vaulted ceiling and back.

I bounce and bounce and yell and yell.

"Everyone would love me! Love me! Love me! Me! Me! Me!"

Unable to see where I am, I bounce off the back of the sofa and crash to the floor, cracking my head on the piano. But I'm okay. I'm going to be loved. Sometimes the rise to the top is painful.

I lie on the floor and rub my head. "Everyone will love me."

The soft tapping on the window startles me, and I sit up, smacking my forehead on the bottom of the piano.

"You okay?"

Four wolves peer in the window, two in human form, naked, of course, and two as giant dogs.

"Are you all right?" Charles yells.

"Fine. I'm fine." I rub my head. "Thanks. How is it outside? Cold?" I perch on my knees and face them, smiling the biggest smile I've ever smiled.

"It's not bad," he answers and frowns, his gaze darting toward the other wolves then back to me. Tommy has the same expression on his face.

"Do you want to come in?" I nod and point toward the door.

"No!" He and Tommy shout at the same time. The other two wolves howl and back away.

"We gotta go," Charles says, turning toward the woods to follow the others. "Just wanted to be sure you were all right." He and Tommy shift back into wolf form as they run toward the trees.

I move to the window. "Funny, it looked like it might have been cold." I watch them fade into the woods.

One little mistake and no one wants to come near you. People never forget. It happened fifty years ago. How was I supposed to know? It's not like I'm a werewolf. I don't know everything about them. You'd think I'd purposefully tried to hurt Sheila. I only wanted to know if the whole silver and werewolves thing was true.

I can imagine how it appeared, me with the giant rubber gloves sneaking up on her. But it was only a trial. I had asked. And she said, "Yeah, right. I can wear silver." I distinctly remember the words. They're branded in my memory.

Is it my fault I didn't quite get the sarcasm in her answer?

Anyway, for the record, it's true. Silver will definitely burn a werewolf's skin. It's almost as bad as silver on vampire skin. She had a lovely scar around her neck in the shape of a thin chain until she died. You couldn't really notice it, if she wore a scarf, which she usually did.

Just so you know her death wasn't my fault. Well, not directly. How the hell was I supposed to know she couldn't swim? What dog can't swim?

I want to celebrate. I'm on the verge of having friends. Friends. I tie my hair up into a bun and head back to the office ready to get to work. I love friends. I so rarely have any. It's lonely being a vampire. I mean, I always have Stefan.

He loves me. Obviously. He married me. That was in 1831, three days before he changed me. I've never asked him if he'd do it again. I'm not quite sure he'd say yes. And I don't want my feelings hurt.

But other than Stefan, I'm pretty much alone. Except for my new cyber friends. They love me.

I plop down in front of the computer and log onto the web design page. My package comes with five pages and one of them is already designated as a home page and one is the blog. That leaves three blank pages for me to design.

"Tips for Today's Vampire." My fingers click the keys with speed that would make any transcriptionist jealous.

"Advice for Wannabe Vampires." I can't help but grin. Wannabes and soon-to-bes.

"Dispelling the Myths." This may actually be one of the most important web pages ever to be designed. Myths and lies have held us down, made us go underground, caused us to be feared and hated. But I'm going to change all that. And when I do, Stefan will see just how important I really am. And not just to our territory, but to vampires everywhere

CHAPTER THREE

-Eva Prim Writes-

October 25th

Updates from Eva

The web design is coming along nicely. The new pages should be ready for viewing in another night or two. In the meantime, I'd like to respond to a question I received offline.

"Eva, do you think a real vampire would be sexy or look like Nosferatu?"

I will not reveal the identification of the inquirer, as I want to encourage participation and conversation.

The answer, quite simply, is both.

Thanks for asking. Feel free to comment here or send any questions too personal to ask on the blog to mistress@evaprim.com. *Eva.*

I had very little time on the computer this evening. I haven't told Stefan about my own personal blog or the website. Not because I want to keep secrets. It's just that he's not a big fan of blogs or cyberspace, and I want to show him I can make friends on my own, and I can help people and make a difference and positively impact someone, for once.

Besides, I'm using a pen name. He wouldn't understand the choice. He thinks Chryssie is a perfectly acceptable name. I think it's a name for a wimpy twelve-year-old.

Eva is much more impressive.

Eva Prim.

When the website is a success, then I'll tell him. When I have lots and lots of friends and bloggers and everyone likes me, he won't have to worry or feel badly or anything like that. It will be wonderful.

"Are you ready, darling?" Stefan exits the bathroom, buttoning the fourth and fifth buttons on his royal blue silk shirt. The tails hang low in the back, covering his perfectly round ass. The front lies open from his collarbones to mid-belly, displaying a muscular chest and rippling abs.

He's wearing different cologne tonight, L'Instant de Guerlaine pour Homme. I inhale and smack my lips. He smells yummy, like lemon with a hint of anise.

I lean into him and rub his chest, pulling the shirt open and peeking in to see the trail of dark hair beginning at his belly button and ending inside his black leather pants.

Okay, I have to admit I love him in a business suit, looking powerful and sophisticated. But I adore his other side, the kinky silk and leather side with boots that lace up his shins. This side doesn't just carry an air of sexiness, no, it radiates from every pore, every glance, every movement. He is pure sex.

And I love it.

He grins. "You are quite ready."

I nod and pull him by his shirt back to the bed.

"I thought you wanted to go out."

"Later." I unbutton numbers four and five and slide the shirt off his shoulders, kissing my way across his chest from left to right and up to his neck.

I focus on the main artery, pulsing a quick, even tempo. He's ready for me, too.

My tongue slides along his neck while my hands unlace the front of his pants. Years of practice have made me a master at undressing him, even when he wears the most intricate pieces of clothing.

Seconds later I've peeled the leather skin from his waist, down his legs to his knees.

"You're leaving them there? I'll have better leverage—"

Before he can complete his sentence, he's on his back, blinking up at me.

I lean forward and kiss him. "You won't need leverage." I'm hungry, and for more than one thing. I pull my shirt over my head too forcefully and rip it up the back.

"Damn it."

"I'll buy you another," he says, unhooking my purple lace bra. His hands come straight to my breasts, thumbs rubbing over my nipples. "Perfection."

Of course, taking off my own jeans while I'm straddling him turns out to be far less sexy than in the movies. Even if I try to do it as fast as possible, he's still going to see me struggle.

I roll off him, lie on my back, and wiggle out of them. "This just ruins the effect," I complain.

Before I can hop back into position, he's out of his pants and boots, and he's on top. "Ah, much better leverage."

"Hey! I was on top."

A devious laugh muffles against my skin as his mouth comes to my neck, his tongue working just above the vein. Slowly he licks me in long, pressing licks. With gentle, yet urgent tugs, his mouth latches onto me.

His fangs pierce my skin as he drives himself into me.

My hips work with his, pumping up and down while he moves in and out. The long, slow strokes quicken as my muscles grab onto him, holding him, never wanting him to pull out. He plunges deeper and deeper with each thrust, and my body shakes, aching for *the* moment, *that* moment.

Finally it washes over us, together.

"Stefan!"

His only reply is a groan that tells me he's pleased, too.

*****

"This is out?" I bang my head against the headrest of the Mercedes. "You said we were going out."

"Darling, we are out." After nearly a full minute of holding his hand in front of me, waiting for me to take it, Stefan reaches in and lifts me from the car to place me on my feet in front of him.

"I wanted to go out. Not come to one of your..." I point at the neon sign reading The Blue Moon at a complete loss for how to say what I want to say without sounding too crass. But I'm pissed off, so what the hell. "...fucking businesses." I shake my head. "You said you'd take me out. You didn't say you'd take me with you to work. What the fuck, Stefan? I'm not sitting through another stupid business meeting with you and Paul, Vinnie and Titus, and that idiot manager. They don't even like me."

"Chryssie, there are things occurring that must be managed."

I get back in the car. "Take me home. I did not get dressed up to come here." I look damn good—tight blue jeans, black leather stiletto boots, green v-neck sweater with the V plunging quite nicely and a mink bomber jacket. I'm not wasting my night here.

"You always liked coming to work with me before."

"Take me home." I slam the door.

"Chrysanthemum."

That name has always irritated me. It's long. It's ugly. And it's nearly impossible for a child to spell. Not to mention the Chrysanthemum is not the prettiest flower.

Well, two can play the name game. "Stefanos." I lock the door.

"I will not stand here and argue with you."

I turn my cheek and stare out the driver's side window.

"Chrysanthemum."

When he uses that tone with me, it's like fingernails on a chalkboard. The very way he stresses the "an" part makes my blood boil. It's exactly the way my mother said it when I was child.

I pop a piece of gum in my mouth and chomp away, snapping it as loudly as I can.

"Do not push me."

Push him? Who does he think he is? Push him?

I flip him the bird before turning my back to him and using my phone to surf the Internet.

CHAPTER FOUR

So…here I sit, beside Stefan, right beside him. We are positioned thigh-to-thigh, hip-to-hip, shoulder-to-shoulder on the couch in his office. For the first thirty seconds I wasn't sure how I got here. But now that I think about it, everything's coming back to me.

The sound of metal bending and glass breaking. The feel of cold wind gusting into the Mercedes. His barely comprehensible lecture as he tossed me over his shoulder and carried me through the restaurant and down to the subterranean level.

I recall something about not testing him, something else about not getting in the way, and then something about not behaving like a sailor. "Is it too much to ask that you act like a lady?" That's the last thing he said in English. The rest of the lecture was in rapid, angry Greek, which I've never been able to understand.

So, here I sit, pretending to be as demure as I can when really I want to rip his head off his shoulders.

"But you believe he's no longer in Canada. Has he crossed over to our territory?" Stefan's voice pulls me from my internal rage.

"Yes, sire. I'm certain he's breeched the border. Vermont and New Hampshire are both strong. It's Maine where the line continues to be weak."

I don't immediately recognize Rob Soldati. The Alpha Werewolf has grown his blond hair past his shoulders. A mustache and beard cover his face. And he doesn't smell like himself. Usually, he smells like Polo Black by Ralph Lauren, a woodsy-incense-y fragrance mixed with his usual wolf scent.

Tonight he smells like a dirty wolf who's been living in the wild without any water or soap or deodorant.

My eye twitches. My nose crinkles. Then I give up on demure and just cover my mouth and nose with my hand.

"Where are your men?"

I elbow Stefan.

"And women," he adds.

"I called back the troops from the north when Cletus was sighted in New Hampshire, outside Concord. Word is he intends to work his way south, though it is unclear how quickly."

"Wait a minute. Cletus is attacking us?" I ask through my hand.

"We have not been able to determine any pattern. His behavior is erratic at best. He's completely unpredictable." Rob scrubs his hand up through his hair. "He hasn't been seen in four days."

"Not since he escaped capture in Canada." Stefan walks to his desk. "Has Tarek been notified? We may need him to hold the Canadian border while we focus on the search."

"Yes. I notified his wolves at the border. They sent word to their alpha, O'Brien. He's fortifying their line." Rob sinks onto the couch. Bags puff under his green eyes. Dirt cakes his nails.

I try not to gag.

"You've done well," Stefan says. "Go home, rest. Come back tomorrow evening. Cheng and Martin will have reported in by then, and I will have decided our strategy." He leans back in the chair and surveys Rob.

Stefan's expression doesn't change, but the power flowing from him does and I can tell he's proud of the werewolf. He's always trusted the Soldatis, every generation of them, and not just to defend our territory, but to personally ensure both his and my safety.

Rob nods. "A good night's sleep will do me well. My men—"

"And women," I mumble through my hand.

Rob smirks and nods. "—and women know how to reach me. If anything changes between now and tomorrow, call. We'll be ready, Stefan."

"I know. Go home. Get some sleep," Stefan says as Rob opens the door to the upper level.

"Bathe first," I say. "You stink to high heaven. Someone spray the couch." I dart over to the desk and perch on the edge at Stefan's elbow, smiling. "I can help."

"No." He opens up the V Mail System. "Too dangerous."

His mailbox is full; twelve messages from me, one from each of the six captains overseeing the New England states, one marked urgent from Tarek and one with the nightly news update from the Federation. Then there are four penis enlargement offers, six magazine bill reminders and eight receipts for Amazon purchases, Victoria's Secret, Nordstrom and SexCandy.com.

"I told you to stop using my vmail address when you buy things. Vmail is for vampire business only, not...shopping. What is this one?" He lets the cursor hover above the SexCandy message.

I glance across the room. Paul, Vinnie and Titus watch us.

"Never mind. We'll discuss it at home." He deletes the four penis enlargement ads.

"Okay. But I can help. Let me go with you. I promise not to get in the way. I'll just help. I can do reconnaissance work." I lean over the keyboard and bat my eyelashes at him.

He leans around me and clicks on the message from Tarek. "No."

"Why not? I just want to help. I'm good on the Internet. I can wo-man the V Mail System or even the phones." I pull his hand off the keyboard and hold it in both of mine.

He doesn't stop reading.

"I could be very useful on this mission. You could assign me to work with Cheng and Martin. We're good together."

He nods at the computer. "Tarek has guaranteed his assistance in holding the Canadian border. He's met with Gabe and Liam but has had no word from Francois."

"I feared Francois was our weak link, sire," Paul says, pacing the floor in front of the desk. "I knew something wasn't right when we left Maine."

"Old alliances fall hard. Francois is lost to us," Titus says.

"Is he dead?" I squeeze Stefan's hand, hopeful. I never liked Francois, not from the moment Stefan took Maine from Aaron. I told Stefan Francois was too loyal to Aaron, and we couldn't trust him. But Stefan said something about Francois pledging an oath and making the blood bond.

"Not yet," he answers as he reads the message from Francois.

His fangs descend, jaw tensing, eyes fading to red.

"Francois allowed Cletus free passage through Maine." His hand balls into a fist in my palm, and I let go. "He claims Cletus is possessed. He could not restrain him and was severely injured in the battle."

"Tsk." I roll my eyes. Vampires don't get possessed. Weak. That's what Francois is. "If Gabe oversees New Hampshire, didn't he notice Francois buckling, couldn't he tell Francois was wimping out?" I huff.

"Chryssie, Francois did not send out a notice announcing his situation," Vinnie says.

"I'd have known if I was allowed to be a captain," I say. And it's true. I'd have known all about Francois. "I told you that you couldn't trust him. You should listen to me. I can be very helpful."

"No."

"You never let me help!" I argue. "I'm a very good fighter. And I know all about Francois and his slimy ways. I told you he was stealing from you last summer, and I was right. I told you he was too rough with the wolves. And I was right then, too. And I'm the one who told you he was scheming about something. I thought he was trying to change humans to vampires, but partnering up with Cletus is just as bad. Worse!"

I jump off the desk and jam my hands on my hips. "You need me. I'm coming with you, and that's final."

CHAPTER FIVE

I try the front door one more time. It's only the fifty-sixth time I've tried tonight. It doesn't open.

I don't know how Stefan does it, but somehow he manages to lock me in the house. I try the windows, all thirty-two of them, not one budges. In fact, when I take a running leap at the six-foot window in the parlor, it bows, like a rubber bubble, slowly dipping out, giving me plenty of time to look all around and notice the four sets of wolf eyes watching me from the woods. Then it snaps back into place, shooting me across the room. I crash into the opposite wall and slide to the floor.

"Fine! Be that way! But I could have helped!" I yell and march into the study. "At least I have the place to myself. Me, myself and my blog."

The high-back leather chair behind the desk is so big I can sit Indian style without cramping my legs. It's high enough in the back that you can't tell I'm sitting in it. The desk is the size of a dining room table. And it's waiting for me and my laptop.

I boot up the computer and pull the afghan my mother knitted for Stefan and me across my lap. It's held up well for a nearly two-hundred-year-old blanket. "They just don't make them like they used to," I say and tuck the ends under my legs.

I log on in gleeful anticipation of hearing from my cyber friends.

-Eva Prim Writes-
Twenty-Eight Comments

Shocked is an understatement for how I feel when I read the messages.

Margaritaman says...

Eva, babe, what kind of answer is both? You've been so good up until now. Strong answers, no wishy-washy non-sense, not afraid to define your opinion and stick to it. Both? That sounds like a woman who doesn't want to upset anyone. Which is it, really? Don't wimp out on us.

Fangman333 says...

Both.

Sleepslikethedead says...

Both. Definitely both.

Goldenrae says...

Come on! Both? They're either blood-sucking monsters or they're hot sex gods. No way are they both. I'm disappointed in you Eva. I want the hot sex god for my vamp fantasy.

PenPro58 says...

Oh, I agree with Eva. Both is the correct answer. Sometimes vampires just don't look good. Everyone has a bad day, er, night. Other times, oh, well, they're very, very alluring. He makes you want to be with him. You feel like you're his whole world. He makes you feel like the most beautiful woman to ever exist.

Mac says...

Spare me. I'm not buying the Hollywood BS idea that something as vile as a monster that bites you and sucks all the blood from your body is sexy. I'd never do it with one of them. No one sucks on me, not like that, anyway. Creatures of the night living on your blood are hairless with fangs and claws and bad breath. They smell and rip your throat out. Why would anybody want to have sex with one? I have the same question about werewolves. What's with the excitement about them? Who wants to get hairy every night?

Moongirl2nite says...

Not all the time. Just sometimes. Usually vampires look decent and try to smell good. Many are highly sensitive about the odor issue. No one wants to smell like they're dead. Werewolves don't get hairy every night, unless they want to. It's the full moon that forces the change. You might find you'd like one if you'd give her a chance.

Fangman333 says...

Both. It's definitely both. Logic. How is a vile creature of the night going to lure dinner home if he's vile?

PenPro58 says...

That's a very good point Fangman333.

Mac says...

No. I wouldn't like it. I just need a costume for a party next week. I don't need a first hand experience with a vampire or a werewolf. Let's think about this. Why would I want to get near either of them? First, they're not real. Second, if they were—I don't want to be bitten by either.

Goldenrae says...

So do you think a vampire looks exactly human when he's not looking creepy? I mean is his skin whiter than a normal guys? Are his eyes red? Does he never smile because he has fangs? I know a guy who's sort of pale and fang-y.

Margaritaman says...

Wow! That Bloody Vlad is awesome. TY Fangman333.

Sleepslikethedead says...

Paler. Definitely paler. Shouldn't be too creepy and should be able to smile without fangs. Eyes should be a regular color. If he's too pale, creepy, smiles with fangs and has red eyes, he's either a new vampire or he's some idiot who thinks he's a vampire but really he's just a human with a weird fetish.

Moongirl2nite says...

Oh. Ok.

Studmufflicker69 says…

FUCKING IDIOTS. FOR ONCE EVAS RIGHT. BOTH. BOTH. BOTH. IM GOING TO FIND YOU AND BITE EVERY ONE OF YOU. AND I THINK QUITE A FEW OF YOU KNOW WHAT THAT MEANS.

Goldenrae says…

Did anyone send Eva the instructions? Someone needs to ban that freak. What is wrong with you?

Mac says…

Man, come on! It's a fun blog. Not a war zone.

Fangman333 says…

I accept your challenge.

PenPro58 says…

My husband will not like this.

Moongirl2nite says…

When my brothers hear about this you're in big trouble.

Sleepslikethedead says…

Bring it on. I bet your half stuck in The Shift.

Margaritaman says…

Dude! Have a Bloody Vlad and loosen up. Anybody got any recipes for snacks? I've got the munchies, man!!!

Studmufflicker69 says…

NOBODYS BANNING ME. HERE I COME SLEEPSLIKETHEDEAD. IN A FEW DAYS YOU SLEEP WITH ME.

PENPRO58 AND MOONGIRL2NITE TELL YOUR HUSBAND AND BROTHERS IM COMING FOR THEM TWO.

Mac says…

Try something spicy with the Bloody Vlad. We had nachos and buffalo wings.

Fangman333 says…

You are a Lesser Vampire. I accepted your challenge first and you have chosen to advance on a woman. I will find you myself. When I do, you will sleep with no one.

Goldenrae says…

Ok. Let's relax a bit, boys. It's just a blog. No need for killing anyone or biting each other. Again, does anyone have the instructions for banning this freak? And what's The Shift?

Studmufflicker69 says…

HA! DONT WORRY FANGMAN333 YOU'LL HAVE YOUR CHANCE. I LOOK FORWARD TO THE NIGHT.

IM NOT STUCK IN THE SHIFT. BITCH.

Sleepslikethedead says…

Yes you are.

Holy shit!

This is wild. They're discussing vampires and The Shift and drinks, and that asshole is threatening everyone. This is huge. They're confused and frightened and angry. And all because of me.

They need me.

It's wonderful.

Oh, and I think some of them might be real vampires. I might actually be connecting with other vampires. Some of them are definitely humans. But the rest are all vampires.

They are all my friends! My friends. Humans and vampires.

Eva says…

Good Evening, My Friends. (Not you Studmufflicker69.)

I know "both" seems like a cop-out answer, but it is correct. Vampires typically look good, except when under extreme duress, dealing with high levels of emotion or unfathomable thirst. Certainly, when you first become a vampire it's very difficult to maintain an acceptable appearance without the strong support and guidance of your master. That is to say, he has to maintain it for you until you develop the strength to do it alone.

Of course, there are vampires who don't care how they look. They even like to present themselves the other way on purpose. I don't recommend spending any time with them. They are not your friends. They are thirsty or angry or just plain crazy. Stay away from them.

"The Shift" is what it's called when vampires go from looking good to the other way, which Mac did a nice job of summing up. But to be sure you recognize a vampire in "The Shift" let me describe one. The vampire may or may not get bigger. The more powerful the vampires, the bigger they get. The hair thins out to straggly strands sparsely hanging on the head. Ears elongate to high points. Eyes fade to red, blocking any of the original color. The skin pales to a chalky white. Hands shift to claws with long nails. And the breath is disgusting. It takes on a life of its own. It actually announces your arrival minutes before you enter a building.

Oh, and one other thing. This will be most upsetting to the women. You grow nose and ear hair. You lose the hair on your head, and it sprouts in your nose and ears. You literally develop the hair growth abilities of an eighty-five year old man. It's disgusting. Try as you may, you can't get rid of it. If you rip it out, you bleed, and it doesn't all come out. It's very, very difficult to perform fine motor tasks with claws and dagger-like fingernails. And it just grows back the next time you shift.

Also, for those of you who have self-control issues, stay close to your masters. If you tend to get upset, or angry, or hurt feelings, if you're somewhat temperamental, overly self-conscious, or just plain miserable to begin with, you're going to spend a lot of time learning to cope with The Shift.

This may not be a bad thing. In fact, it might actually be helpful as you begin your new existence as a vampire. You'll become accustomed to the downside of life.

Mac, I hope this was helpful to the costume planning.

Margaritaman, I like dark chocolate with my Bloody Vlad, but then I like dark chocolate with everything.

Goldenrae, if you're wondering if your man is a vampire because something's just not right, then something's just not right with him one way or another. If he can't keep The Secret, then he's not stable. If he's not keeping The Secret because he wants to tell it, then he's dangerous. Dump him.

Have a good day. Until the evening, Eva

P.S.—Vampires can't drink an entire human dry in one sitting, at least not alone. Come on, how much can anyone drink in one sitting?

P.P.S.—Would a picture help?

I log off the blog and onto the V Mail System.

The daily news briefing flashes another picture of Cletus Shiftbottom. Someone saw him in Boston last night.

"Boston! Boston!"

I pull my knees under me, click on the article and begin reading.

Vampire terrorist and demon-lover, Cletus Shiftbottom, was photographed leaving O'Neill's Pub at six-thirty in the morning. The master vampire showed no fear of the rising sun. Instead, he stood in the street waving it into the sky.

In typical Cletus fashion, he stopped The Shift midway through the process, allowing only his claws, red eyes, and pointed ears to appear. The seven-foot monster lurched down the street, terrifying innocent human onlookers.

The Master immediately sent troops to the area to sanitize the human minds. The Federation will surely issue a bounty for Cletus's head. Not keeping The Secret is punishable by death.

With the late hour and the pandemonium Cletus created, it was difficult to find a vampire to interview, but as always we Federation reporters get the job done.

"Where is the Master? He's supposed to keep us safe. Where is Stefan?" Marjorie Roughtiron cried from her hiding spot.

She wasn't easy to find, but we managed to drag her out from behind a dumpster in O'Neill's back alley, her fully shifted body the result of overwhelming fear.

"Of course, they found her. Her breath would be hard to miss even if she hid in the dumpster. Wimp."

I copy the picture of Cletus and paste it onto my website on the "Tips for Today's Vampires" page. Underneath it I type, "Half-shifted vampire, Cletus Shiftbottom." Above it I type, "Dangerous. Keep away."

On the "Advice for Wannabes" page I type, "Someone to be avoided" and add a link to the picture.

Then I scroll through my photo album. There isn't one picture of a fully shifted vampire in any of the files.

Well, why would there be? Who wants their picture taken when they look like that? I plug in my camera to charge. I'll just carry it around with me for a couple days. Someone will have to lose control at some point. They always do.

I log off my computer and slip it back into its drawer before heading down to bed. The sun is just beginning to peek over the horizon, casting a muted glow about the room. Running past the windows, I shoot down the hall, open the door to our bedroom and bolt down the stairs, happy to be wrapped in the cool darkness of our basement boudoir.

Curled into a little ball, I lie in bed. What the hell is Cletus doing in Boston? And, why doesn't Stefan know about it, or does he? And, where is he? Usually, he tells me if he's going to be home after dawn. He always calls if he isn't going to make it home, which is very, very seldom. In nearly two hundred years we've only slept apart three days because of his work. He makes it a point to come home.

On the other hand, we've slept apart more than three hundred days because of something that occurred due to something that I may have had something to do with in an unintentional, well-meaning sort of way.

Glancing at my charger, I realize I've left the phone up in the office. So he may have called, but I've missed it. I roll over and stare at the clock.

Six ten.

Six forty-five.

Seven eighteen.

Seven twenty-one.

Seven forty-eight.

At eight fifteen, I drag my exhausted body out of bed to search the house or at the very least find my phone and call him. If he hadn't fortified the outer walls of our bedroom with silver, I'd be able to sense his presence. Instead, I'm left with no choice but to will my lethargic ass up the stairs. Oh, how I hate the idea of going to look for him. But I have no choice. Without him I can't sleep so up I go into the light.

I hate to burn. Vampires really do burn in the sunlight. We don't immediately combust. It takes some time, but we begin to smoke and sizzle, literally. You really can hear yourself sizzling. Once the sizzle starts, it grows into a roaring inferno in a matter of minutes.

Just the thought of it sends a shiver up my spine.

I enter the code unlocking the door and turn the handle.

I happen to know about the sizzling and smoking based on first hand experience. I just had to know if the rumors were true. Titus was the one who told me. Of course, I didn't believe him. I mean, come on—sizzle? How can being in the sun make anything sizzle?

So, I stood on a beach as the sun rose. I love the beach. The water. The waves. The feel of the sand on my feet. It's wonderful.

I do not, however, enjoy the sun. That giant ball of heat burns like a mother-fucker. My skin blistered and bubbled and smoked.

When the sizzling began, I remember very distinctly thinking, what is that sound? I stuck my fingers in my ears to make it stop. That only made it worse.

Thank the devil for Stefan. He saved me. He's really a good egg, when he's home in bed and not out gallivanting after sunrise!

I shove the door open and stumble forward.

A stink that could only mean one thing hits me like a brick to the face.

CHAPTER SIX

I gag.

Out loud.

It echoes down the hall. The sounds of my gasping coughs are magnified by the cavernous space. I can't hear anything other than the hacking, retching sound of my own attempts to keep from vomiting on the Persian rug.

"Are you ever going to grow up?" Titus snarls.

I bend over, cover my mouth and wave Titus away. My eyes bulge. I wheeze, gasp and cough, but somehow, I manage to keep my intestines inside my body.

He's slightly taller than his usual appearance of six feet two inches and a whole lot beefier. He looks like a gargoyle on steroids. Giant ears protrude above his head. Red beads glow in his eye sockets. His nose crooks to the left. Dragon claws replace his hands.

"Honestly, you're acting like a twelve-year-old." He turns and marches down the hall. "Stefan wants you to join us."

Titus is, without a doubt the stinkiest shifted vampire I've ever, ever met. Think of vomit, shit, and stale blood mixed together. That's what he smells like, not that any other shifted vampire smells much better. And based on the fact my foyer smells like the town dump, I'd say there are several shifted vampires in my house.

I stare after Titus, trying to decide what to do. I now know Stefan is home. I also know he's not alone, which means he's working. However, he's working with some seriously stinky guys.

When I focus, and believe me, it's a difficult task, I'm able to discern seven distinctive odors. Five of the captains and Rob are here with Stefan. Something big is going down.

I'm torn. The chance to be included in something huge and important is very, very exciting. However, the fact that I will need to tolerate The Stinkies in order to be included really makes this situation a lot less appealing.

Then, it hits me. I know exactly what I'll do. I run down the stairs to prepare.

*****

"We can't leave any portion of our territory unguarded," Titus says. He paces the floor in front of the desk, stopping only when Stefan speaks. "We don't know for certain Maine is Cletus's home base. It's not safe to move too many of the wolves to the northern quadrant. It will leave this area too vulnerable. He'll expect that."

"Yes, he will," Stefan replies. He sits perfectly still behind his desk. No business suit this time. Instead, he's wearing a leather jacket, open over a black T-shirt. His black trousers are tucked into combat boots. A silver-bladed knife with a thick ivory handle rests on the desk in front of him. He's been doing reconnaissance work. Only his eyes move as he surveys his men.

"He will not expect us to leave the higher ranks here," Rob says. "I'll go with two senior wolves to lead the northern quadrant. That will allow us to leave my brothers here to guard the southern and western borders."

"I agree with Titus. Stefan, we shouldn't move too many wolves. We really..." Paul shakes his head. "I can't concentrate. Tell her to take it off." He points in my direction.

Stefan glances at me.

I'm perched on the desk beside him. I imagine I look like a vampire concubine in my red silk jammies with matching nail polish on my fingers and toes. My legs are tucked to the side, and I'm leaning on my elbow, my head close to Stefan's.

He smiles at me. He is not shifted. Thank goodness. Every so often, if I'm daring enough, I inhale as deeply as I can tolerate and breathe in a slight whiff of him. He's not wearing cologne. It's just his scent, so faint, I can barely recognize it, but I cling to it with every last olfactory cell I have.

I straighten my shirt. I'm not looking that bad. My bed-head's not too wild considering it's trapped under the straps. Granted, I don't have on makeup, but what can they expect? I was in bed.

"Chryssie, darling, maybe you could take it off."

My eyes widen. "No." My voice sounds like it's coming from a tunnel. I shake my head. "Don't make me. They stink." My lip curls at the thought of it. My stomach flips.

"Darling, it is a bit distracting." His fingers trace circles on the back of my hand.

I glance across the room.

Titus shakes his head. Paul, who in this state could easily be mistaken for Titus, stares at me. If not for the fangs, I'm sure he'd be frowning.

Gabe and Liam each sit on opposite ends of the giant couch across the room, watching and waiting.

Vinnie sits on the leather chair in the corner, his ankle resting on his knee. He's the only one wearing shoes, and they're enormous.

"What size are those?" I ask, pointing at his feet. "Do you carry an emergency bag in your trunk for when you shift? Your feet aren't usually that big."

"You've got to be kidding. Stefan!" Titus growls. "If she's going to stay, she has to remain on task."

"I'm only asking. Geesh. No need to get upset." I sit up straight, legs folded.

Rob turns away to face the window, and based on the fact his shoulders appear to be vibrating, I know he's laughing.

Vinnie's foot taps, and my eyes are drawn back to the boats he has for shoes.

"What are they—a size twenty, maybe a twenty-two?" I ask. "They must be specially made. Where'd you get them? Did Raoul get them for you? He has ridiculously large feet on a normal day." I shake my head. "You know, I wonder if it's true, what they say about men…and feet." I stare at Vinnie. Then my gaze drops to the floor, and I look at everybody's feet.

"All right, darling. You've gone far enough. Take it off." Stefan reaches for me, but I see him coming and zip to the end of the desk.

"Okay. Okay." I wave my hands in front of me. "Let's just say we leave some of the wolves here and let some go north. If you leave Rob and two of his alphas, you could also leave Vinnie, seeing as he's the captain for Rhode Island. You can take the other alphas, who'll be able to take command of the betas. I don't see why you can't just call back Cheng and Martin for a few days." I turn to face Stefan. "With the three wolves and the three vampires I should be able to run Rhode Island, Massachusetts and Connecticut just fine in your absence. Then, you can hunt Cletus in Boston. You do know he's in Boston, don't you?"

My gas mask fogs because I've been talking too much. I blow on it and that just makes it worse. I tilt my head to the side to see past the clouded area but the last inch of unfogged mask disappears in a cloud of my hot, rapid breaths. The tension in the room shoots to the ceiling.

"You cannot be serious," Titus yells. "You actually believe we should leave you in charge?"

"Oh, no. Absolutely not," Paul says.

"She's a walking disaster. Anything she touches turns to…to…" Titus doesn't finish the sentence.

"Shit," Paul says.

"Yeah. That's it," Titus agrees.

An exasperated huff escapes me, further clouding my mask.

Before I have a chance to respond, Stefan is out of his chair, pinning both men to the wall. "I am the Master of this territory. I decide who is in charge of what areas."

He hasn't fully shifted, but his hands are now claws, clenched around their necks. And I don't have to see his face to know his fangs have descended.

I hold my breath, pull my mask off, wipe the inside with my sleeve and cram the mask back on my head.

"I do not turn everything to shit." I bite my lip, trying to hold back what's bubbling inside me. Titus and Paul focus on Stefan whose grip loosens, though he doesn't remove his claws from around their necks. "I'll admit to the occasional error in judgment, but I do not turn everything to shit."

Even with the mask on I can hear what my voice is doing. But I refuse to crack in front of them. I'm not giving them the satisfaction of seeing me crumble. No way. Not this time.

"If I had a little support from you guys, I'd be very, very successful. I'm perfectly capable of running the Tri-States." The mask scrunches my hair, sending a jolt of pain shooting through my head. I yank a handful of hair free, leaving a wad bubbling up between the straps.

Stefan releases Paul and Titus, but doesn't turn around. "I will consider my options. If Martin and Cheng were available, I would leave them here with Paul and Vinnie and a small contingency of wolves. But with my two best men chasing demons…"

Now he turns to face me. As if he has to make the point. Like everyone in the room doesn't know who let the demons loose. They all look at me.

I huff. My mask fogs again. "Honestly, can't a girl make one mistake?"

"One?" Vinnie asks.

Stefan growls, and Vinnie shakes his head.

"Without the two, I require a different strategy," Stefan says.

I grab my cell phone off the desk and scroll through the numbers. When I find what I know I'm going to need, I type a quick text and hit send.

"You have to admit, no one would expect you to leave Chryssie in charge," Rob says.

The captains all turn to Rob and hiss in unison.

Stefan licks his lips and sighs. "This is true." He steps in front of me. "Darling, you're not ready yet, not without Cheng and Martin to…"

"To what?"

Cheng and Martin. Cheng and Martin. Cheng and Martin. It's all I ever hear.

And what for? What can they do I can't? What good are they? It's not like they're superhero vampires. They're just Cheng and Martin.

"To advise you in my absence," Stefan finishes.

"Advise? I don't need advice. I know perfectly well how to manage a small area." I sit up straight, put a hand on my hip and stare at him.

His fangs are still visible, his eyes red, but his hands are no longer claws.

"It's a bit insulting you think I need Cheng and Martin to advise me. I have proven I can run things for a short period of time in your absence."

His hands rest on my neck, thumbs stroking my skin.

"I ran The Blue Moon for you when you went away that weekend." It wasn't even a full weekend, but still I did it. "No one was killed. No patrons were bitten. No unwanted guests arrived for dinner. And the building remained intact."

I performed quite well. Everything turned out perfect. Piece of cake, even.

It was Vinnie who cracked under pressure. He seemed very busy that night, rushing around like it was the first restaurant he'd ever opened. We had a list, a To Do List. By the way, I should say I love To Do Lists. You can't go wrong if you've written it all down, can you?

I checked the list. Food. Check. Lighting. Check. Heat. Check. Security. Check. Vinnie double, triple, and then quadruple checked everything I checked.

He stationed guards at every entrance on both the interior and exterior of the building. He even had a guard follow me around. Something about wanting a full security detail just in case someone got out of hand.

It was really very sweet of him, though utterly unnecessary. I've always been perfectly capable of defending myself, in spite of what Stefan might believe.

Anyway, with all his running around and looking after me, I'm pretty sure Vinnie might have stayed awake for the full thirty-six hours. He kept saying something about the culmination of events and the alignment of the moon and stars and the fifth dimension opening up above the restaurant. I think the lack of sleep made him loopy.

"I oversaw the opening night of The Groove." I nod and grin. "That was a great night, remember?" Stefan has a rule of presiding over the opening night of all his businesses. I think he does it to make sure the managers don't screw up, but he claims it's a show of support for them. He's only missed a few, and since I'm his proxy in a pinch, I was in charge that night, which meant it was Vinnie and me again.

It was so much fun. Stefan was ordered to report before the Federation regarding some incident involving three new vampires who'd misunderstood something they overheard.

It wasn't my fault. Everyone knows you should not eavesdrop and when you do, you may hear things you don't understand. Anyway, he was forced to dispose of them, promptly, which he did.

But in his absence, I opened his new business without a hitch.

"Didn't you develop the 'No Sex on the Dance Floor' policy after that night?" Titus asks Vinnie.

Vinnie inhales, holds his breath for a second, not long enough if you ask me, and then exhales. "Yeah." He closes his eyes and shakes his head. Vinnie manages The Groove.

"Every opening night has minor glitches that get worked out," I say, leaning away from Stefan and frowning at Vinnie.

There is truth to the notion vampires have very active libidos. How the hell was I supposed to know combining vampires with music and the energy of a bunch of horny humans who've become less inhibited due to alcohol consumption would turn the dance floor into a sex fest? It's not like I'd ever hosted an orgy before.

It was my first bar opening. Besides, everyone was happy that night. That's all that really matters.

"We also gained a great new recruit that evening. Need I remind you of Gianni?" He's been a vampire since the seventies, Saturday, September 16, 1972, opening night to be exact.

Vinnie groans. He'd had no choice but to change Gianni in spite of his desire to remain carefree and unencumbered by a fledgling. Stefan ordered him to do it after we discovered Gianni nearly drained in the parking lot and the responsible parties nowhere to be found. It was meant to be a punishment for allowing the sex fest. But as much as Vinnie complains, he can't deny Gianni was a good catch.

"Oh! And what about the boutique? I ran it for an entire week without so much as one overcharge or an unhappy customer." I beam.

The boutique was a trendy little shop on the East Side of Providence. We made a killing during the first week. Rich East-Siders came in to check us out and dropped tons of money. I thought sales might have been my future.

It was my second, no third, attempt at a career in sales. Let's not think about the other two.

"You can't take credit for that. You cheated, doll," Liam says, his accent catching my attention. He's British. I love the way he speaks. His accent alone could almost make me agree with him. For that reason I have to pay close attention to everything he says.

"You really did, Chryssie," Gabe agrees.

Rob nods.

I glance up at Stefan. He raises one eyebrow.

"You can't count it as cheating. You didn't explain the rules before you set me fr…before you let me work there." I bite my cheek.

Stefan's fangs disappear. "You're right. I was not explicit in my expectations of you." His eyes fade from red to sparkling coals. "I made an assumption. It was foolish of me."

I hook my fingers into his belt loops. "You know what they say about assuming."

For a vampire, Stefan runs amazingly clean businesses. He neglected to tell me that charming the customers into buying things was against the rules. When I ran out of merchandise in less than a week, he figured out what had happened. It wasn't until several months later, when I wanted to open another store that he explained my "promotion" to an office job meant I couldn't go back to sales.

"Well, you can't really count the boutique as one of your successes," Rob says.

"Yes, I can. It can't count as anything less than a success. Everyone was very pleased with their purchases and there were no returns." I swing my feet in circles on either side of Stefan's legs. "Obviously, a success."

"A success," Stefan agrees. "Even so, it does not prove you are ready to manage the Tri-States alone."

"I won't be alone. I'll have Rob and Vinnie and Paul." I rest my hands on his waist and gaze up at him, my eyes as wide as I can make them, my lips turned to a slight frown. Usually it works to some extent though the presence of the gas mask may alter the effect.

"No. I'm sorry, Chryssie. It's too dangerous without…"

My phone chimes.

I hit the button, and the message that pops up thrills me. I grin at Stefan and shove the phone up at him.

"Problem solved."

CHAPTER SEVEN

Well, things didn't quite turn out as I'd hoped. Having Cheng and Martin text back their support of my bid for the position of interim captain of the Tri-States didn't secure the nomination. Even so, I'm in a better situation than I'd expected. I am in charge of Central Command: Operation Cletus.

Duties of the central commander include monitoring the V Mail System and keeping the troops aware of any Cletus sightings, reports of attacks or humans gone missing. My updates to the troops are to be made via Stefan, the five captains and Rob. In an effort to hold the ranks in order, I am not to communicate directly with any of the underlings. It seems the frontlines have a tendency to misconstrue information so it's best they only receive filtered briefings.

Communications are to be made via text message or vmail. I *am* allowed to call Stefan. Let's face it. He'll worry about me. He loves me. And this being the first battle when I've ever been given an actual post is good reason for us to stay in contact.

Although, I don't know why he'd worry. As part of my job I'm forbidden to leave the house, which means once again the doors and windows have been hexed or something. My lack of presence in the Command Center could cause chaos. As he explained it, the captains will be waiting for me to relay vital information, and if they call into Central Command and I can't be reached, well, pandemonium could ensue.

I can't let that happen. I definitely will not desert my post. Unless of course I have to leave the post in order to help the cause, in which case, it's not deserting.

I lace up my boots, tuck my T-shirt into my fatigues and pull my hair up into a ponytail. My bowie knife is tucked securely into my shoulder strap. It's my only weapon. I wanted a sword like Cheng has, but Stefan said no. Something to do with difficulty explaining an accidental decapitation. He also nixed the gun idea. However, I did manage to get him to agree to a ten-inch bowie instead of the Swiss Army knife, which was really, really too small. What can I kill with a pocketknife?

The office is now set up in accordance with my needs. I've logged onto Stefan's computer, leaving the laptop in the bedroom in case of emergencies during the day. My cell phone is on the desk beside the landline. A map of New England covers the far wall. Giant pushpins mark the locations of the captains' offices. Smaller pushpins mark Cletus sightings. Tiny "X's" painted in red nail polish mark the places where Stefan and I have vacationed. I wanted to be sure Cletus didn't do any damage to my favorite New England spots. Maine is outlined in brown, signifying Cletus has infiltrated the area.

An assortment of dark chocolates fills a desk drawer from Godiva to Dove to Ghirardelli to Callebaut to Hershey. I lie on the desk, pluck a truffle from the Godiva box and pop it into my mouth.

There's nothing going on according to The System. Cletus hasn't been spotted since his appearance in Boston the other morning. Another search of the database and I still haven't found any new information about him. No unusual reports by humans, no attacks other than the typical muggings and no vanishings. There were a few comments about foul odors in Boston, but that might just be the way the city smells.

So far this job is boring as all hell.

The Nightly Reports from the captains and Rob arrive in The System at half past one or 0130. Everyone reports all clear. I send out the response.

Roger that. Nothing new to report here. Over and out.

Immediately six vmails arrive.

Are you kidding?

Don't be so dramatic.

Come on.

Really?

I told you all this was a bad idea.

Here we go.

So I respond.

If you're so busy in the field, how do you have time to bitch at me? Obviously, none of you is focusing on the situation at hand. Get back to work!

It's not easy being central commander of a bunch of doofuses. I roll over on the desk and eat another truffle.

Stefan's vmail arrives and it's addressed only to me.

Darling,

Please be sure to keep a record of the reports via a timeline. We'll want to track any changes in order to anticipate Cletus's moves.

Stay safe.

~S~

I quickly input all of the reports into a spreadsheet and send a message to Stefan.

S—

I've deployed a process.

Central Commander

I check the V Mail System once again. Nothing. Now I'm bored to tears. I've color-coordinated the pushpins by state. I've alphabetized my chocolates, eating half the "G's." I painted my fingernails and toenails hot pink or as Revlon likes to call it, Lava. I thought if my fingernails matched the "X's" on the map, it would be distracting during briefings so a change was in order.

I run downstairs, bring my laptop back to the office and log onto my website. What good would I be if I couldn't multitask?

After uploading the picture of Titus, which I snuck as he headed to one of our guest rooms, and two more pictures of Cletus, one un-shifted and one fully-shifted, I add a few more Tips for Today's Vampire. Floss and brush your teeth, including your fangs. Gargle with mouthwash. Chew sugarless mint-flavored gum. Keep breath mints on hand. The tips seem pretty basic to me, but not everyone has good hygiene.

On the Advice for Wannabes page I type, "Exercise. Stay in shape. Take care of your body. It's not true you become a hot supermodel when you become a vampire. If you're ugly now, you'll be ugly for eternity."

One last review of the spelling and links to pictures proves the website is ready to make its updated debut.

I click the word "launch."

I'm so excited I can't help but squeal when it goes live. In a rush to tell everyone, I log onto the blog.

~Eva Prim Writes~
Thirty-three Comments.
Mac says…

If you can find a picture of anything that looks like that I'd love to see it. That's a great description. Exactly what I thought a vampire would look like. Monstrous.
Goldenrae says…

Eeewww. Nose and ear hair just put it over the top. So much for the Hollywood vampire.
Sleepslikethedead says…

Yep. It's the worse part.
PenPro58 says…

Oh, it's terrible. The breath is quite distressing but the nose hair. Oh…
Fangman333 says…

You get used to it.
Margaritaman says…

Is the nose hair so long it makes drinking a Bloody Vlad impossible? Now that would be tragic.

Moongirl2nite says…

I don't think a shifted vampire drinks from a glass. You know the claws and all.

Mac says…

The nose hair can't be that long. Seriously? How would a vampire bite anyone if his nose hair covered his mouth?

Sleepslikethedead says…

The longer you go around shifted, the grosser you get. So the nose hair is longer for some.

Fangman333 says…

It does not get in the way of feeding.

Margaritaman says…

I'm going to try to give my girl a hickey with two straws in my nose.

PenPro58 says…

Oh, it's not that long for most. If it is long, you really don't care because you're one of those who likes it. The hair remains shorter, if you try to look normal.

Goldenrae says…

Is there a possibility the hair could become longer when the vampire is not shifted? Like, if he looked human could he have nose hair that was maybe sticking out of his nose by say an inch or so? One nostril might be slightly longer.

Moongirl2nite says…

He'd just bite through the hair. He wouldn't care at that point. Vampires with really long nose hair aren't worried about hygiene or appearance. And nose hair really isn't a barrier to feeding.

Sleepslikethedead says…

What do you mean sticking out of his nose? Is it just a few stray hairs or are you talking enough to look like he's growing a mustache into his nose instead of down over his lip?

Fangman333 says…

Goldenrae, tell us more.

PenPro58 says…

What else does he look like?

Margaritaman says…

It's impossible and now I have a bloody nose to go with my Bloody Vlad.

Goldenrae says…

Yes. It looks like his mustache is growing up. The hair on the right nostril is slightly longer. It's not always like this. Sometimes he trims it or something. Though he does get a lot of bloody noses so he tends to leave it. He's pale, very pale.

Mac says…

That is disgusting. What about snot?

Fangman333 says…

What color are his eyes?

Sleepslikethedead says…

How tall is he?

PenPro58 says…

Are his ears pointed?

Moongirl2nite says…

How's his breath?

Mac says…

How low are your dating standards? Why are you even bothering with a guy with this much nose hair?

Goldenrae says…

I can't remember what his eyes look like. He's tall, maybe six feet six inches. His ears aren't pointed but they have little tips at the top. Now that I think about it, I'm pretty sure he drinks Scope. He carries a flask in his pocket and he swigs from it a lot.

I don't date him. He's my neighbor, and he comes over every night to borrow something. Last night he wanted milk. The night before he wanted eggs. God knows what else he might want. Why doesn't he bother some other neighbor? Maybe that's what he's doing right now. Maybe he's scaring the hell out of the old lady across the street. I don't like him, but how do I tell a neighbor to leave me alone?

Oh, and he's cold. Not just personality-wise. I mean he's literally cold. I thought it was from being outside, but he seems colder than the outdoor temperature. And even after he's been in the house for while he doesn't seem any warmer.

He reminds me of a man I met last summer only he's a lot uglier.

Margaritaman says…

I just bought a nose hair trimmer online. All this talk about nose hair has made me paranoid.

Mac says…

He sounds like a real treat. Tell him you have a boyfriend. He'll get the hint.

Moongirl2nite says…

Uh-oh. Don't open the door. Keep it and the windows locked.

PenPro58 says…

Have you invited him in?

Sleepslikethedead says…

You didn't invite him into your home, did you?

Goldenrae says…

Well, I did let him in the first night. I mean, at the time he seemed harmless and didn't freak me out and what kind of neighbor would I have been to slam the door in his face? But, now that I think about it, he doesn't even ring the bell anymore. The last couple visits he's just let himself in without asking. Yesterday, when I came out of the bathroom, I found him sitting on my couch.

Fangman333 says…

Goldenrae, you must rescind your invitation immediately.

Mac says…

Woo-hoo. Get the garlic bulbs and hang the crosses in the windows.

My eyes pop. Goldenrae needs me. She has shifted vampire problems, and I'm sure she doesn't know how to deal with them. If she did, she'd have never let him in to begin with. Of course, there's a simple way to handle this.

Eva says…

Good evening, everyone.

You're having quite a chat on this blog. Goldenrae, I think Fangman333's advice is quite prudent. You should rescind the invitation. It only takes one "come on in" and a vampire can keep entering your home until you tell him he's no longer welcome. Rescind the invitation, and then do as Moongirl2nite advises and lock all the entryways to your home. Until this is sorted out, you should also try to be in the house before sundown as an added precaution. If you're religious, you might consider wearing some sort of talisman or charm representing your faith. If you're not religious or have fallen away from your faith, now would be a good time to find it.

Also, for the record, garlic does not work. It stinks, but then shifted vampire breath smells far worse. And most likely, he'll only eat some of the garlic to frighten you.

I think I'll add the garlic info to the Myths page of my website, which I have updated. The new pages are at www.evaprim.com. Check it out. There are a couple pics of shifted or partially shifted vampires on the site and some info on the Tips for Today's Vampire page. There's even a little something on the Advice for Wannabes page and soon there'll be a myth on the Dispelling the Myths page, too.

Goldenrae, keep us posted.

Until tomorrow evening, Eva

I check The System once again. Still nothing. Boring. However, in my vmail there's a message from Cheng.

Chryssie—we're on our way and we're bringing you a surprise. Cheng

A surprise! I love surprises!

Cheng—What is it? Tell me. Give me a hint. Can I eat it? What color is? How big is it? Is it alive? Does it have fur? Is it a puppy? I'd love to have a puppy. Oh, a puppy would be perfect. Don't tell Stefan. He doesn't want another dog after the last incident. But if I have it and then he finds out, he won't make me give it back. I know exactly what I'll name him. Is it a big dog or a little one? You know I like big dogs. Oh, I hope it's a Labrador. But I'll be happy no matter what it is.

Before I can finish my response, another vmail appears in my box. This one's from Martin.

Chryssie—it's not a dog. Martin

Oh, shit. I start the message over.

Cheng—What is it? Give me a hint. Chryssie

My phone chimes as a text message arrives.

No, you can't eat it. Sometimes it's alive. Sometimes it's not. Its color changes.

What the hell could it be?

When will you be here? And maybe I wasn't going to ask about that.

The phone chimes. *If all goes accordingly—2morrow. And who R U kidding? That's what U always ask.*

Ooh. A surprise tomorrow. What could it be? What could it be? I hop off the desk and bounce up and down.

"A surprise. A surprise. What could it be? What could it be?" I chant and jump, arms swooping up above my head then slapping down to my thighs.

The activity on the laptop screen catches my eye and one particular line jumps off the page. Turning to read it, I nearly give myself whiplash.

Goldenrae says…

Hey you added a picture of my neighbor to your website.

CHAPTER EIGHT

Fangman333 says…

Which picture?

Sleepslikethedead says…

Cletus?

PenPro58 says…

Oh, this is bad. Very, very bad.

Moongirl2nite says…

My brothers are in Boston.

Mac says…

Eva, where did you get those pictures? They're unbelievable. Do you have friends in the movies or are those Photoshopped? You are so talented. How am I going to create a costume that cool? Where do I get that kind of makeup? How do I make the hair stick to my ears and nose?

Goldenrae says…

Yes, Cletus. Though, I have to say that picture is much better than what he looks like now.

I swallow hard and stare at the screen, unable to move.

Margaritaman says…

Does anyone else think the hair coming out of his ears looks like pubes?

Sleepslikethedead says…

That picture is very old and from a database, requiring certain clearances.

Eva says…

Goldenrae, has Cletus come by tonight?

PenPro58 says…

This conversation needs to come offline.

Fangman333 says…

Agreed.

Goldenrae says…

No. I haven't seen him since yesterday. But I'm not home. I'm at a friend's. How do I get rid of him? Can I just tell him he's not allowed into the house? Can I yell it from behind the door or do I have to open the door? What if he steps in before I can get the words out?

Fangman333 says…

Let us each email the mistress with our contact information. Eva, you will need to be the central command for this operation.

Mac says…

Funny joke, Goldenrae. Your neighbor sounds like a winner. But he's not a real vampire. They don't exist, people.

Eva says…

Got it. Email me at mistress@evaprim.com.

Cletus! I'll need to gather the troops and send them straight to Goldenrae's house. Quickly! Goldenrae's humanity is depending on me. I click over to my email and wait to hear from everyone. Then I check the desktop for any Cletus reports, grab a pen and walk in circles around the middle of the room.

Exactly how am I going to save Goldenrae? I can't leave the house. I don't know where my cyber friends are located. They could be anywhere in the world. Anywhere could mean not near Boston, although Moongirl2nite's brothers are in Boston, so maybe we could use them. But I don't even know what they are. If they're human, they're no use, just another worry.

I pull out a notepad and draw a line down the middle of a sheet of paper. "Liabilities—A.K.A.—potential casualties" titles one side. "Troops" heads the other. Goldenrae, The Brothers, Goldenrae's entire neighborhood all go in the Liabilities column. Mac is obviously human, but I don't know where he is. Margaritaman, I can only hope continues to enjoy Bloody Vlads in his house, wherever that may be. When it comes down to it, they're both liabilities. They land on the left side.

In the Troops column I write Eva, Fangman333—just because I'm guessing he's not really some crazy wannabe but an actual vampire. How else would he know about The Shift? Sleepslikethedead is another pretty strong guess, if you ask me. I mean, she seems to like the idea of provoking Studmufflicker69.

The unknowns go across the top. PenPro58 worries a lot, even though she seems fairly knowledgeable. Moongirl2nite is a complete unknown. Based on her mushy comments, I can't tell if she's human or anything else. One thing I know for sure, she is soft.

Why is the first column fuller?

I study the map. The last Cletus sighting was in Boston's Back Bay. The two previous to that occurred in Maine where he managed to take control of Francois. He must have some idea Stefan will not lie down and let him take over New England. He can't possibly still be in Massachusetts. That would be ridiculous. He has to know Stefan will hunt him across the entire state.

The ringtone on my phone startles me with the chorus from Blue Swede's rendition of Hooked on a Feeling. I selected the ringtone for Stefan's number. Let's face it. He can't stop how he feels about me. I answer before the chanting ends and the first line begins.

"Hello."

"How are things at Central Command, darling?" Stefan's smooth voice flows through the phone.

"Fine." I click the desktop for a news update. "Where are you?"

"Quincy. You've been monitoring The System?"

"Yes. Ooh, bring me back some kettle corn."

"Anything new there?

"Nope." I scroll through the news briefings. Not one report of Cletus has occurred since yesterday. "No new sightings and nothing in my vmail."

"Have you been investigating other sources?" he asks.

"Well, I was going to call Tarek, but you said not to call anyone but you, so I didn't."

"Tarek has no news."

"I can't leave the Command Center so I can't go gather any intelligence. You've really limited my ability to be helpful in this mission. You underestimate my skills, Stefan. If you'd let me into the field with you, I'd be able to make a huge impact."

"I know."

"Well, unlock the doors so I can help." I could help everyone, if he'd only set me free.

"Chryssie, I have received a report of a Cletus sighting and I'm wondering why it did not come from you." A slight edge cuts through "you."

I purse my lips, scrunch my eyebrows and ask, "Where?" My fingers click the keys, searching for any information on Cletus even though I know there's nothing new in The System.

"You should be searching outside The System as well." That edge slices through his entire sentence.

"Don't get so huffy. I'm looking." I open up Google and search, "Cletus Shiftbottom."

When the page returns with one entry, I gasp.

Photos of Cletus Shiftbottom. *www.evaprim.com*

"It sounds like you have found this Eva Prim link. I'd like you to research this site. Find out all you can—who owns it, where the pictures came from, who are the people participating on the blog. Everything."

I click the link to my website and connect straight to the page of Cletus pictures. "Human Cletus." "Half-shifted Cletus." "Full-on Vampire Cletus." Below these pictures is the other one I posted.

"I want to know where the picture of Titus came from and how it got on the Internet. Do you understand?"

Through the phone line I can not only hear, but actually feel his rage. My ear burns, and I swear I hear sizzling.

"Got it," I say.

"When I find out which of my underlings has posted a picture of my Massachusetts captain in his shifted state, that vampire will pay with his life." He growls the words through clenched teeth.

"Okay. Don't worry about the kettle corn." I hang up.

CHAPTER NINE

Now, I know I should be worried. I am worried. Sort of. The one thing I know without question about Stefan is he is not going to kill me. He's not going to be happy, and it may take quite a while for him to calm down, but he won't kill me, especially not when I save the day. Of course, if I don't save the day, I'll definitely be facing some sort of punishment. But I'm pretty sure he won't kill me. There have been plenty, plenty, plenty, plenty of opportunities for him to kill me. And he never has. Oh, he's come close.

It happened in 1878. We slept apart for fifty-six days. It was necessary. He needed his space. I slept in a mausoleum in Connecticut. It was rather uncomfortable, but better than facing him. On night fifty-seven he found me and brought me home. At that point he was so worried he forgave me. Unfortunately, I'm still not allowed in New Orleans. Actually, the entire gulf coast region is off limits. That's just another item on my Fix-It List.

Of course, that incident didn't involve humans, only vampires and a few, some, several werewolves. But no humans. It was contained to the Gulf Coast.

I click over to my email and find six messages already waiting. Immediately I recognize Goldenrae, whose email address is *goldenrae@yahoo.com*. Then there are four I'm not sure of—*charlie@nightlife.com; nightshift@harpercars.com; blondeone@tigerspace.com;* and *mastergardener@nocturnaledge.com*.

 It's the sixth one that jump starts my heart, and then nearly gives me heart failure.

hitmanm@neterritory.com

The sound of my panicked breathing fills the air. Shallower and shallower, the breaths come. Faster and faster I try to pull in a deep lungful until finally I sound like a honking duck.

My body tingles as The Shift begins.

"No. No. No. No. No."

I pace back and forth, shaking my hands, shrugging my shoulders and rolling my neck.

"Relax. Relax. Relax. It's gonna be fine. No need to worry."

When I turn at the edge of the rug and step back toward the desk, I walk smack dab into it. My breath. The sound that escapes me mimics a foghorn.

I gag.

My ears grow. I grab the tips and try to scrunch them back into themselves. "No. No. No."

The first twitch in my nose occurs, and my ears itch.

"SHIT! SHIT! SHIT!"

Before the claws appear I rip the nose hair from my nostrils. Blood drips down my chin, and I swipe it away with the back of my hand. I never manage to pull out any of the ear hair because my nails become daggers.

My feet tear through my leather boots leaving only my ankles and shins covered. My pants shred up to my thighs, converting to shorts with long strips hanging to my calves. My bra pops off and remains stuck under my T-shirt, which is now stretched to the point of barely covering the rock-hard pecs replacing my breasts.

A red haze appears, indicating my eyes are no longer brown. I glance down and confirm my nose is much larger than it should be, making it very easy for me to smell my breath.

I cover my mouth and run to the bedroom. The gas mask won't fit. Even the extra large one won't go over my nose. It's time for my homemade contraption.

The reality is I don't have to breathe. I'm a vampire. We don't have to breathe unless we're talking. It's the only reason we need an air exchange.

The problem is I never quite mastered the art of standing around without breathing. It's just not natural. So I breathe. Even in this state.

I grab the longest scarf in the closet, a plastic bag and an air freshener, the kind you hang from your rear view mirror. After securing the bag in several folds of red silk I tie the scarf over my mouth and around my head. The air freshener slides into place behind the fabric and under my nose. Now I'm ready for action.

I learned this trick a number of years ago. I look like an idiot, but my breath doesn't smell as bad.

Back in the office, I sit behind the desk. The sound of the plastic bag crinkling back and forth with each breath masks the clicking of my dagger-nails on the keyboard as I type, using one finger at a time. At this rate, I'll be here all night.

I open the emails, beginning with hitmanm, knowing exactly who it is even though he's signed his name fangman333.

Eva, send out one email linking all our addresses so we can communicate. Fangman333

Do you know how annoying this message is? I know what I need to do. I don't need him to advise me.

I open each of the other emails. Almost everyone has signed a web name, making it fairly easy to navigate the situation.

Charlie@nitelife.com is Moongirl2nite. *Nightshift@harpercars.com* is Sleepslik-ethedead. *Blondeone@tigerspace.com* is PenPro58. Goldenrae is Goldenrae.

The only one I'm not sure of is *mastergardener@nocturnaledge.com*. He signed his email as Damien. Who the hell is Damien? I click "reply" and type, *Who are you?*

Of course typing those three words takes forever. I finally hit send after starting over four times.

I open another email and copy everyone's addresses into the address box. In the subject line I type, "Connection." However, before writing a message, I realize I could be setting Goldenrae up for something even less pleasant than nightly visits from Cletus.

For instance, Fangman333 will not intend to kill her. But he won't take any prisoners in an effort to eradicate the world of Cletus. And, if she isn't killed, she won't be the most stable individual when the melee has ended. If she remembers any of it, it will be traumatic. If Fangman333 helps her forget, she'll probably have *mush brain.*

I pace the floor. My excitement makes me breathe heavier, which is just plain disgusting, and I have no choice but to add another air freshener to my scarf.

Since Goldenrae's already dealing with Cletus on a nightly basis, it's a fair guess he's been taking a nip each evening. This fact only complicates the matter. The vampire bond is a difficult one to explain. But suffice it to say when a vampire repeatedly feeds on the same human, there's a bond.

A one-time drink doesn't equate to anything. It's like a one-night stand. The parties involved are both willing and usually neither wants to run into the other in the light of day. The last part is doubly true for vampires.

Yeah, I know what you're thinking. What human could be willing, right? News flash—ninety-eight percent of humans are willing. This recent vampire craze has really helped us out in the dining arena. Humans think vampires are sexy and one bite will feel great. And it does as long as the vampire isn't brand new. Newbies have less control and zero skill in the orgasm department. Everything takes practice.

I sit on the edge of the desk and kick off my shredded boots. As Central Commander of Operation Cletus, the CCOC, which now involves two sectors, the New England Territory, NET, and the Friends of Eva, FOE, it's my responsibility to keep everyone as safe as possible, which, at this moment means not allowing them all access to each other. I cancel my email to the group and begin one to Goldenrae.

Goldenrae, where are you located? Are you wearing any religious pendants? Eva.

Then, I address an email to PenPro58, Moongirl2nite and Sleepslikethedead.

Hello friends. In an effort to keep Goldenrae as safe as possible I have emailed her separately for information. Where are you all located and what is your battle history? Eva

The last email I send is to Fangman333, knowing it's not going to go over well. It's fair to say he'll probably kill something when he reads it. But I have no choice other than to stall. Also, it would be helpful to have some information for planning purposes.

Fangman333, thanks for the advice on connecting the group. However, for security purposes, I will need to know your precise location and your ability to participate in a battle in the New England area, should one occur. Eva

The computer chimes as responses appear in rapid-fire succession in my inbox.

Moongirl2nite writes…

To all: I'm in Rhode Island. I've never fought in a real battle. Only sparred with my brothers. I have eight of them, and they serve the Master.

The sister of eight brothers serving the Master in Rhode Island could only be Charlene Soldati. The Soldati Family has served Stefan for hundreds of years, following him from Greece and Italy to the United States. The Alpha Werewolf is the oldest Soldati brother, Rob. I knew Moongirl2nite was a wolf. Young. Inexperienced. I still don't know which column to put her in. She won't get killed as easily, but she won't know what she's doing either.

It would be helpful to have someone who could move Goldenrae during the day. The only problem is, when you're as closely aligned to the Alpha Wolf as his baby sister is, you can't keep secrets or disobey him so her abilities are definitely questionable. I circle her name on the pad.

Sleepslikethedead writes…

I'm in New York, traveling north to assist with the Cletus battle. The Nightly News Briefing reports Cletus to be in Boston. I can be there in a day. I've fought many battles in my three hundred years and am more than willing to take on Cletus.

PenPro58 writes…

Hello everyone. I'm home and afraid getting to Boston would be quite a challenge, though I'm working on it. My battle experience is limited, however, I'm thoroughly and properly trained.

Goldenrae writes…

Eva, I live in Providence, Rhode Island, but I'm hiding in Cranston. I haven't told any of my neighbors where I am. The doors and windows are locked. The lights are off and I'm hiding in a closet. I have a cross but I can't seem to put it on. He's a real vampire. I just know it. I don't want to die. Can you help me? Goldenrae

Rhode Island! Rhode Island! I jump up and send the chair flying into the wall. Cletus is in Rhode Island, twenty-five minutes away from my home.

I respond to Sleepslikethedead, PenPro58 and Moongirl2nite.

Eva writes…

Troops, Cletus has not been in touch with Goldenrae this evening. But based on her response, I fear he's bonded with her. If he doesn't visit her tonight, I'm sure he'll do it tomorrow. I can't imagine he'd be able to resist her for more than one night. Goldenrae is located in Rhode Island. Eva

Sleepslikethedead writes…

Bonded? She'll defend him to the death. We have no choice but to kill her, too.

Sleepslikethedead has a good point, but it doesn't mean we should kill our new friend immediately. We should at least give her a chance to resist Cletus's call. It's the whole human-servant thing, a very old trick handed down from Vlad. He really was a sneaky bastard, the cause of our current status in society. Before him, we were able to mingle with humans without issue. But he was greedy. Really screwed us.

PenPro58 writes…

Bonded? This is very, very bad.

Moongirl2nite writes…

What exactly does being bonded mean?

Eva writes…

I'll explain bonding on the blog. It's helpful information for current vampires and wannabes. Let's not plan to kill Goldenrae on sight. Let's give her a chance to prove her allegiance.

Fangman333 writes…

Eva, I am located in New England, Exeter, RI to be exact. I am battle-ready at all times. Now, where is Goldenrae?

Exeter?

I click reply and fire off a response in hopes of figuring out what he's up to before I go to bed.

Martin, what are you doing in Exeter? Aren't you supposed to be out of the country?

It's five-fifteen. I feel terrible not to be able to assist this evening, but our only shot is a young, inexperienced werewolf whose brothers hover around her like she's a fragile Faberge egg. She'll never be able to help Goldenrae today.

Eva Writes…

Goldenrae, based on the late hour we are unable to assist you. Cletus is powerful enough to walk in the early morning light so stay hidden until mid-morning. I'll contact you tomorrow evening about a plan for meeting. Eva

After gaining a consensus from PenPro58, Sleepslikethedead and Moongirl2nite to meet back on email immediately following sunset, I prepare and post my latest article for my blog.

Just as I'm about to log off the laptop one last email arrives.

Fangman333 writes…

Now, Eva, how would you know who I am and where I'm supposed to be? I wonder how you could possibly have such classified information, Little One?

Chapter Ten

That foghorn sound fills the room, and I can't think. The scarf crackles incessantly as I desperately try to breathe. I rip the contraption off my face and fan myself with the air fresheners.

What is wrong with me? Why did I type his name? Stupid. Stupid. I wasn't thinking. He knows it's me. I know he does. What if he tells Stefan? I'll never be able to help Goldenrae. Stefan will… Then he'll… I'll be… ACK!

Stefan's going to kill me this time. If he finds out, he's definitely going to kill me. I know it. I just know it. This is it. The end.

I shut down the computer. I don't just send it to sleep. I shut it down and unplug it and bury it in the bottom of my candy drawer.

Then I dart down the hall to the bedroom and hide under the covers, waiting for Stefan to come home. There is no chance I'm going to be able to shift back to my other self. I can't get my body to relax enough to stop panting, never mind convert back to my human form.

The more I pant, the worse the room smells, the more upset I get, the harder it is to gain control, which continues the panting. It's a living, breathing hell.

The door opens at the top of the stairs.

I hold my breath and force my heart to stop beating.

"Darling, are you awake?" Stefan says, sliding into bed beside me. His hands move across my skin.

My heart thunders in my chest. A gasp of polluted breath escapes me like a hot steam valve exploding on a cold winter morning.

"What has left you in this state?" He moves closer to me, pulling me against him and offering me his wrist.

Hmm. How to answer?

"Just nervous about the Cletus situation," I say, my voice shooting up twelve octaves. I bite into him.

It only takes a second before I shift back to my much more feminine, less stinky, not-hideous body, but I don't stop drinking. At this point, I'm parched to the edge of literal dehydration. Being a bundle of nerves for hours can make anyone thirsty.

"Don't worry about Cletus. We'll find him." He kisses my neck. "Did you get very far on the website research?"

I clamp down on his wrist.

"Ow!"

"Sorry." I kiss the bite mark and rub my thumb over his skin. "Not yet. I'm sure I'll have more information tomorrow. I was kind of worked up over not realizing I should be googling Cletus information." Oh, and the idea you might figure out I'M EVA!

"Well, you've only had the computer a few weeks. You'll get the hang of it." He tucks the blanket up around us and settles in behind me.

"Any word from the front?" I ask. If I wasn't already dead, I'd swear I was having a heart attack. A tightness like I've only experienced eighty to ninety other times grips my chest.

He yawns. "Hmm. Cletus appears to have left Boston, heading south. Let's talk about him in the evening."

I clear my throat. "Any word from Cheng and Martin?"

"Why is your heart racing? Are you frightened Cletus will attack them? Your heart usually only beats like this when we…" He nuzzles my ear.

"No. They texted me they were bringing me a surprise, and I just wanted to be sure they'd be here tomorrow." My voice is considerably squeakier than usual, and I think my heart just exploded.

"Don't worry. Your surprise will be here tomorrow." He chuckles.

"You know what it is?" I turn to face him.

"I do. But you know I won't spoil it," he answers before falling completely silent.

It always amazes me he can cease to be alive without exhibiting any clue it's coming. I have no time to consider the surprise because as soon as he sleeps, I'm pulled into slumber with him.

*****

"Do you believe this?"

Titus's voice roars down the stairwell, echoing through the stone passageway. I pause halfway up the stairs and debate crawling back to bed. However, instead I trudge forward and shove the door open, knowing I need to clear everyone out of the house so I can check on Goldenrae.

I scent the air. Titus is shifted. I gag.

"Knock it off," he shouts. "Stefan, if she wears that mask…"

"Chryssie, darling, come and help us." Stefan's calm voice floats in the air. His scent, deep and manly, acts as a mask filtering Titus's stench.

Wandering down the hall to the office, my heart already beating like a marathon runner's, I wrack my brain trying to figure out how to convince them to leave.

Rob, Gabe and Liam are also present. Gabe and Liam study a map on the coffee table. Rob stares at his phone, texting. Titus paces. Stefan greets me at the door, kissing my cheek. His dark gaze washes over me, sending a wave of warmth through me. He loves me.

For a brief moment, something different glitters in his eyes. Something probing. Something powerful.

I gulp and try to smile, though I'm only able to force the left side of my mouth upward. "Hi."

"Good evening, my flower." His fingers brush my cheek. "Come in. Join us." He leads the way to the desk.

"The Vampire Bond," Titus shouts. He's so angry drool drips from his mouth. He's the exact image of the photo on the website.

He paces the office, reading or rather, shouting my blog. His shadow looms beside him on the wall, cast there by the flames from the fireplace.

"Only three reasons exist for a vampire to bind a human to him. The first is stupidity. An idiot may repeatedly feed from a human who tastes particularly good or who is an easy catch based on the limited powers of said idiot.

This idiot would have no idea of what he's done. The Bond isn't one-sided. It's not as though the human is bonded to the vampire like a lovesick teenybopper chasing the movie star of the week."

He stops pacing. No one moves. Stefan stares at his computer screen. Rob sits on the sofa. No one even reacts to this angry reading of my work.

I'm perched on the edge of the desk nearest the door, ready to bolt at the first sign any one of them is going to accuse me of writing the blog. My hand covers my mouth. My nerves are at it again. I can't help but breathe, which makes it impossible to ignore Mr. Stinky.

"She's calling the vampire an idiot. Does she not realize she's the idiot? Let me continue. Let's see what other pearls of wisdom she has to share," Titus yells. As he stomps across the room, his feet pound into the rug, his toenails gouging the fibers to shreds.

"Oh, no. The Bond is double-sided, like double-sided sticky tape made from the strongest glue ever created. When a vampire bonds with anyone, The Bond is a constant presence, ever hovering in the back of his mind. Even in battle he'll think of her, worrying about her safety, her life, her death. He'll wonder why he didn't change her. If he thinks she's dead, he'll let himself be destroyed, possibly engaging the sun to kill him.

It's very Romeo and Juliet in a dark and twisted sort of way. Sometimes, Hollywood gets things right. Vampires are romantic. Who'd have thought?"

Rob chuckles.

Titus's head snaps up and he glares, snarling like a rabid gargoyle.

"Come on, man. You have to admit, that was funny," Rob says, not in the least bit concerned about Titus's reaction. "Vampires are romantic? Hollywood gets it right. This chick's a riot."

Liam's lip twitches, and Gabe turns away from everyone to face an oil painting of the Greek Isles, every detail of which I'm sure he's had committed to memory for the last two hundred years. I'm not sure if they're laughing at Titus or my blog. I sit quietly and watch.

"I don't have to admit it's funny. It's not funny. She's outing us. It's not your picture plastered all over the Internet for millions of people to see. Maybe tomorrow she'll discuss werewolves. Who'll be laughing then?" He kicks an empty chair and sends it smashing against the wall.

"Which brings us to the second reason a vampire bonds. Love. When a vampire falls in love, he bonds with his mate. Again, very romantic, if the mate is willing. An unwilling mate could kill a vampire or drive him to kill himself. It's a sticky situation.

"Option number three involves emulating Vlad. By bonding humans to him, Vlad created an army of human-servants who killed themselves to save him. Unconsciously, the human-servants cared for their vampire-master, even loved him.

"Egotistical, maniacal vampires try to follow in Vlad's footsteps, hoping to gain power, strength and security. During the day when the master's influence is weaker, the humans don't think of him, don't even remember him, but they protect him, unaware their every move is made to ensure his safety. At night when he rises and comes to them, they offer themselves freely.

"These are the reasons vampires bond with humans."

Titus crumples the paper in his fist. "She has to be stopped. We must find and destroy her. First The Shift, then The Bond. Next it will be The Change." He throws the ball into the fireplace and glares at the burning blog.

"Chryssie is working on it, Titus," Stefan says, glancing in my direction. "Darling, do you think you'll have any information for us tonight?"

The entire room turns to face me. Every one of them is depending on me to figure out who this evil vixen is. Who is the dastardly vampire creating such a ruckus in our world? How do we stop her?

"Yeah, Chryssie. Do you think you could produce some amount of intelligence tonight?" Titus demands, curling his lip over his fangs.

"Hey! It's not like you've produced anything helpful in the hunt for Cletus. So back off!" I jump off the desk, fangs descended.

"I'm the one who found the website!" he yells, stalking toward me.

"Big deal. Have you found Cletus?" I lunge for him.

Stefan appears between us. "Chryssie, cut him some slack. It's his picture this new enemy has posted."

Enemy? Enemy? He thinks I'm the enemy. Tears build in my eyes, and I turn away.

"What's the matter, darling?" He catches my chin and turns me to look at him.

I shake my head. "Nothing. I'm fine." Oh, my husband thinks I'm the enemy, that's all.

The front door bangs open and something crashes into the foyer. Stefan leans past me, grimaces and shakes his head. After some scuffling and growling, two strangers appear, a very tall and beautiful, however awkward blonde woman and an incredibly short Mexican-looking guy. Their movements are so jerky, I can't help but stare.

They look like rickety robots trying to maneuver. With each step their bodies lurch forward. The sight of their wobbling heads makes my neck hurt. Think of bobblehead dolls in need of a good lube job.

"Who the hell are you?" Titus asks.

Cheng glides into the room behind them. "This is Cynthia and Jackson," he says with a slight bow.

A grin plasters itself across my face, and my fangs disappear. I've missed him. Cheng's always been so kind to me, teaching me to spar, throw and catch daggers, shoot pistols and he's even tried to teach me to move with the stealth of a master vampire.

His hair is pulled back into a long braid hanging down his back, just the way he always wears it when he hides a knife in it. His dark eyes glitter. He's dressed in navy trousers and a loose fitting maroon shirt. I'm sure he's hiding an arsenal of weapons on him.

"Chryssie, Cynthia and Jackson are your surprise," Cheng says.

I turn toward the robots. "You're giving me dysfunctional humans?" I'm confused. What do I do with them? I'm fairly certain I can't fix their jerkiness. "You don't expect me to change them, do you?"

A lesser vampire must ask her master's permission before changing anyone. And though I've asked, repeatedly, I've been denied. Something about too much work to manage one in the first year and my lack of patience causing a difficult situation and it not being a good way to begin a relationship and ultimately the safety of the region being of concern.

"No. You can't change these guys," Cheng says, resting a hand on Jackson's shoulder and wrapping his arm around Cynthia's waist. At five feet eight inches tall he appears to be about a foot shorter than her. The Mexican's almost a full head shorter than him.

"What do I do with them? I thought you said I couldn't eat them." Not that they appear particularly appetizing. Something in their faces almost looks dead. At first glance I didn't notice it, but the more I study them the more I see the flatness in their eyes. I tend to like my meals less dead looking...more...alive.

Stefan chuckles. "No, you can't eat them." He walks over to Cheng. "It's good to see you."

"Same here, sire." Cheng offers his wrist to Stefan, who simply nods at the gesture.

It's not often he takes Cheng or Martin up on the formality of strengthening their bonds when returning home from an extended journey.

"I take it Martin is still pursuing the others?" Stefan studies the tall blonde. His gaze locks with hers, and her eyes nearly cross.

There's a funky smell in the air and it's not just Titus. I lean toward the robot-humans and sniff a couple times. It's a charred sort of smell, like burning hair or burning flesh or something.

"Why do they stink?" I rub my nose.

"Chryssie, Cheng has brought you two demons." Stefan makes the announcement as if he'd just said Cheng brought back Florida oranges. Not a care in the world.

"Demons?" I swallow. "These are two from…the, um…you know, The Book." I point at them and frown.

"Yep," Cheng says, squeezing them both like he's testing fruit.

"Stefan, what kind of punishment is this?" I glare at him. "You said you forgave me. It was your damn fault with those stupid books. Why did you even have them? You still haven't explained." I pull my bowie knife out and run across the room straight for the demons.

The one thing I know about demon slaying is that if you can remove the heart from the host body before the host is dead and the demon has left the body, you can kill the demon. It's apparently quite difficult which is probably why Cheng and Martin are the only two vampires I know who can do it. But I'll figure it out, if that's what they want.

"Chryssie." Cheng catches me around the waist and lifts me off the floor, spinning me away from the demons and disarming me. "You're not supposed to kill them. They like you."

"Darling, they're two friends for you," Stefan says. At six feet four inches tall he's just a bit shorter than the blonde.

"What?" I hear my question in stereo as Rob jumps up from the couch.

"You're not serious, are you?" he asks.

"Demons? You think I can't make friends with anything normal?" I ask, fighting with Cheng to give me back my knife.

"Stefan, we can't have demons near the wolves. We're not vampires. We're alive. Demons have tried to possess wolves hundreds, thousands of times. It's dangerous. They can't stay in the territory." Then he does something none of the Soldatis have done in hundreds of years. He pulls his cross from under his shirt to lie exposed on his chest.

In general, the sight of a cross is not problematic to a vampire who isn't really, really evil. I know, hard to judge, but still. However, the sight of a cross has a very different affect on two demons.

CHAPTER ELEVEN

As soon as the gold cross flashes in the firelight, Jackson and Cynthia go wild. The giant blonde turns on Stefan, trapping him in a chokehold. Jackson lunges. Titus couldn't have moved faster, but the stumpy robotic demon catches his giant feet and sends him tumbling into Rob.

The Alpha Werewolf kicks the demon, snapping the poor host's head to the side.

Jackson growls and bites Titus's chest.

"Get him off me!" Titus howls, pulling Jackson's hair in an effort to disengage his bite.

Rob kicks Jackson again.

The demon growls and clamps down even harder on Titus's chest and a flood of blood gushes down his face.

Liam grabs Jackson around his waist and tugs, but long claws grow out of what used to be Jackson's hands and dig into Titus, who howls in agony.

"He's a strong one, mate," Liam says and attempts to pull an arm loose as Rob kicks Jackson again.

Jackson's legs encircle Titus and his claws dig in deeper, making the shifted vampire howl again as he desperately pulls at Jackson's arms.

Across the room, Stefan is now in a seated position, still in a headlock with Cynthia's legs clamped around his waist. If he was human, I'd be concerned she was going to snap his body in half.

Cynthia looks like she's going to cry. Her big deep blue eyes are wide as tennis balls and brimming with unshed tears. She looks absolutely terrified.

And she should. Anyone dumb enough to attack Stefan should have the good sense to realize they're going to die. But here's the question. Will Stefan kill my new pet? And, if he kills her, isn't he also killing an innocent bystander? It's a lot to consider.

I'm less interested in the second question and more interested in the first. Now that I see demons can force a host body to shift into a monster and attack Titus, I kind of like my surprises. Though, I am going to have to do something about the odor.

I crinkle my nose. "Can you put me down?"

"Yes." Cheng places me on my feet and walks over to Stefan. "Sire, this has all happened so quickly. I could not have foreseen the wolf's reaction." He shoots a menacing glare at Rob who is still trying to keep out of Jackson's reach but kick him in the head at the same time. "If you'd like, I can dispose of these two."

I zip across the room and drop to the floor to kneel between Stefan's legs. "No. Don't let him do that." I shake my head and rub Stefan's thighs. "I like them. I want to keep them. I'll take care of them. I promise."

Titus roars behind me. Cynthia whimpers. Stefan's hands dig into her arms as she tightens her hold.

"Darling…" He chokes before somehow managing to pull Cynthia's arms off his windpipe. "I'm not sure they're safe for you to keep."

"Oh, but they haven't really done any damage," I say.

"Chryssie!" Titus growls. "This damn demon is clawing my intestines."

Jackson hisses.

"Like I said, they haven't really done anything wrong. Rob started it. He pulled out the cross. Everyone knows demons don't like crosses. Even I know." I nod and scoot closer. "Please. Please let me keep them."

I know what you're thinking. But listen, these two aren't easy to destroy. If a werewolf-vampire tag-team can't pull one to shreds, there's an outstanding chance I can't kill it either.

"Chr—" Stefan scoots lower, forcing Cynthia's forearm off his Adam's apple. "You can't control them."

"Do you want me to snap her arms off?" Cheng squats down beside Stefan and grips Cynthia's arm around her bicep.

Gabe kneels on the other side, holding the other arm in the exact same manner. "If we move quickly, sire, Cheng could do his thing."

Stefan's gaze meets mine.

I shake my head. "No! She doesn't mean it, and she's not really hurting you." I rub her forearms.

The dam breaks and tears flow down her cheeks, running into Stefan's hair.

"Well, he's killing me!" Titus yells.

"I wonder, if I stop trying to pull him off, do you think he'll relax and let go?" Liam asks Rob.

"It can't hurt to try," Rob says, leveling another kick at Jackson before bolting across the room.

"Don't just leave me like this." Titus wrestles to dislodge Jackson.

"Titus, look at Stefan. They haven't touched Cynthia and she doesn't have claws. Maybe this guy just needs to relax," Liam says, patting Jackson on the shoulder.

"Cynthia, please let go of him," I say.

In a voice as deep as any man's she says, "Okay." Her jerkiness returns, and she struggles to untangle herself from Stefan, who at the first sign of freedom is up and standing across the room beside Rob with me in his arms.

"Darling, I'm not sure these demons will be the best friends for you after all," he says.

I squirm out of Stefan's embrace and walk back to Cynthia, who was left alone on the floor.

I heft her back onto her feet and prop her against the wall. "What's wrong with you?"

"This is my first body in more than two thousand years," she says. "I'm a little rusty."

"What's the deal with your man-voice?"

"I haven't figured out how to use the higher chords." She's not even a smooth bass. She sounds like an old Barry White album played way too slow and backwards.

"Oh," I say. "What about the smell? You really stink."

"Demons stink." She shrugs.

Another voice, even deeper than hers, comes from Jackson. "When we enter a host, the skin burns. That's why we smell like burning flesh."

Cynthia nods. "What he said. You can stop him, you know." She points to Jackson.

"How?" I ask.

"You're our master. You control us."

If I didn't know better, I'd think I hear angels singing.

"I what?"

"Whoever summons the demons, controls them," she answers.

Collectively the room groans.

I am a demon master. "Yes!" I raise my hands to the ceiling in victory. Finally, a master of something. I wouldn't care if they were two Chihuahuas. The fact that I'm their master is awesome!

I can barely control myself. I jump into her arms and hug and kiss her. She's mine. I love her, even if she stinks.

"Chryssie, you really should call Jackson off Titus," Cheng says.

"Oh, right. Jackson, heel."

"He's a demon, not a dog," Cheng says.

"Jackson, release."

Still no response. My eyes narrow.

"How about just 'let him go?'" Cheng offers.

"Jackson, let go of Titus," I order.

And no sooner than I finish the command, he's standing beside me, a bloody, smelly mess, but he's no longer attacking Titus.

I'd hug him, too, but at the moment he's too gross.

"Thank you, Cheng. I love them." I hug Cheng.

I'm going to bathe them and dress them and teach them how to walk in their bodies and figure out how to get their voices to sound normal and then take them into public and show them to everyone.

Friends. I have two friends. Real, live, maybe not alive, but in someone's living flesh, friends.

"You're not letting her keep them, are you?" Titus demands.

Chapter Twelve

"Quit squirming." I dunk Cynthia in the tub once more, scrubbing her hair to rinse out the suds.

"Can't breathe!" She chokes and water shoots out of her mouth.

"You breathe?" I yank her head above the water.

"Yes. It's a human body. It breathes," she snaps in a super-low growl.

"Don't get snippy. How was I supposed to know demons breathe? Vampires don't breathe." I pick her up and set her on the bath mat before putting Stefan's robe on her and wrapping her hair in a towel. "You smell a little better."

"Hey," a deep voice calls from the doorway. "Why can't I wear this one?" Jackson holds up a bottle of Eternity Cologne. He's naked, which makes watching his jerky movements painfully amusing.

I snatch the bottle from his hand and replace it on the counter before rummaging through the collection of colognes and picking Millesime Imperial by Creed. The melon base note isn't one of my favorites, but I don't hate it, and somehow I think it will complement the faint odor of burnt hair. "Because only Stefan wears that one. I don't want you ruining the scent for me."

"You're breathing right now," Cynthia says as she tries to rub her hair dry with the towel. It's like watching a model having a seizure.

Jackson attempts to help. Together they appear to be having a tug of war over her head.

"All right. Stop that. You'll pull her head off." I comb and dry her hair. "I don't really breathe. I mean, I breathe, but I don't have to. It's an old habit."

After getting them each dressed in a pair of Stefan's jeans and a shirt, which by the way, look a hell of a lot better on him, although Cynthia doesn't look half as bad as Jackson, I carry them up to Command Central. Letting them walk down the stairs took too damn long. Going up will waste the whole night.

Surprisingly, the house is empty except for the demons and me. I'd had my doubts Stefan would actually leave me in peace with Cynthia and Jackson after the hullabaloo.

It took nearly an hour of arguing and tremendous self-control not to give in to a fierce desire to order Jackson to attack Titus and Cynthia to possess Rob before I finally convinced Stefan I could be trusted with the demons. Of course, the doubt in his voice was very clear. He drove the point home by announcing he was hexing the house. *Again.*

Out of habit I try the doors just to be sure and find them sealed from the outside.

"Practice walking," I tell Cynthia and Jackson, motioning to the area in front of the desk. "You need to be able to fit in, sort of."

I boot up the laptop and check my website.

My email is on fire. Goldenrae sent a message and my troops had a complete conversation.

Goldenrae writes…

What now? Can you meet me? Can I hide at your house? Please help me. I think he's angry. I can feel it. He's coming for me.

Of course I want to meet her and hide her and help her. But it's going to be awfully difficult with the hexed house and Stefan. I shake my head. I click reply.

Eva writes…

Goldenrae, do you know how to get to Exeter?

Moongirl2nite writes…

Demons! In our territory. My brothers said this may be worse than Cletus.

Sleepslikethedead writes…

Ladies, I'm headed toward The Groove. Let's try to meet there.

PenPro58 writes…

The Groove is out of the question. You'd think I was asking for a fledgling. Apparently, we have issues to address at home and some dire need to maintain our borders. Is it really too much to ask that I go on my own?

Moongirl2nite writes…

Oh, The Groove. I've been there before. It's not a favorite place for me, but I'll be fine as long as there aren't any demons.

Sleepslikethedead writes…

Fine. Whoever can should meet at The Groove tomorrow at midnight. I'll keep a watch tonight for Cletus.

PenPro58 writes…

I'll try to be available on email, though I'm being required to work on the issue here so I may not have much time.

On the blog Mac and Margaritaman are arguing with Studdmufflicker69 and Margaritaman is still looking for variety in his Bloody Vlad.

Margaritaman says…

Do you think adding rosemary to the Vlad will help with vampire breath?

Mac says…

Can a vampire bond to a human without the human's knowledge of the attack and how does one ensure it doesn't happen?

Studmufflicker69 says…

NO YOU IDIOT.

Mac says…

Hey, man. There's no need to be a jerk. I'm not talking to you.

Margaritaman says…

Okay. How about mint? Would that be weird with the tomato?

Studmufflicker69 says…

IM NOT TALKING TO YOU EITHER

Margaritaman says…

WTF? There's no need to be an ass. I'm just asking.

Studmufflicker69 says…

I KNOW WHO YOU ARE. AND IM COMING FOR YOU

Margaritaman says…

What is wrong with you? Who are you? I'm not afraid of you, you freak.

Studmufflicker69 says…

NOT YOU.

Mac says…

Don't threaten me. I'll put a stake through your heart so fast you won't know you're dead.

Studmufflicker69 says…

IM ALREADY DEAD. WHERE YOU AT? ILL COME GET YOU NOW.

Another email arrives in my inbox with a quick ding, and I groan.

hitmanm@neterritory.com writes…

Eva, where is Goldenrae?

I hit delete. Maybe, if I ignore him, he'll go away.

I begin another message to Goldenrae but before I get very far a crash and the sound of shattering glass pull my attention away.

The demons have left the room.

I bolt out of the office and run down the hall to find them in the kitchen. A juice carton is imbedded in a glass cabinet and orange juice runs down the wall and over a counter. Glass shards lie scattered across the floor. Crushed condiment bottles and lids are strewn everywhere.

Cynthia has climbed halfway into the fridge and Jackson stands beside her holding a jar of pickles in one hand and pouring hot sauce down his throat with the other.

"What the hell are you doing?"

"…hungry…"

I can barely understand the word, and I can't guess which of them said it.

You know, Cheng could have given me an owner's manual for these two. Who knew demons ate?

"You're making a mess and give me that." I yank the hot sauce out of Jackson's hand. "That's not food. It's a condiment. You don't drink it." I push him out of the way and pull Cynthia out of the fridge.

A turkey leg sticks out of her mouth.

"Eww, you are disgusting." I try to dislodge the turkey leg but she bites down and growls. "Let go."

She shakes her head.

"Yes." I tug the leg back and forth, and her head follows like a dog holding onto a pull toy.

She growls.

I glare and clench my teeth. "You're wasting my time. I need to get back to…" I pinch her nostrils shut and wait.

She crosses her eyes and looks at my fingers. Her cheeks turn bright pink.

She gasps and coughs, and the turkey leg comes flying out of her mouth along with some stuffing, the last of the cranberry sauce, a few carrots and a lump of mashed potatoes. All of which lands down the front of me.

Oh, if only I'd thought this through a little more.

From head to toe I'm covered in Vinnie's practice Thanksgiving meal. This time I growl. "Grrrooooosssssss!"

Energy buzzes along my skin as I fling food bits to the floor.

"She's mad." Jackson slips, landing on his ass in a puddle of milk.

I clench my teeth and curl my lips back to keep my fangs from cutting me. "I'm going to…" I heft Cynthia off the floor with the intention of snapping her long, skinny host body in half. "I don't have time for this. I have work to do." My vision fades to red. My ears and nose twitch. The Shift has already begun.

"Sorry, master." The deep voice cracks above my head.

"What?" I stop moving.

"Sorry," she repeats.

"No, what did you call me?"

"Master."

I put her on the floor. Lettuce falls from her hair. A ketchup stain the size of a volleyball marks her shirt and clumps of horseradish roll down her arm. Her giant blue eyes blink, not in unison. Staring at her is making my brain burn.

"Why can't you work the eyes right?"

"I'm trying." They begin to flutter like butterflies on speed, each dancing to a different beat. It reminds me of the old movie reels with the subliminal messages to buy popcorn.

The next thing I know I'm lying on the kitchen floor and two demons are leaning over me.

"You're going to be fine," a deep voice croaks. Cynthia sits beside me pressing a cold compress on my head.

"Is that cider?" I ask.

"Yes," Jackson answers. "Is it helping?"

"She's pressing a cold apple cider compress to my head and you're wondering if it's helping?" I sit up. Either I just received two of the dumbest demons on the planet or the world's assessment of demons as evil, terrifying monsters is completely wrong. They're morons.

"It works on humans," Cynthia says.

"Pressing apple cider to a human's head works for what?"

"It makes them feel better," she answers.

"Apple cider?" I'm so confused. I don't know what she's talking about.

"I panicked." Jackson slumps against the counter. "You were shifting and then you passed out, and I panicked. I never saw a vampire pass out before. So I used apple cider."

"Oh, I thought you said apple cider would work." Cynthia turns to face Jackson who's still holding the now crushed jug in his hand.

"No. The cold compress, not the cider," Jackson says.

"Oh." Her head bobbles.

"That's it. Are you both retarded? Are you rejects from the underworld? Did something happen to the two of you? What's the story? I can't take this. I have Cletus Shiftbottom to worry about. He's attacking our territory and bonded with my friend for devil knows what reason…"

"Maybe he's building an army," Cynthia offers. "Vlad did it. Mikhail did, too, we heard." She tries to pick something out of my hair and ends up twining her fingers in the waves and ripping out a clump.

"What the fuck?" I shove her back and jump up. "I'm trying to like you, but you're killing me."

"I'm only trying to help," she croaks. "We want you to like us. We've been trapped in The Book for so long. Then you released us, and we don't want to go back. We want to be with you." Tears stream down her face and she punches herself in the head as she tries to swipe them away.

Ugh!

"Stop that. Stop crying. I don't want you to cry. I just don't have a lot of time for this. Goldenrae is in danger. Stefan's territory is under attack. I have to figure out how to get out of…and I can't meet her looking like…" I glance down at my hands and realize they're hands, not claws. My vision is crystal clear. "How? How am I not shifted?"

"Oh, I didn't want you to be mad. I know you don't like that other look so I stopped you," Cynthia says, clinging to the counter as she tries to stand. Her feet slide in opposite directions, and she ends up in a split.

"You stopped me? How?" I pull her to her feet.

"I just did it." She shrugs. Her eyes still don't blink correctly.

"You're our master. When you need help, we must provide for you," Jackson says, ripping the door off the fridge. "You don't like being shifted so she stopped you. Sorry about this." He hands me the door. "I meant to close it."

I nod, prop the door beside the fridge and grin. "I need some help getting out of the house. Can you do that?"

CHAPTER THIRTEEN

"If he finds out, he'll be mad," Cynthia says from behind the scarf covering her face.

"Don't worry about Stefan. I'll take care of him. And how's he going to find out? He's in Boston tonight. He won't know." I shove a hat on her head and zip her coat. "We'll go out, find Goldenrae and be back before he gets home."

"I don't like the hat," she calls as I run back to the desk to get Goldenrae's address.

"And I don't want to wear a coat," Jackson complains.

"This must be what motherhood is like." I grab my car keys from the table and slide into my jacket. "You're wearing them. One of the rules of the vampire world is to blend in. When it's cold out, humans wear coats. Your hair's wet so you need a hat."

I shake my head. The fact I just took a shower with two demons boggles even my mind, but we'd already wasted enough time.

Still grumbling, they hobble toward the door.

"Okay. Do your thing." I wave at the door. "Get us out."

"He's going to know," Cynthia whines. "Then, he'll be mad and the last time he was mad we ended up in The Book."

"Just open the…" I turn to face her. "The last time he was mad you ended up in The Book. *He* put you in The Book?"

She nods and glances at Jackson. "I don't want to go back to The Book."

"I thought you'd been in The Book for thousands of years," I say.

They nod.

"But Stefan is only five hundred and…" I have to pause to do a little math. "eighty-six."

They shake their heads.

"Are you telling me he's been lying to me for two hundred years?" My eyebrows pull together and dip. My jaw locks. "Is he creepy vampire old? Older than Vlad?" The really old vampires have the personalities of statues and some very, very weird habits.

"Not exactly," Jackson says and attempts to pat my shoulder, which sends me tumbling forward. "Sorry."

"Exactly what are you saying?" I bounce back up off the floor. "He told me he's been a vampire since the 1400s. How could he have put you in The Book two thousand years ago?"

"Maybe he wasn't always a vampire," Cynthia suggests. "Maybe he was a human." Her head bobbles.

"Are you telling me he was reincarnated? A lot?" My eyes widen.

"No." She shakes her head.

"Are you saying he never died? Was an immortal and not human?"

"Nope." The headshakes and bobbling merge, and I'm fairly certain her head's about to bounce off her shoulders.

"What the hell are you saying?" I reach up and grab her chin.

"I'm saying he might have been a demon trapped in a human body that was changed to a vampire five hundred and eighty-six years ago." She smiles. "Yeah, that's it."

"Eeeeewwwww." My lip curls. My nose crinkles. "Impossible. I don't believe you. Stefan is a demon? No. Uh-uh. No." I suck my cheeks in and pace in a circle between them. "My husband is not a demon."

"A demon-vampire," Cynthia corrects.

The entire thought of it repulses me. The idea he was a body snatcher before a vampire is very upsetting. This may seem like a foolish point, but the fact is I would not want my body possessed by anyone else. I mean I made the conscious decision to become a vampire. Demons don't give you a choice.

"Odd, you didn't notice before," Jackson says as he presses his hands to the door. "With your weird fetish for smells and all. He has that slight burnt scent as an undertone." He slides his hands along the door and closes his eyes. "It's unmistakable. To demons anyway."

Stefan does have a slight, very slight, burnt scent. A bit of a fire-like smell, like smoking wood. I've always enjoyed it.

I rub my hands over my face. "That doesn't make him a demon."

"No. The smell doesn't. The fact he commands Ta Biblia Daimon means he's a demon," Cynthia says.

"No, controlling The Demon Books proves he's powerful. The mark proves he's demon," Jackson says and pulls Cynthia toward him. "Press here." He points to a spot on the wall to the right of the doorframe.

"Oh, you found it?" She shuffles into position beside him. "The lock?"

"Yes. I'll counterbalance the opening," he answers as he places her palm against the wood.

"What mark? Does he have a triple six somewhere? I'd have noticed. I've seen him naked nearly every day since I met him, and he doesn't have a mark like that." A slight grin tweaks my lips, and I sigh.

"Not a triple six. That's funny. The mark of Satan on him." Cynthia laughs.

"Pay attention," Jackson barks at her.

"Okay," she groans.

"What mark?" I'd have noticed a mark on him. I know every inch of him from the bite mark that made him a vampire to the scars on his back where he was whipped in 1412 to the little burn on his thigh he received trying to save his family in…

"The burn. You must have seen a burn mark somewhere on his body. A perfectly shaped star. It's probably not pink, probably slightly darker than the rest of him." Jackson's hands hover over the door directly opposite Cynthia's. "There it is. Steady, Cynthia. Don't pull away or we won't be able to open it. If he senses a change, we won't get a second chance."

"This hurts. He really doesn't trust you," Cynthia says over her shoulder as she starts to pull back. "He's going to kill us when he catches us. I just know it. He's not going to send us back. He's going to kill us." Her lips quiver in her bobbling head.

I shove her back toward the door. "Don't you dare let go." I'm getting out of this house, if it's the last thing I do. My husband's a lying demon. My friend's in danger. My territory's at risk. I'm not staying trapped on the sidelines. "Get this door open!"

Chapter Fourteen

"Who is this Goldenrae and why are you putting us in danger for her?" Cynthia asks from the backseat.

I push the pedal to the floor and the dark blue Marquis vaults up the on-ramp to the highway. Air whooshes through the open windows, sending my fuzzy pink dice bouncing against the windshield.

My head is still spinning from the idea Stefan is a demon and not just a vampire. I tap my fingers on the steering wheel. "How many times am I going to have to explain this?"

"Don't get annoyed. We don't know *everything*. We've been trapped in a book for two thousand years," she says, her deep voice sounding like a croaking bullfrog.

I sigh. "All you have to remember is Goldenrae is my friend, and I don't want her to get hurt. Nothing else."

"Easy for you to say. He won't put you back in a book when he finds out you left the house even though he'd hexed the doors and windows. He'll send us back," she says. "He'll know *we* did it."

"Cynthia." I glance in the review mirror expecting to see the road behind me and maybe the left side of her face. Instead, the entire mirror is filled with her big blonde head. "You really should sit back and put on your seatbelt."

"I'm a demon. I don't need a seatbelt."

"I can't see behind us."

"Use the side mirrors." She leans over the seat, closer to Jackson. "I want to sit in front next time."

"Sit back." I glare into the mirror.

She turns around and looks behind us. "There's no one back there. Jackson, I want to sit in the front next time." Her fingers wrap around his arm.

He smiles at her and nods. "Next time."

"I thought I was the master," I say.

"You are," they answer at the same time.

"Then why won't she sit back?"

"You're not serious about the command," Jackson answers, still watching Cynthia.

"What?"

"You don't really want her to sit back. It's not an actual command. It's more of a suggestion. We're not good with suggestions. They leave us to make the final decision which can be confusing for some."

"The whole room for interpretation issue," Cynthia adds, smiling at Jackson.

"What are you saying?" I ask.

Cynthia turns to me and rolls her eyes. They spin in her head. "If you want to be in charge, you have to be the dominant one in the situation. You can't be wishy-washy." She tries to push her hair back from her shoulder and ends up chopping herself in the neck, causing her to make loud choking noises.

"For devil's sake." I glare into the mirror. "Sit back!"

She throws herself against the backseat, coughing.

"You don't have to get so mean," she croaks.

Leave it to me to end up with the only two demons in history capable of misinterpreting commands for suggestions.

The car launches down the exit. I'm forced to slow down as we pull into a residential area.

"You might be too late," Cynthia says, pulling herself up to lean on the front seat again. "Cletus may have already killed her. If we get caught sneaking you out of the house only to find her dead, you're going to have a lot of explaining to do.

And he's going to put us back in The Book." She drops her head onto the top of the front seat and whines, a low moaning whimper.

"Why are you so negative? She probably didn't respond to the instant message because she was hiding. She's not dead. Cletus doesn't know where she is." I turn onto Oak Street. "And Stefan is not going to find out we left the house. Now look for number five."

Her head pops up. "She's bound to him, a human servant. I know it. He's probably making an army to defeat Stefan. That's what he'll need, an army of peons who love him enough to die for him because Stefan will kill them all." Her arms hang over the seat, and Jackson holds her hand. "Then you know what he'll do to us."

She's right. Cletus will need an army to defeat Stefan. A Cletus-Loving-Army-of-Peons. The CLAP. Just what I need.

"What are you going to do, find out where all his servants are and try to save each one of them? It'll never work. You'll have to tell Stefan," she says.

"I'm starting to like Jackson a lot more than I like you," I answer as I put the car in park outside the dark house.

"That's not very nice," she says and inches closer to Jackson.

I scent the air and don't notice any hint of anything stinkier than my demons. "Stay here." I slink around the car and up to the house, peering in the windows. Nothing moves. I listen.

A single rocking chair sits in the corner of the small porch. A broom lies on the floor beside the closed door. The wood creaks with each step I take. Outside the door I concentrate, listening for any voices or movements or breathing. Faintly, a heart beats.

I inhale. A foul stench comes from inside the house, seeping out from under the door. I turn the knob and crack the door open.

The familiar stink of Shift permeates the house. It's too weak for anyone to still be here, but strong enough to signal a recent presence.

"Hello," I call, hoping the owner of the barely beating heart will hear me and think the words "come in." Nothing, not even the ticking of a heating system responds.

"You want us to go in?" Cynthia asks. I lurch forward, hit the open threshold of the house and tumble backward. Without an invite, I'm not getting in. Even if two demons scare the vampire right out of me, I'm not able to cross the damn threshold.

"How did you do that?" I growl through my now descended fangs. No one sneaks up on a vampire, especially not two clumsy demons.

She grins. "It's a gift. Do you want us to go in?"

"I told you to wait in the car."

"Fine. But you're wasting time. Stefan is going to come back from Boston and find us gone, and then he'll pu—"

"Fine. Fine. Fine. Go find the human and bring her out. And don't break anything. And hurry up." How did I end up with a Nervous Nelly for a demon?

"We know. We want to get back before Stefan comes home. We still have to figure out how to reset the hex," Jackson whispers, which sounds like, well it sounds exactly like you'd expect a whispering demon to sound. Just plain creepy.

I peek in the garage. Nothing there but a car and some old tools. Then I check the perimeter, probably should have done this before sending the demons in, but what could happen to them? They're demons.

When I arrive back on the stoop, two bodies are piled in the doorway, a middle-aged man and woman. Bite wounds mar their necks. They haven't been dead for very long. They're still a bit warmer than room temperature.

"Where's the live one?" I call in.

"We're coming," Cynthia yells back.

"Hurry up."

"Quit complaining. It's not like she was lying around waiting for us. We had to dig her out of the basement."

They come around the corner covered in dirt and carrying a woman bent in the most inhuman sort of way with her feet up and her head back near her ass. I cringe as they whack the poor thing's golden-blonde head into a wall before dropping her at the door. Her body falls half in and half out of the house.

"Honestly, she's heavier than she looks," Cynthia complains, wiping her dirty hands on Jackson's back.

"You know…" I snarl through my teeth. "She's still alive. We're here to rescue Goldenrae, not kill her." I bend down and pull her out.

"Who are you kidding? She's as good as dead." Cynthia's foot comes up as though she's going to step over the man lying to the left of the dirt-covered blonde. Instead, her foot gets caught in his shirt, and she trips and tumbles out of the house, landing on the older woman.

"She's not going to die," Jackson corrects, pulling Cynthia to her feet.

"Yes, she is," Cynthia argues. "She's been drained."

"She's not drained." He props Cynthia against the railing.

"Jackson, this is not a body we could possess. She has been drained." Cynthia tries to put a hand on her hip and shoves herself sideways.

"She's not drained." He rolls the body over. "She's been rejuvenated. See?"

The sound that comes out of Cynthia is a cross between "Ack" and "Oooh" and "Gross." "Graoohckss!"

CHAPTER FIFTEEN

"I don't understand why we're taking her," Cynthia says. "She's going to awaken looking for her master. How are you going to explain why you have a fledgling vampire in the house?"

The ride home seems to take longer with the nonstop babbling of a worried demon. At least she's in the backseat with Jackson.

"You won't be able to convince Stefan she's yours." A loud click punctuates her statement. "She's not going to want you. There'll be no way to trick him. He'll know."

"She's not allowed to have a fledgling anyway," Jackson adds.

"How do you know?" I glance back. Cynthia's head appears in the mirror. "Put your seatbelt back on."

"Cheng and Martin told us a few things," Jackson answers.

Cynthia's bobblehead nods.

I press my lips together. Does everyone know?

"You have to admit, you are a bit of a…" Cynthia begins, her fingers drumming the headrest.

My eyebrow creeps upward.

"…disaster," she finishes and leans into the front seat.

"That's it. I'm returning you to The Book myself. Now sit back." I jerk the mirror to the side so I don't have to see her. "I can't believe they decided to give me two insolent demons. It's as if they set me up to fail."

"I was supposed…" Her knee comes up over the seat.

"I don't want to hear it. We have more important things to do than worry about who sits in the front seat. Now get back there," I command and push her back. Wind whooshes through the open window sending my hair flying across my face as the car speeds down the highway. "Jackson, you're sure you can reset the hex?"

"I haven't done this before, but I think I can manage," Jackson answers.

"You have to do it. Stefan will put us…" Cynthia's voice cracks, and she begins a low moaning whine that makes me want to drive the car off a bridge.

"Stop her," I say to Jackson as I straighten the mirror.

"I'll figure it out. We won't go back. Stop crying." He rubs her arm, and she nods, slumping against him.

"Cynthia does have a point, Chryssie. How will you explain the fledgling?"

"Her master will track her. He'll come for her, and then what?" Cynthia adds.

"Goldenrae won't rise until tomorrow night. She'll stay in the trunk during the day and then we'll get her to The Groove to meet the others, and everything will be fine." Of course, I had hoped she'd remain human, but since that's no longer an option, my new goal is to keep her out of Cletus's army.

"You don't think Stefan will notice a fledgling sleeping in his house?" Jackson asks.

"She'll be in the garage," I say.

The wheels of the Marquis squeal as I take the exit. We fly down Route 102 as if we'd never left the highway.

"Oh, that's different. He'll never sense anything in the garage," Jackson says.

"Is that sarcasm? You're supposed to be helping me. Sarcasm does not help." I glance into the rearview to find Cynthia's head again.

"Why aren't you in your seatbelt?" I turn up our mile-long driveway, speeding as if the sun was on the horizon.

She blinks slowly, both eyelids work together and long lashes fan over deep blue irises. She's quite lovely when she controls herself. "What if she…" Cynthia hitches her thumb toward the trunk. "…is not Goldenrae? Then what?"

"Cynthia has a point. We don't even know for certain we took Goldenrae," Jackson agrees.

I slam my foot on the brake, and Cynthia lands ass-up in the front seat.

"Of course it's Goldenrae. Who else would it be?"

"It could be any blonde." Jackson yanks on Cynthia's legs.

"You don't know what Goldenrae looks like. What if the other blonde, the dead one we left on the porch, was Goldenrae?" Cynthia's arms flail about, reaching for anything and finding my shoulder. "What if it wasn't Cletus who bit her?" She digs her nails into me for leverage.

"Yes, what if this is another vampire's work?" Jackson pulls Cynthia up beside him. "What if we just stole someone's approved mate?"

"We did not just steal a stranger. I'd know if Stefan had approved a mating change. He'd have told me." I flip Cynthia back over the seat and turn around to look at them.

Their expressions say it all. Neither of them believes me.

"He never keeps those kinds of secrets from me. I always know."

They glance at each other, and then back to me.

"There's no reason he'd keep that sort of secret. He never has."

"How can you be so sure?" Cynthia asks. "You didn't even know he was a demon."

The reminder makes me sneer. I squeeze my lips together and close my eyes. As much as I know I'm going to regret saying this, I say it anyway. "Because I get to interview anyone who is changed."

"Interview?" Jackson asks.

"AAAHHH. For the position of Friend. Okay? Everyone tries out for the damn position. No one has accepted the offer, but everyone tries out. Are you happy now?"

Does everyone, including my demons, have to remind me I haven't had tremendous success in the friendship realm?

"Ooooohhhhhh," Cynthia says and nods, each blinking eye again keeping its own beat.

Our heart-to-heart conversation is interrupted by Blue Swede's chanting rendition of Hooked On a Feeling. I've always loved this song, though hearing it right now doesn't really make me happy.

"Uh-oh," Cynthia says and slides backward to sit beside Jackson. "Don't answer it." She shakes her head, eyes focused on the phone.

"He'll only call back." I hit send.

"Where are you?" Stefan's voice is calm, deep and calm. Too calm.

We're only twenty feet from the garage in my estimation. So, "home" seems like an appropriate answer. I mean why tip him off I might be hiding something in my car by saying, "sitting in the car?" I'm certainly not about to say outside.

"Where have you been?"

It's funny how a man's voice can actually get deeper from the start of a sentence to the end. You can literally hear the tone drop, lower and lower with each spoken word. My voice, of course, goes *up* in exactly the same measure with my response.

"What do you mean?"

"Chrysanthemum." One word. Four syllables, each one an octave lower than the last.

"Yes?" A squeak.

Silence.

I glance at Cynthia and Jackson. She's curled in a ball with her head on his shoulder, shaking like she's just washed down a pound of chocolate-covered coffee beans with four shots of espresso. He stares at me wide-eyed.

I purse my lips and wait for Stefan to speak. He called me. It's not like I'm the one looking for him. Of course, this waiting is uncomfortable. Soon I'll feel The Summons.

It's a pain in the ass. The Summons. The Call. They're one in the same. A master can "call" his progeny to him. It's part of The Bond. I'll blog about it later. But for now I need to block him, if I can.

"So, I'm going to let you go now. I've got some stuff to do." I hit a button on the remote, and the garage door opens, revealing three large wolves.

Cynthia gasps.

And there are more. On either side of the car wolves emerge from the woods, stalking toward us, snarling.

"This is a bit of overkill. Don't you think?" I say.

"Not really," Stefan growls. "Where have you been?"

"We'll discuss this some other time. And if any of your wolves get hurt, it's on your own head. I have demons, you know!" I end the call, dropping the phone onto the seat. "Hold on!"

I wrench the gearshift into reverse and floor it, sending gravel, dirt and leaves flying as I cut the wheel to the side and turn the car toward the street. I gun it down the driveway, wolves howling as they chase me to the end of the darkened drive.

Cynthia screams as a wolf lands on the roof and another clings to the door.

"Get off there!" I bang on the ceiling. "If you scratch my paint job…" I pull the wheel hard to the right, spinning the car out and sending the wolf on the roof flying. The wolf clinging to the door manages to pull himself halfway into the car through the open window. "Stop him! I can't drive and deal with wolves!"

With his face morphed into a long snout, giant canine fangs protruding and black eyes glowing, Jackson leans forward and growls.

The wolf yelps and falls out of the car, tumbling into the trees.

I peel out of the driveway and take off for the highway.

"What the hell was that?" I ask.

"It's what he'd have looked like, if I possessed his body," Jackson answers, sliding back into his seat beside Cynthia, who is still curled up whimpering.

"No wonder they don't like demons," I answer.

He nods. "Cynthia, it's all right."

"No it's not. He knows. He knows. He knows. We're going back. She can't stop him. I don't want to go back."

I hate when she cries. I hate when anybody cries. I'm not good on the crying-front.

"Okay. Knock it off. He won't send you back. I won't let him," I say, almost believing myself. "You're mine. He's not going to take you away."

"You weren't supposed to leave the house and we let you out. He's not going to forget what we did." She wipes her eyes.

"Couple of things—first, I forced you to let me out of the house; second, and maybe this should be first, he should not try to keep me in the house. This new control thi—"

"It's really not new," Jackson interrupts.

"Whatever. This control issue he's got needs to end. I'm not staying on the sidelines while he runs everything. I'm not some flunky. I'm his wife. And I'm an independent thinker, woman, thinker. Whatever. I'm free to do as I please. And I'm pleased to say I will participate in this situation." I grip the steering wheel with both hands, ten o'clock, two o'clock, and grin.

"Great. But where are we staying today? We need a place to keep your friend back there and a place for you to sleep." Jackson points out the passenger side window. "In case you haven't noticed the sun is rising."

In the distance a peachy-red glow creeps along the horizon. And as fast as I can drive, I know I can't outrun the fiery giant ball lighting the morning sky.

CHAPTER SIXTEEN

I hate motels. They never quite seem to hit the mark. I prefer a fancy hotel with room service and a gym and spa. But when you're in a hurry to get to bed before the sun crests the horizon, or your husband, the Master, figures out where you are, you don't waste time searching for a Hyatt. Not to mention, toting along two dysfunctional demons and one dead-to-the-world fledgling who's bound to awaken with a thirst no one wants to experience would probably draw unwanted attention in an upscale hotel.

"One room, two beds," I say, knowing where I'll be sleeping won't be comfortable.

"I'll need a credit card to hold the room." The attendant appears older than me in literal years. His hairline begins behind his ears, and four, no, five long scraggly hairs cling to his skull like worms. He has more wrinkles than a prune. Even his eyelids are wrinkly.

"I'm paying cash."

"I'll still need a credit card." He slides the room contract in front of me and points to the little box marked "credit agreement."

"No, no credit card."

"No room."

"You know, I'm quite thirsty."

"There's a vending machine around the corner. You'll see it on your way out."

He turns back toward his office-bedroom. His hand moves to grab the doorknob but meets my hip instead.

The look on his face is priceless. His wrinkly eyelids smooth in an attempt to keep his bulging eyeballs in his head. His jaw drops open in a breathless gasp.

"How did…"

"I do prefer my men a bit younger, but…" I pull him into his room and slam the door behind us.

*****

The closet's not very big. Big enough for one, but two of us? It's a three by three square. No. It's definitely not big enough.

"It wasn't very nice. That's all I'm saying." Cynthia plops down on the bed nearest the bathroom. She manages to remove Stefan's sneakers from her feet without using her hands.

"You're getting better at controlling certain body parts," I say, trying to figure out how in the world I'm going to sleep in the closet with a fledgling vampire.

If I was at any vampire or werewolf owned establishment, I'd be able to sleep on the bed, completely secure in the knowledge no one would dare disturb me. But here, not so much.

I pull the hangers from the bar inside the closet and toss them onto the floor before slipping Goldenrae into the coffin-sized cubby, leaning her unconscious, dead weight, okay dead all around, body against the sidewall. She slides forward, and I catch her before she ends up doing a face plant onto the skanky carpet.

"Don't change the subject," Cynthia says. Her shirt comes flying off, followed by her, actually *my,* bra. Stefan's jeans land in a heap beside the bed.

Jackson rips his shirt pulling it over his head.

"Try to be more careful. You're going to have to wear those this evening."

"Sorry," he says as he struggles with the jeans.

"You're sure you locked the door?" I push Goldenrae to the back of the closet. Her legs buckle and she slumps in a heap.

"Locked it and hung the sign out." Jackson fumbles with the button fly.

Cynthia begins helping him with his jeans. "Meanie." She tosses the insult my way, not even bothering to look at me.

"Oh shut up. I was thirsty. He was being difficult. It's not like I didn't pay him." I yawn.

"You should have given him a better tip." She tugs Jackson's jeans to the floor, and pulling both feet out from under him to remove his boots, sends him flying onto his ass.

"Woah!" he yells and lands on the bed.

Cynthia pounces on him with nearly cat-like movements. "I've missed you." The grin on her face sends ice-cold, creepy-old-man-vampire chills down my spine. If I didn't know better, I'd swear she was about to eat him.

"How could you miss him? You've been together for thousands of years." I shove Goldenrae's legs into the closet. They fall out of the door, and I roll my eyes. I'm never going to get any sleep.

"We haven't *been* together," she says in a purr that makes my right eye pulse and my throat close.

Jackson responds with a low growl.

I jerk Goldenrae onto her back and push her legs up the wall. It doesn't look comfortable, but at least she's in the closet. I step over her and glance back into the room. "You're not actually going to—" Too late. They are.

The high-pitched screams come from Jackson. The wild, angry-bear-like groans come from Cynthia. The furniture bangs up and down. The TV and the radio blare to life and someone shrieks, "Yes! Yes! Yes!"

I lunge into the closet, slam the door shut, pinch my eyes closed and plug my ears.

I'm not a prude, not by a long shot. But it is really hard to watch my jittery, wobbling demons fuck. And listening to it is no better. In fact, it may actually be worse.

After humming The Battle Hymn of the Republic eight hundred and twelve times, I nearly lose my mind. "Will you please hurry up and finish?" I yell.

"Just go to sleep," Cynthia yells back.

"If I have to come out of this closet…"

"We opened the curtains and the shades. Sunlight's pouring into the room," she threatens.

The damn closet is so small I can barely turn to peer down at my feet to see the crack of sunlight creeping below the door, just about to touch Goldenrae's fingers. I crouch to grab her hand.

"You're going to set Goldenrae to flames!"

"No we're not," she answers. A fourth spring pops and joins the other three in one of the most painful quartets I've ever had the displeasure of hearing.

I wedge my feet under Goldenrae, attempting to turn her onto her side. The crack of light slides forward.

"Listen, you rotten, horny demons. If you don't draw those shades…"

The closet door suddenly opens and a blanket lands on top of me.

"Cover up with this. We haven't made love in the sun in… What would you say, Jackson, three thousand years?"

"Two thousand eight hundred and sixty-two. But who's counting?" His husky voice is accented, like a Spanish lover's, and his laugh reminds me of…Stefan. I shudder to think of it.

My fangs descend. "Did you just toss the dirty motel comforter on me?" Do you have any idea what happens on these things and how often they don't get washed? "I hate you, demons. When I see Stefan, I'm demanding he send you back."

"You won't be in any position to demand anything," Cynthia answers between grunts. "He's so angry he's even trying to call us back to him. You're screwed. I think this time you may actually end up in The Book with us."

"I'm not going into any book. And what do you mean he's calling you?" My head and butt hit opposite walls as I bend over to cover Goldenrae with the blanket. I end up in a squat, tucking and shoving the blanket around her. All the while, my breathing gets heavier. I'm fairly certain I'm going to suffocate in here. Goldenrae may actually die a true death from my breath.

There's a long, not quiet pause before anyone answers me. I'd swear something was vibrating. The sound coming from outside the door begins low and grows until it sounds like a washing machine about to shoot off the ground.

"What the hell are you doing?" I focus on the sound, but don't bother to decipher it because the next thing I hear explains it all.

"AAAAHHHHHH. YEEEESSSS! YEESS! YES!" They scream together.

"Oh! Fantastic," Cynthia says. "Where did you learn that?"

"Well, if you recall, I've done it before. Do you remember Athens in 1022?"

"Oh, right. The night in…"

"AARRGGHHH! For devil's sake! Shut the fuck up! I'm trying to sleep!" I bang on the closet door.

"Fine! But I'm not answering your question," Cynthia taunts.

"The sun will set. And when it does, I will come out of this closet. I will find you both. And I will rip you limb from limb. Then I'll take your parts to Stefan and tell him to put you in The Book."

My breath has now created even less space in the damn closet, and there's no place to turn to avoid it. Faintly, I see a red tinge. My fingers begin to tingle.

"Sorry, master," Cynthia calls from just outside the door. She taps lightly. "Don't shift. Just relax." Her voice is squeaky and high and not at all as confident as it was just seconds before. "He's trying to call us because demons serve their demon master. But you're our master so he can't. He can only control us, if he can control you."

I blink. So, basically, I need to stay the hell away from him so he can't control me and them.

"Don't take us back to him." Her breathy whisper almost sounds feminine. "He'll use us to find the others."

The others? "What others?"

"The other ten. Our brethren who weren't captured are waiting for you to claim them," Jackson answers. The closet door creaks. "They want to be with you, too."

Both my demons are now pressed against the door, whispering their answers.

"Ten more for me?"

"Yes," Jackson answers.

"So, am I their master, too?" My heart picks up speed.

"Yes," Jackson whispers in a voice so low, so soft that if I weren't a vampire, I'd have never heard it.

Ten. Ten more demons. My own little army. I could defeat Cletus and save our territory. I would be a real master!

"I want them," I say, my heart beating wildly.

"You have to call them," he says.

Even with this new bit of excitement, I'm unable to maintain complete concentration. I'm exhausted. The sun is well above the horizon. I have to rest. And my demons must keep me safe.

"You'll explain when I awaken. For now, no more sex. Be quiet. Don't leave the room. Don't make a lot of noise. This includes the TV, radio or anything else that makes noise. Don't answer the phone. Don't let anyone in. Don't eat anything." The last sentence slurs past my lips. My head droops, and I topple forward to crack my forehead against the wall as I plummet into sleep.

CHAPTER SEVENTEEN

My neck hurts. And my left shoe is wet due to the line of drool hanging from my lip. I hate sleeping in closets.

"Master, are you awake?" Cynthia whispers.

"Yes." I push myself back, unable to lift my head. "I need a neck rub."

The closet door flies open and Cynthia jerks me out, tosses me on the bed and climbs onto my back. "Let me help you." Her fingers dig into my neck as though she's kneading dough.

"Am I lying where you… No! NO! *No!*" I bound off the bed, sending her flying. "You're killing me." I rub my own neck.

She blinks up at me like a frightened china doll. Her eyelids are at it again.

"I thought you figured out how to work the body." I roll my shoulders then stretch my neck to the side.

"When I'm relaxed, it works fine," she answers in her not-even-remotely-silky baritone voice.

"Where's Jackson?"

"Here," he answers coming from the bathroom, naked, body parts bouncing.

I turn away and end up facing Cynthia. "Maybe you could put your pants on," I say, motioning toward him. Cynthia's dressed, backwards, but dressed. "How's that shirt working for you?" The collar comes right up under her chin. She's buttoned up nice and snug down the back.

"It's not as comfortable as when you dressed me." She tugs at the chest, and I realize her bra is on backward, too.

"Where are the buttons for the jeans?"

"Here." She lifts the shirt and proudly shows me the fly. At least she's managed to put those on correctly.

Jackson sits on the floor to pull on pants.

"Honestly, I think Stefan gave you to me as a preemptive punishment for something." I spin her around and unbutton her. "Because I'm fairly certain I have yet to do anything that would warrant giving me two demons with absolutely no common sense or ability to dress themselves."

"When is she going to wake?" Jackson asks as I button his jeans for him and lace up his boots.

"Soon." The sun has barely set.

The one great thing about fledglings is they're late sleepers. It's really the only good thing. Let's face it. Ravenous, illogical, impossible to control, scared, usually angry bloodsuckers are not the most fun to be around. Also, it's worse when they aren't bound to you.

"I haven't forgotten your antics from this morning." I shoot as terrifying a gaze as I can at Cynthia and Jackson.

They freeze, looking as guilty as bank robbers when a teller points a gun at their heads.

"So about the other ten demons. How do I get them?" I also haven't forgotten about my own army. With a dozen demons I could get a lot accomplished.

"Okay, well, you see," Cynthia begins. Her head moves faster than her mouth, eyelids flapping like juiced-up butterflies. "First you have to know who they are. No, wait. You don't have to know who they are."

"It does help, though." Jackson sits on the bed.

"Right. It helps, but it's not required." Cynthia sits beside him. "It's probably way too much to expect her to call all of them now with her…" She points to the closet. "…about to awaken and Stefan after us. Don't you think?"

"Probably."

"I think we should discuss this when you have less on your plate." Cynthia bounces around on the bed until she's facing me.

My fingers curl around my phone as though they're practicing a neck throttle. I want to grab her by the throat and...

"Just tell me what I have to do." I mentally count to ten and remind myself I still need her. And I like her.

"You have to repeat some of the words from The Book backwards and focus on the other ten. Then they'll come to you." Cynthia grins. "It's really easy. Stefan used to do it all the time."

I grimace. "You know I don't have access to The Book." In fact, the damn book is locked up so secure at this point I'm not even sure Stefan could remember how to gain access.

Cynthia shrugs. "I don't know what to tell you." She flops back on the bed and smiles at Jackson. It's a very similar grin to the one that got them going this morning.

I pick her up and drop her in the chair across the room before the slurping begins.

I just need to work out a few details before we leave. I turn on my phone and log onto my website.

-Eva Prim Writes-
Twenty-one Comments
PenPro58 says...

Ok. So has anyone heard from Goldenrae? What about Eva? Do we know if Eva was able to find her?

Moongirl2nite says...

I'm not sure, but maybe we should discuss this off the blog.

Fangman333 says...

I agree.

PenPro58 says…

Very well, but we need an easier way to connect. And where is Eva?

Studmufflicker69 says…

WHERE IS GOLDENRAE? WHAT HAVE YOU DONE WITH HER? ILL FIND HER AND THEN ILL FIND YOU! EVA PRIM YOU ARE GOING TO DIE. BRING HER TO ME!

Sleepslikethedead says…

You're not getting her back. We know it's you, Cletus. We'll find every one of your fledglings and destroy them all. We're coming for you.

Studmufflicker69 says…

COME. IM WAITING. ILL TAKE YOU FOR MY OWN. YOU AND EVA WILL JOIN ME. BRING GOLDENRAE. SHE IS MINE.

Mac says…

I thought this psycho was banned. Eva, just go to your controls page. Get him out.

Margaritaman says…

Dude, do you really have that much nose hair? That's gross. I don't think Goldenrae likes it. I'm pretty sure no girl likes it.

Studmufflicker69 says…

FUCK YOU. SHE LIKES ME JUST FINE.

Mac says…

Margaritaman, don't encourage him. Eva, where are you? Get this freak out of here.

Margaritaman says…

Ouch. Dude, chill. A visit to a good salon will make you feel better. My friend Betty could wax you and trim you. Get some eye drops for the redeye. And if your breath is as bad as it sounds, you should see a doctor. Then you probably wouldn't have any trouble with the ladies. But wear a hat over those ears. The vampire vibe is a big hit with the chicks right now, especially if you're good in the bedroom. ☺

Mac says…

Jesus, Margaritaman! Stop encouraging this freak. Anyone who goes through this much trouble to look like that and scare the shit out of women isn't safe.

Moongirl2nite says…

No, Mac. Cletus is real. It's no trouble at all for him to look this way.

PenPro58 says…

Oh, no, Mac. Cletus is real. He's causing havoc in the New England Region. It's all over the news.

Studmufflicker69 says…

WHERE IS SHE? YOU BITCHES ARE GOING TO PAY! EVA—YOULL BE THE FIRST TO DIE.

Sleepslikethedead says…

Where are you? We'll come to you. I can't wait to deliver your death.

Moongirl2nite says…

Wouldn't it be best if we told the Master? Shouldn't he be in charge? Doesn't he want to know what's happening? Should I call my brothers?

Fangman333 says…

Yes Cletus. Where are you? We'd all like to know.

The Chef says…

We will dine well tonight.

Studmufflicker69 says…

IM RIGHT IN YOUR OWN BACKYARD WHERE THE HUNTING IS EASY.

Interesting. Well, at the very least everyone appears to still be heading in the right direction. In an effort to save time and ensure everyone gets the message, I use the blog, too.

Eva says…

Good evening, everyone. Those of you who are participating, we're still on track for our planned rendezvous. There's been a slight change in the status of our target, though she's still comfortable for the moment. Our objective has changed and we will need to take a more aggressive approach to managing the cargo. I will require immediate assistance upon arrival as I don't anticipate having control of the target for too much longer. Please arrive armed and well fed as you will not have the opportunity to feed once we meet.

Looking forward to seeing you. Eva

P.S.—It may be quicker for you to park two blocks over rather than circle the lot for parking. Please do not delay. Oh, and Moongirl2nite, don't call your brothers.

The last thing in the world I need is for the Soldatis to show up at The Groove.

"All right. Let's go," I say.

"I'm hungry," Cynthia says.

"Me, too," Jackson adds.

Come to think of it, so am I. "Okay, we'll get something at the fast food place around the corner."

"What kind of food? I like turkey," Cynthia says.

"It's burgers. You'll like it." I try to unfold Goldenrae without dislocating any of her of her joints.

"I want turkey."

"You're getting a burger."

Goldenrae flops out of the closet and lands on the floor.

"Turkey."

"Why is she wet?" Jackson asks.

"I don't know." I scratch my head. Her shirt is soaked down her left side. We both stare at her. Then it hits me. My lip tugs up and to the left.

"What is it? Do you know?" He touches her shirt.

I do know. But I'm not admitting I drooled on my friend all day. No way.

I shake my head. "Let's get going."

With Goldenrae secured in the trunk, I pull out of the lot and around the corner to the burger stand.

"Why can't we have turkey?" Cynthia whines.

"We're in a hurry. Stop whining. It's annoying." I pull up to the drive-thru and order two of the largest burgers they have with fries and two large sodas.

"Do you want those to be diet?" The kid's voice harps through the speaker below the menu.

"No."

"Diet? What's diet? I want diet. Yes, diet," Cynthia yells and leans across me to stick her head out the window, positioning her lips inches from the speaker. The horn blares when she leans on the steering wheel. She screams and jumps, whacking her head on the roof.

"Get off me! What is wrong with you?" I shove her back onto her side. I knew it was a bad idea letting her sit in the front. "Put on your seatbelt!"

"So, one diet, one regular?" the voice calls.

"No."

"Yes," she yells.

"Fine!" I snarl, ready to punch her in the head. "I'm pulling over to the side to get my money together. Can you bring it out to the car?"

"Sure," the kid calls back.

As I pull out of the lane and head toward a spot in the corner of the lot away from the lights and out of sight of the window, Cynthia starts with fifty questions.

"Why are you doing this? Your money's in your hand. Why are we parking so far away? I can't see inside. What if he can't find us? I'm hungry. We need to eat. I want turkey."

Honestly, I debate biting her. I've never knowingly bitten a demon, never even wanted to, but right now, at this very moment, I'm more than slightly tempted to bite her. I turn to face her, my lips curled back over my fangs, my eyes fixed to a glare.

"Master?" She presses her back against the passenger door.

"Not another word." I breathe the words, trying to keep from lunging at her.

"I'm…"

"Quiet!"

"Here's your food. That'll be $12.67," a voice mumbles from outside the car. I turn, money in hand and smile.

His cry of alarm is short-lived. I snatch the bag, toss it at Cynthia and pull the guy into the car. His feet flail for only a few seconds as I quickly calm him, gazing intently into his eyes, sending soothing words to him.

Relax. I'm not going to hurt you.

He nods.

I just need a drink, only a sip. You won't feel a thing.

"Okay." He dips his head, offering me his neck.

My fangs pierce his skin, and warm, unpure blood fills my mouth. I taste immediately what he's been smoking. This is why I don't eat fast food. It's just not good for you. And unfortunately for me, marijuana slows my reflexes. My instinct to stop drinking doesn't kick in until I've gulped five or six mouthfuls, swallowing down his tainted blood.

I pull back from him, blood dribbling down my chin. "Damn it. Why do you smoke that shit?"

"It feels good, man," he mumbles, eyes closed, lost in a haze of marijuana and vampire seduction.

I stare down at him, trying to figure out what to do next. His neck has a slight bruise, okay not so slight. I'm usually much neater and rarely leave any evidence. But like I said, pot affects me, too. Why? I don't know. It doesn't seem to have much effect on other vampires, just me.

Same with wine. I love a good Chianti. But I'm forbidden from drinking wine without Stefan. It seems to have a powerful impact only he's able to tolerate. Beer, not so much of an issue. And I do love a good beer.

Pot, a definite effect. I'm already feeling a bit sloppy. I smack my lips and sigh.

"You oghafs…kay?" Jackson asks with a mouthful of something.

I close my eyes and nod. "Yeah." I can feel myself grinning. My cheeks feel tight as though they've been grinning for days. My lips are numb. I lick them and taste the heady flavor of marijuana and blood.

"You don't smell like a smoker." I pat his cheek. "You smell like a fry daddy." I giggle.

He laughs. "You're funny." His head lolls backward and presses on the horn. We all jump, and he and I laugh hysterically.

"Uh-oh." Cynthia stops eating. "This isn't good."

"No. Not good at all," Jackson says as he eats the burger wrapper with the last bite of his super-deluxe-jumbo-three-quarter-pounder-triple-cheese-bacon-onion-lettuce-tomato-pickle-big-boy burger.

I snort. The kid hoots. My head drops back and tears run from my eyes. We both gasp between peels of laughter.

Cynthia has French fries sticking out of her gaping mouth. "I've never seen a vampire stoned."

I lean over and rest my head on the kid, howling uncontrollably. "She has French fry fangs."

He curls up into the car laughing so hard I lose my grip on him and he slides onto the floor.

I fall over sideways, laughing, my head resting on Cynthia's lap.

"Well, what do we do with her now?" Cynthia slurps down the remainder of her diet soda, making that funny whistling-sucking sound.

The kid points at her and laughs. I scream and slide off the seat to the floor.

"I'm gonna pee my pants," he announces, holding his side and laughing.

I try to catch my breath. "N...n...not in the car," I manage before laughing again.

"Can you drive?" Cynthia asks Jackson.

"I've never done it, but how hard can it be?"

They climb out of the car, pull the kid and me off the floor and shove me into the backseat, leaving the kid in the parking lot.

"Hey, I want to come." He points toward the car.

"Yeah, we can't leave him." I climb out of the window to grab him. Stoned or not, I know I can't leave him. He might remember something and that would be very bad. I giggle.

CHAPTER EIGHTEEN

Twenty minutes later, after being screamed at by two irate demons who've shifted from a dysfunctional blonde supermodel and a Mexican gardener into monstrous beasts with scales and claws and fangs and snouts, the kid and I are still laughing hysterically, but Jackson has figured out how to work the car and Cynthia is manning the GPS as we speed down the highway toward The Groove.

"You know what? I'm hungry." The kid rubs his belly. "Let's order pizza." He pulls out his cell phone.

"Oh, shut up. You're not getting anything to eat. In fact, you're getting eaten later," Cynthia snaps as she attempts to smooth her hair back into place and ends up with a clump in each hand.

Jackson grunts as his claws shift back into hands and he holds the steering wheel with a death grip.

I laugh. "I'm not eating him. He's not good for me."

The kid laughs and slips the phone into his shirt pocket.

"No, but we might need him for who's in the trunk." Cynthia nods toward the back. Or was it just an uncontrolled head-bobble? I'm not sure, but she's redirected my attention. Suddenly, I remember Goldenrae.

I sit up straight. "She can't have him." I try not to care about my food, well not care about it this much. I mean, if I cared too much, I'd never eat. But, when someone makes me laugh as much as the kid, I can't very well let him get killed. He's damn funny. Just looking at him is funny.

He's got an orangey-red Afro. He's a white guy with an Afro. That alone is funny. Plus he has about a million freckles and the greenest eyes I've ever seen. "What are you?" I ask.

"What?" he answers, rolling his head to the side to face me.

"You have an Afro. Are you black?"

"Do I look black?"

"No. You look like you might be Irish, but you have an orange Afro. How big is it, like six inches off your head?" I press my hand to his hair and let it spring back.

"Cool, huh?" He grins.

I like him. But he is one of the ugliest guys I've ever seen. Though, I think I'll keep that fact to myself.

"Never mind about him," Cynthia orders. It sounds like an order, and I don't like it.

"Don't tell me what to do," I say, slouching on the seat, arms folded over my chest.

"Yeah," The kid adds, nodding at her.

I giggle.

"Jackson, do something," Cynthia says.

"Chryssie, exactly how are we getting our cargo into The Groove without Vinnie noticing you have an unawakened fledgling, and everyone finding out you're Eva Prim?"

What happens next snaps me out of my lethargy and fires me full-throttle into complete unfiltered awareness.

"Oh, my God! You're Eva Prim? I'm Margaritaman, baby! Woo-hoo. EVA!!" The kid sits straight up, pumping his arms in the air, hooting. "Let's check the blog." He reaches for his phone.

I start to laugh, but stop abruptly when a growl rumbles from the trunk. If I hadn't been the one to put our cargo in there, I'd think we had a trapped grizzly bear behind us.

Everyone, including Jackson turns to look at the trunk.

"Uh-oh," Cynthia says.

"What is that?" Margaritaman asks.

"Goldenrae," I answer as the car swerves onto the median. "Jackson! The road!"

He jerks the wheel and sends the car spinning across the highway. Everyone screams, Jackson, Cynthia, Margaritaman and me. From the trunk, we hear Goldenrae bouncing around. "Get me out of here," she hollers.

I lean into the front seat and grab the wheel to stop the spinning. "The brake, gently, apply the brake. Slow us down."

Jackson complies and we land back in the high-speed lane without so much as a scratch on the car. However, we have attracted the attention of Rhode Island's finest.

Lights flash behind us.

"What do we do?" Jackson asks.

"Get me out of here!" Goldenrae bangs on the trunk.

"Be quiet," Cynthia yells.

The state trooper tailing us orders, "Pull over."

"Shit," Margaritaman says.

Fingernails shred through the lining of the trunk.

"Hey! Knock it off in there," I yell. "Don't you do that!" I bang my hand on the backseat.

Goldenrae doesn't listen. More shredding ensues and soon fingers jab through my seats.

"PULL OVER!" The officer's outrage is quite easily detected in his bellowing command.

"Knock it the fuck off!" I yell at Goldenrae and pinch the fingers jabbing through the seat. She growls and her fingers vanish back into the trunk.

A second set of lights joins the first.

"Pull over, Jackson." I turn around, debating whether I should climb into the front seat and take over.

"What are we going to do? I don't have a license," Jackson says, literally making a right-hand turn on the highway to park the car perpendicular in the breakdown lane.

"Somehow, I think that's the least of our worries," Margaritaman says before a hand from the trunk shoots through the seat and grabs him by the hip, jerking him back against the leather. His high-pitched scream interrupts the orders being barked by the officer outside the car.

"I'm only going to say this one more time. Put your hands in the air where we can see them."

"Get her off me!" Margaritaman pounds his fists on her hand while I work as fast as I can to loosen her grip.

More shredding comes from the trunk.

"Are you biting your way through the damn trunk? Stop it!" I hit the seat where I think her face is.

It doesn't deter her. She presses harder, and I feel her teeth moving against the leather.

"HANDS IN THE AIR!"

Another set of lights arrives.

Damn it all!

"Put your hands up," I say and jerk Goldenrae's arms into the air.

"Exactly how are we going to explain this?" Cynthia asks, waving her hands above her head.

"Jackson, you distract the officer on your side. Cynthia, you take the one on our side. I'll try to keep Goldenrae under control. Margaritaman, you're going to need to drive the car away, when the opportunity arises."

"But there are at least…" Margaritaman glances toward the right. "… four police cars. That's a minimum of four officers. More likely eight. Distracting only two will not make it possible for us to escape. I should have stayed at work."

"I told you," Cynthia says.

"Shut up, Cynthia." I tighten my grip, trying to keep control of Goldenrae's flailing hand.

"Oh, my God. What's that?" Margaritaman says, staring at Goldenrae's hand, which is now morphing into a claw. "Why is that happening?"

From inside my jacket pocket my musical ringtone plays and the sound of Blue Swede chanting about being hooked on a feeling fills the car.

"Really?" Now? Now he decides to call.

"I'll get it," Cynthia says, and before I can tell her no, she's in the backseat ripping my jacket pocket, digging around for my phone.

"Hi Stefan," she sings into the phone.

"STAY IN YOUR SEATS! HANDS IN THE AIR!" I'm pretty sure the officer is shouting into his bullhorn.

"He sounds angry," Cynthia says.

"He sure does," Jackson agrees.

"Oh, nothing. How are you?" Cynthia asks.

I sit perfectly still, not breathing, not blinking, barely conscious. Stefan and Cynthia converse as though they were discussing gardening. The fact he's an enraged demon-vampire who is also The New England Territory Master and my husband locked in the midst of a battle for control of his region while we, a band of misfit helpers, run wild through the state of Rhode Island with a fledgling vampire shifting into a not very attractive version of herself trying to escape from the trunk of my Marquis, doesn't even seem to matter. His low, calm voice hums through the phone and I hear every word he says.

Cynthia's eyelids vibrate, not flutter, vibrate like her finger is stuck in an electrical socket. Her teeth chatter just as quickly as her eyelids move. And her voice whines, "Ooooooookkkkkkaaaaaayyyyyyyyy."

That's the response to, "If you've told her more than you should, The Book will seem like paradise when I'm through with you."

"DRIVER! OPEN THE DOOR SLOWLY!"

"You have told her more than you should, or no?" His Greek accent laces each word, and anyone would swear he'd just learned to speak English.

Jackson stares into the mirror. Even he knows what the sudden arrival of Stefan's accent signals.

"Chrysanthemum." Stefan's voice floats to me as if spoken through a magical intercom. "I know you hear me."

Hear him? I practically see him. He's flooding my mind with his presence, with his anger, outrage at what I've done. What I've done? He doesn't even know the half of it. How can he possibly be this angry?

He's home. I can sense him sitting at his desk, eyes red as a box of Queen Anne Cherries, fangs descended, angry enough to allow the points to pinch his own skin, and claws, sharp as hawk's talons. I feel the rapping rhythm his nails make as he drums them against the wood. An angry habit he has. Of course, it only ever becomes apparent when he's angry with me.

"Come home." Two words. A simple command.

I'm not very good with commands or orders or directives. I'm only now learning how to give them so they stick. I've certainly never been good, and don't have any intention of becoming good, at taking them.

"I'm a little bit busy at the moment. I'll catch up with you later," I say. "Hang up, Cynthia."

"DRIVER! NOW!"

"Open the door, Jackson." I point an elbow toward the driver side door. "Cynthia, hang up."

She doesn't move. Neither does Jackson.

"I don't want to get shot," Margaritaman says.

"Who is with you, Chrysanthemum?" But he's not really asking me. I feel the change in his focus. He's asking Margaritaman, engaging him, luring the kid to him.

"Never mind. Now stop doing that. We're in a bit of situation here."

"I'm Margaritaman," the kid says, leaning toward the phone as though he might press his lips to it.

"Stop it! Stefan!" I let go of Goldenrae to grab the phone.

Goldenrae claws Cynthia, who jerks away, tossing the phone out the window as she dodges another swipe of the daggers.

"Uh-oh." Cynthia sticks her head out the window to look for the phone.

"STAY IN THE VEHICLE!"

Goldenrae's claws flail wildly, slashing in every direction, and before I can regain control of her, she swipes across Margaritaman's back.

He doubles forward. "Aarrggghh!"

"Damn it, Stefan! This is all your fault!" I yell, grabbing the claw with one hand and the waist of Cynthia's jeans with the other. "Get in this car! Are you crazy?"

"HANDS IN THE AIR! DON'T MOVE! HANDS IN THE AIR! GET DOWN ON THE GROUND! HANDS IN THE AIR! STAY IN THE VEHICLE! DON'T MOVE!"

"Oh for fuck's sake. Which is it?" I growl.

"I can almost reach it," Cynthia says and wiggles a little bit further. "Got it." She shimmies back through the window, but before she reaches the safety of the front seat, gunshots stop her.

Chapter Nineteen

"No!" Jackson howls, reaching toward Cynthia's slack body. A snout with canines protruding up, down and sideways replaces his gentle, round face. Spit drips from his jaw. He lunges over the seat and drags Cynthia back into the car.

"I'm bleeding. Oh my God. I don't want to die," Margaritaman cries. His bloody hands press against his abdomen doing very little to stem the blood flow.

Goldenrae's heavy breathing reminds me of a bull preparing for attack.

"Stay calm in there." To keep her from ripping Margaritaman to shreds I kneel on her claws.

"You're going to be okay," I tell him, but as soon as the words come out of my mouth I don't believe them. Goldenrae has clawed through his body, breaking ribs and shredding some of his innards. His belly makes a squishy sound when he clutches his wound.

My stomach turns. This a little too gross for me.

"HANDS IN THE AIR! HANDS IN THE AIR!"

"Cynthia? Cynthia?" Jackson's rough voice goes from anger to a sob so fast I'm not sure what to do. "Help her, Chryssie. Help her!"

Goldenrae growls and snarls, and her claws gouge through the leather seat.

"Oh, God! I'm too young. I shouldn't have smoked so much. Oh God." Blood pumps from Margaritaman's wounds. He lies back against the seat looking paler than an albino. "Oh, God! Why didn't I go into accounting like my mom said? Why didn't I travel more? What was I thinking?"

"HANDS IN THE AIR! WHY AREN'T THEY LISTENING? DAMN IT PEOPLE! HANDS IN THE AIR!"

My vision fades to red. My breathing quickens and tiny currents buzz through my fingertips and ears. *No. No. No. No. No. The Shift.* I'm scared.

"Chrysanthemum."

Stefan.

Cynthia never disconnected the call.

"My flower, listen to me." Stefan's voice is muffled against Cynthia's palm.

"Stefan? Help me. I don't want Cynthia to die. Or Margaritaman. And the police are getting closer and madder." My nose twitches and my ears itch. "I don't want to hurt anyone."

My voice cracks.

"Remain calm. You are capable of resolving the situation in the car." His voice is smooth with only the slightest trace of an accent. He's focused, working, unemotional.

"How?" I twist Goldenrae's arm so her nails dig into the seat.

"You must feed them both."

Such a simple idea. Just feed them. Leftover French fry, anyone?

"I can't." I shake my head.

"It's the only way."

No one but Stefan has fed from me. No one. I mean no one. The idea of anyone else latching onto me and…no one.

"Chryssie. Please?" Jackson sobs.

"Can't she just go into someone else?" I offer.

"No. As part of the deal to remain out of The Book we have to stay in these hosts," Jackson answers, holding Cynthia's barely conscious body in his arms. "Please. The host is almost…" He buries his face in her neck.

Something squeezes my heart, like a vice-grip crushing a water balloon.

"Chrysanthemum, you're wasting time. If these are your friends, you must care for them." So simple. "Your wrist."

"Oh! All right!" I bite into my right wrist and push it toward Cynthia. Jackson grabs it and smashes Cynthia's mouth to my skin. She wastes no time latching on and drinking.

"I'm not sucking on your arm," Margaritaman manages to say as I bite into my left wrist.

"Listen, I'm not happy about it either, but, uh, you're dying. That thing sitting in your lap, it's your guts." I point toward his legs.

"I don't want to drink vampire blood."

"And I don't want to be a vampire keg, but it appears no one's getting what they want right now. So drink." I shove my wrist at his mouth and he dodges me. "You're not seriously being difficult on your deathbed, are you?" I try again and he slides off the seat. "Well now you're fucked. How are you getting off the floor?"

"DRIVER! OPEN THE DOOR!" the cop with the bullhorn hollers.

Cynthia's eyes open. Her lips suction to my skin like a high-powered vacuum, and she slurps.

"Let go," I order. But she and Jackson both hold onto my arm.

"She needs more," Jackson says.

"She's done." I jerk my arm away.

"Margaritaman." I lean down to pull him against me. "You—"

"Give. Him. To. Me," a possessed voice demands from the trunk. "I smell his blood. Give him to me." Goldenrae's claws frantically wave, grasping for Margaritaman.

The car bounces from the force of Goldenrae's jostling in the trunk, and I almost lose hold of Margaritaman.

Jackson kisses Cynthia. "Oh, my sweet Cynthia," he coos and she giggles.

"WHAT THE HELL IS GOING ON IN THERE?" Hidden behind shields, guns raised and brandishing a bullhorn, the cops inch closer.

"Stop trying to grab him. He's not for you." I slap Goldenrae's claws away and bite into my wrist once again before prying open Margaritaman's mouth. My other hand massages his throat to force him to swallow. A few sips and he should be good as new.

"Chrysanthemum, who else is with you?" Do you remember the edge in Stefan's voice when he wondered why I hadn't been scouring the Internet for information on Cletus? Yeah, that edge is back.

Cynthia and Jackson stop kissing long enough to look at me. She shoves the phone toward me like it's a hot potato. I shake my head.

She mouths, "Take it. It's for you."

I mouth, "No. Hang up."

"Don't even think about it," Stefan responds.

"Feed Meeeee!"

"HANDS IN THE FUCKING AIR!"

"Stefan, what about the police?" I ask, hoping he has an answer and that it will keep him busy long enough for me to figure a way out of this mess.

"Well, as you've not told me where you are, I'm forced to assume you're the ruckus on Route 95 near the split to 295. Am I correct?" He's smug. As if he's a genius.

He only has half a dozen wolves on the state police force. Like I don't know how he's figured it out.

"You know exactly where we are."

Margaritaman suddenly seems to be enjoying his drink. I mean, really enjoy his drink. He moans, and his hips wiggle, er, pump, and he has a clear and obvious erection.

"He's had enough, Chrysanthemum." That slight edge in Stefan's voice is now razor-sharp. Apparently, he doesn't actually like it when others feed from me either.

"I want some!" The demonic voice howling from the trunk echoes inside the car.

"Who else is with you, Chrysanthemum?"

Now, I could simply admit who it is and avoid having to constantly focus on blocking his mental interruptions. Giving him the information would allow him complete access to the situation and avoid me having to contend with his squad of hairy coppers. Of course, he'd find me and take her from me under the pretense of doing the right thing for her. I'd put up a pretty good fight because I know better than him about what's right for my friend, but I'd lose. I know this because, well, you probably know why I know this.

Or, I could say, "It was Cynthia. She's still thirsty."

Cynthia's eyes bulge so far she can't blink. She shakes her head with such speed I'm sure she has whiplash. Jackson's face scrunches, sinking inward so much his nose and eyes vanish. With his chunky cheeks you can only guess what body part his face now resembles.

"The demon wants more?" The question is almost incomprehensible. In fact, I think a couple words were in Greek.

"I'm sorry, Stefan. We seem to have a bad connection. I'll have to let you go." I disconnect the call and shove the phone in my pocket.

"Are you crazy?" Cynthia yells. "He'll kill me! He was very clear about not…"

Jackson squeezes her body against his and clamps a hand over her mouth. "We should get going. I think this is our chance." He points past Cynthia toward the flashing lights.

Pandemonium has broken loose on the highway. Shots fire. Shouting ensues. Wolves bound from the woods chasing the officers away from the Marquis, toward their vehicles where they come face-to-face with vampires.

"Shit. I should have known he'd send them," I growl, grabbing our captive's flailing claws and pinning them against the seat. Once again her chopping jaws press against the leather backrest making the seat appear to be alive.

Devil only knows what the inside of my trunk looks like.

"Who are they?" Jackson asks, shifting Cynthia in his arms to watch the situation unfold around us.

"Stefan's Clean-Up Crew. They'll work with the wolves to undo what we've… what's transpired here."

Dahey, Lorcan and Turlough stand amidst the chaos, waiting for the wolves to round up the panicking officers. The three brothers have been with Stefan since the 1700s, when he traveled to Ireland on vacation. I've never known for sure if Stefan changed all three or just one, and then they changed each other, but somehow they're all bound to him.

Together they have a unique ability to cleanse minds without the general confusion otherwise known as *mush brain* most humans experience when a vampire scrubs a little too hard. It's like the brothers use a delicate cleanser to rinse away all the ugly impurities, whereas a typical vampire sanitizes with a Brillo pad and Ajax. It's not pretty.

"We should leave before they square up this situation," I say. "Jackson, you and Cynthia will need to ride back here and control Goldenrae so I can drive."

"I love you, Eva," Margaritaman interjects. His eyes are half-closed, and he's licking his lips as if he's just fought off a killer attack of the munchies with a quart of Heavenly Hash ice cream. His wounds are healed, and although the bleeding has stopped, he's still a gory mess.

"Well, that's so nice of you." I smile. He's not that ugly. "Why don't you climb into the front seat before you—"

"Let me help you." He yanks Goldenrae's claws from me, pinning them against the back of the seat, covering the indentation made by her chomping jaws. "Cool it in there!" he orders. With one hand he holds her down. "We should probably get going." He sits sideways on the seat, resting his head against the window, eyes closed.

"—get hurt again..." My jaw hangs open a bit. Somehow I hadn't ever considered a fragile human being able to control an angry, starving fledgling. But why would I? When has this ever happened before?

Never, as far as I know.

"I'd have never guessed your blood was this powerful." Jackson shakes his head.

"Me neither," I agree. I've only ever seen a human drink from a vampire once before. Well, not including transformations. That whole process is something totally different. But in the case of a human just taking a drink, I've only seen it once when one of Stefan's former captains, Sharisse, fed her lover. What was his name? Phil or Bill or Will or something like that. She did it to save his life, and it worked. But I don't remember him being particularly strong afterward.

When we're in position with the two guys in the back holding Goldenrae's arms, and Cynthia finally getting her wish to ride in the front seat by swearing to remain in her seatbelt, I restart the car.

"Where you going, chicky?" A dirty, naked man standing beside my window leans in, reaching for the keys in the ignition. "He said you'd try to escape."

Wolves circle the car, snapping and growling.

Before I can even form the first word of my answer, Cynthia, with her face morphed into an exact replica of his, leans close to his head and demon whispers, "Boo!"

That's all it takes. One little word and the big, bad wolf cries. Giant tears well in his eyes and he struggles to fall away from the car. "No! No! No!" He shifts back into a wolf and bolts toward the woods, yipping and howling the entire way.

Cynthia giggles. And I do too as I pull the gearshift into drive and gun the gas pedal, scattering the remaining wolves and leaving a rubber-scented cloud in our wake.

Chapter Twenty

"Are you sure?" Margaritaman asks, shoving his fingers into his blood-crusted Afro and scratching away. In the rearview mirror I watch red flecks float in the air around his head.

"Positive," I answer, taking the exit to Downtown Providence.

"It seems a little odd four of us wouldn't be able to handle her," he says.

"Margaritaman, she's a newly awakened fledgling. She's wild and strong and hungry," I explain, still concerned he's sitting in the backseat holding her claws against the leather imprint of her snapping jaws. At some point his newly acquired vampire strength will diminish, and he'll be just as fragile as he was when I met him.

"Master! Help me!" Goldenrae howls from the trunk.

"Not to mention she's not mine and clearly wants her maker." I motion toward the back of the car. I bet if she wasn't a newly awakened fledgling, but rather a normal female, she'd have a completely different perspective on wanting Cletus.

I don't drive directly to The Groove. We can't very well march into the club looking like we do. Everyone is covered in blood and Goldenrae is shifted. She smells like the bottom of an overflowing trashcan after it's been baking all day on a beach in the mid-July sun.

I email Sleepslikethedead and ask her to bring clothes and supplies and meet us a few blocks away in Water Place Park.

Her response is very promising.

Sleepslikethedead writes...

Eva, I'll be there with the clothes and the silver chain. We should be able to get Goldenrae into The Groove without too much trouble.

That's what I like. Positive thinking. We'll see how long it lasts.

Goldenrae grunts and growls while trying to dislodge her claws from Margaritaman and Jackson. But it's a futile attempt. They readjust and pin her down. With her body trapped in the trunk, arms confined in the backseat there's no way she can possibly cause any more trouble. I step out of the car to stretch while we wait for Sleepslikethedead.

We only wait about thirty minutes before a metallic purple 1969 Javelin pulls up. Noelle Harper sits behind the wheel. Her shoulder-length, jet-black hair billows around her head as she pulls the car into a spot behind the Marquis. She's always had the coolest cars. Of course, on this topic we've never had any problem holding a conversation. On most others, well, that's a different issue all together.

"Chryssie?" she hisses. "What are you doing here?" She slams her door with a huff before walking toward me. "Don't tell me you're PenPro58." She shoves her keys into the pocket of her jean jacket.

"Guess again." I pop a piece of gum into my mouth as I slide onto the hood of the Marquis.

"Well, you can't be Fangman333." She stops short in front of me and pulls off her sunglasses, revealing a steely-blue glare. Her pretty eyes have always reminded me of forget-me-nots, though who knows why. She's about as dainty as a steel two-by-four.

"No. But you're getting warmer." I swing my feet.

"Why are you covered in blood?"

"Where are the supplies?" I look past her to the Javelin. "When'd you get the car?"

"A couple weeks back. You like the color?" She opens the passenger side and pulls out a few paper bags.

"Yeah. I love the way the metallic paint changes color from different angles." I sway from one side to the other, letting the moonlight pick up specks of silver and green.

"Cut the crap. Why are you here?" She shoves the bags of clothes at me. "Who's in the Marquis?"

Right on cue a howl echoes from the trunk.

I lift my eyebrows. "Goldenrae." Rummaging through the bags, I take first pick of the supplies. Let's face it. My demons don't care what they wear and Margaritaman is no fashion plate as demonstrated by his burger boy attire.

"Shit." She steps toward the trunk and crinkles her nose. "She's shifted."

"Yep. Cletus got to her before I did." I pull out a T-shirt reading, "Bikers ride it hard" and a man's denim button-down shirt.

I lean into the driver-side window. From the expression on Cynthia's face I'd say my timing was impeccable. Another couple seconds and I'm pretty sure she'd have climbed into the backseat to be with Jackson. "Cynthia, you'll have to get out of the car to change."

Damn horny demons. How quickly they forget what they're supposed to be doing.

"Okay," Cynthia agrees and scooches toward the door.

Placing my phone, keys and lipstick in the pockets of my jeans, I ask Noelle, "Where's the silver chain?"

"Trunk." She nods toward her car. "So who are you?" she asks.

"You're kidding? You honestly don't know?" I drop my bloody jacket into one of the empty bags and pull my ripped shirt over my head. Before my arms are fully into the clean T-shirt, Margaritaman is out of the car and standing beside me.

"Eva, baby, let me help you." His hands shoot out, and it becomes quite clear his definition of help and mine aren't exactly the same. He squeezes and cups and gropes and moans, hips thrusting like a dog humping the air. And we both end up paying for it.

My complete shock drops my guard and sends alarm signals straight to Stefan, who responds with an angry roar that any preternatural being within a hundred-mile radius hears.

Instinctively, I growl and swat at Margaritaman, sending the poor kid hurdling through the air. He lands between the bumpers of the Marquis and the Javelin, body bent in half, knees to his ears. Painful.

Noelle drops her glasses and takes a step back. "The Master." She gasps. "Oh, shit. You're E—"

Before she can finish the sentence I tackle her, pinning her to the ground, face first, my hand clamped over her mouth. "Don't you dare!"

Stefan's angry presence buzzes around us, a black cloud, prickling in the air, searching for me and the cause of my upset. Rage swirls like a tornado picking up speed, defining his very essence.

And I pray my groping friend remains silent. If Stefan finds Margaritaman now, he'll kill him.

No one moves. Even Margaritaman has the good sense to stay still. Noelle and I stop breathing. Our hearts stop beating, and we remain frozen where we landed.

The demons sit wide-eyed and motionless, watching.

Stefan's presence almost has a physical form. He's so angry I think he might materialize right here in front of us.

I focus, sharpening my senses and slamming down my defenses, shoving him back, away, forcing him to leave me. It takes all the energy I have to summon enough strength to block his intrusion. When I'm absolutely sure he's gone, I roll off Noelle and collapse beside her.

"You're Eva Prim?" she groans, barely lifting her face from the ground.

"Yeah." I push my hair back, panting.

She turns her head to face me. "It's true, what they say. He can appear outside his own body. Rumor or legend or something, that's what I thought. But it's true." She presses her face back into the ground. "He's going to kill us for this."

"Probably."

Now, I've always known he could do that thing he does, you know, have an out-of-body moment or two. Of course. I mean, I've seen him do it no less than… never mind how many times. He's never come this close to actually materializing. He sort of was just *there* before. But tonight he was really *there*.

I sniff. "Something stinks."

"You're lying in dog shit," Cynthia says, half leaning out of the car. "Can you help me with this shirt?"

"Well, he won't kill you. But he'll definitely kill me," Noelle corrects, getting to her feet and wiping dirt from the front of her T-shirt and jeans. "We gotta unload Goldenrae before Cletus finds us. Have you questioned her? Gotten any info from her?" She glances toward the trunk and Margaritaman.

"We haven't had a chance. When she woke up, we were in the middle of something else and couldn't really talk to her."

Cynthia's eyes roll. I can't tell if she's doing it on purpose or if she's lost control again.

"I'm assuming you captured her to lure Cletus here so we could kill him and please the Master." Noelle leans into the Marquis. "You okay in there?"

Jackson nods.

Noelle's assumption sounds good to me. I mean, I can totally see why she'd make the assumption, and maybe subconsciously that was my plan. I probably just hadn't realized it at the time. Maybe. Yeah. I'm sure that was it. "Yep."

This time I'm certain Cynthia is mocking me. Her head bobs and her eyes roll, but I can tell she's doing it on purpose—she appears to be controlling some of it. "Knock it off. Just get out of the car."

I stand up and rip the shit-covered T-shirt down the front.

Margaritaman wiggles and thrashes in a mad attempt to free himself.

"Don't move," I order.

Cynthia freezes.

"Not you." I pull her out of the car through the window, tug off her shirt and shove a T-shirt over her head. "Don't you own anything other than T-shirts?" I dig through the bag for another one.

"No. Exactly who are they?" Noelle points toward Cynthia and Jackson. "And what is wrong with him?" She stares at Margaritaman, who is now drooling.

I pull on another T-shirt. This one reads, "I know my way around your tools."

"This is Cynthia and that's Jackson."

"Hi," Jackson calls from the backseat. Sweat beads on his brow as he struggles to hold Goldenrae's arms.

"We're her demons." Cynthia pulls on pants.

"This is Margaritaman." I walk to the back of my car.

"From the blog? How'd you find him?" Noelle stands beside him and grabs his right arm.

I grab his left. "We sort of just stumbled onto him."

We yank him out from between the cars and prop him against the Javelin.

"He drank from Chryssie. That's why he's drooling," Cynthia says as she stands up from pulling on Stefan's shoes. "I did, too. But I'm not drooling."

"Dickies? Seriously. You own Dickies?" I say, realizing Cynthia is now wearing men's sneakers, mechanic's pants that are at least eight inches too short, and a T-shirt reading, "Honk if you want to get greasy."

"I work in an auto dealership. I'm a mechanic. What do you think, mechanics wear pearls and prom gowns to change your oil?" She sneers and turns toward Cynthia. "Why did you drink from Chryssie?"

"You don't actually work there," I remind her.

She grits her teeth. "They pay me for certain jobs. Answer the question, demon."

Cynthia doesn't flinch.

"The owner pays you? What's your salary?" My eyes narrow.

"I'm not having this argument with you again." She stomps to the trunk of her car. "Margaritaman, get over here!" She pops the trunk and instructs Margaritaman to remove the silver chain.

It's a long story. But in a nutshell, Noelle's first (and only) husband, Tom, owns Harper Cars. She neglected to tell him she was a vampire. When he figured it out, he tried to kill her. A divorce would have been a lot smarter, but he went for the stake. Long story, short—he didn't kill Noelle. Instead, she turned him into a vampire. Without permission from the Master and against Tom's will, mind you. He's been pissed for the last forty-eight years.

As his master, Noelle is forbidden from deserting him, not that she could anyway. She still loves him. She works at Harper Cars for free to try to make it up to Tom. If you ask me, I think he really loves her, too. He lets her sleep in the house they own together, and he hasn't taken any other lovers since the change. But, according to rumor, they haven't *been* together either.

You probably guessed it, so let me confirm. Noelle *is* one of my failed attempts at friendship. We tried. Well, not that hard. Just enough to irritate both of us, Stefan, Tom, Cheng, Martin, Vinnie, Liam… You get the picture.

Chapter Twenty-one

"Isn't silver bad for vampires? Exactly how are you going to get the chain around the vampire without burning her skin or your own?" Margaritaman hops from side to side like he's got ants in his pants.

"Demons," I answer. He bounces twice on his left foot and once on his right. "What's your problem?"

He drools at me and smacks his lips.

"No." I point my finger at him.

"Yeeeessss. You called," Cynthia sings, appearing at my side. "Jackson, come here." She bolts to the car.

"Cynthia! No! I wasn't…" I'm not fast enough.

She wrenches open the door, reaches in and jerks Jackson from the backseat.

"But, Cynthia…Goldenrae," he says as she plants a big wet one on his forehead.

Goldenrae bursts through the backseat, tearing the leather seat to shreds, growling and snarling the whole time. The sound of metal bending and breaking coincides with my front seats being jerked backwards into flat recliners. She exits the vehicle through the windshield sending a shower of glass spraying over the sidewalk and into the street.

"What the fuck?" I yell. "My fucking car! You idiots! How is this possible?"

Goldenrae stands on the hood of the Marquis, claws balled to fists, drool pouring from her mouth, roaring like a…well, like a baby lion. Picture a full-grown lion, you know, proper dimensions, but only miniature. She roars like a lion, but it comes out like a lion that's been shrunk. It's more like a high-pitched squeal.

"What the hell was that?" Noelle appears at my side holding a blanket. "She's awfully small."

And that she is. Not just her roar, but her entire body, aside from her giant claws, which are actually pretty impressive. She's at least a full foot shorter than when we found her. Maybe, she's four feet tall, maybe. She's just as ugly as any shifted vampire—stringy hair, red eyes, pointed ears, big nose, atrocious breath. But she's little.

"This is great. She can't be too much—" Noelle stops short. Goldenrae levitates off the car and then wings sprout from her back. Enormous wings, at least eight feet in either direction. They unfold and extend and flap, holding her hovering above the Marquis.

"Wings! She's got fucking wings!" I yell. "Get her!"

We rush her, the demons, Noelle and me. But she doesn't notice our attack. She's focused on Margaritaman.

Goldenrae flaps and flaps, blowing dirt and pebbles everywhere. "Mine!" she barks and dives downward to grab Margaritaman. It's not until she collides with the roof of The Marquis, leaving it no longer driveable or even enterable, that we're finally able to get hold of her.

A flood of emotions crashes down on me. I'm thankful she doesn't know how to use her wings, relieved she didn't get to Margaritaman before we got to her, and enraged by what's happened to my car.

"Get her off there," I shout, grabbing one wildly flapping wing as Noelle grabs the other. I taste blood. My own. I'm biting down so hard my fangs are cutting into my bottom lip.

Jackson grips one of her arms and one leg and drags her off the roof.

"Mine. Mine. Mine." She repeats the words over and over, ogling Margaritaman, who is now hiding behind the Javelin, peering around the back, shaking. "Please. Please. Please." Her claws dig into the car and she pulls the roof off as we drag her to the ground.

"Well, at least she's retained her manners," Cynthia says, lying on top of Goldenrae and pinning one massive claw below her wing.

"The chain," Noelle calls to Margaritaman.

He throws it toward us, sending ten feet of silver braid shooting into the air. Like a slinky snake with a lethal bite, the chain spirals toward us.

For a split second my terrified gaze meets Noelle's. Her pretty blue eyes no longer remind me of forget-me-nots. Instead, two giant plums sit in her eye sockets. Metal jingles overhead. Panic sets in. Noelle and I scream. Goldenrae grunts. The demons howl.

Noelle releases Goldenrae, and I do the same. Ducking beneath the silver whip, we bolt across the grass, leaving Cynthia and Jackson to wrestle with the enraged fledgling.

Smoke puffs from Goldenrae's skin wherever the chain makes contact. She whimpers and growls.

"Are you crazy?" Noelle descends on Margaritaman like a downhill speeding freight train. "When I get my hands on you…"

Margaritaman dives under the Javelin. "Sorry. Sorry. Sorry. Sorry."

Goldenrae shakes off Cynthia and Jackson and yanks the chain away from her body before running into the park. She lurches across the grass, wings unfurling and flapping furiously. Every few steps she gives a little jump as if she's willing herself off the ground.

As the demons and I race after her, Goldenrae picks up speed with each flap and hop. I dive onto her back before she's able to scale the ten-foot stone wall. The demons collide with us, and arms flail as we try to recapture her.

"Noelle!" I yell, dangling from Goldenrae's waist. Jackson and Cynthia each cling to one of her arms.

Goldenrae flaps again and lifts us a few more feet into the air. Granted we're only four or five feet off the ground, but she's gaining height.

Noelle lunges onto Goldenrae's leg, which sets her off kilter and we all tumble downward, rolling across the chain, three of us yelping each time the silver scorches our skin.

"Blankets. Get the blankets from the trunk," I call to Margaritaman.

He nods, climbs out from under the Javelin and scurries to the only part of my car that looks as though it isn't destroyed. He kicks the trunk and it pops open with a click.

Forty minutes later we've wrapped the mini-flying-fledgling in the blankets, secured her with the silver chain, dumped her in the trunk of the Javelin, reopened the trunk and gagged her so we don't have to hear her continued cries of, "Master! Master! Help me!" and climbed into the car.

"Well, that turned out okay." I check my lipstick in the mirror. The little bloodstained puncture marks below my bottom lip have healed, leaving me with my usual perfect smile.

Of course, Margaritaman has a different perspective on everything. Now he's afraid of Goldenrae (finally), and Noelle (makes sense to me), and the demons (he saw Cynthia's face when the werewolf tried to stop us). Not to mention he's asked no less than ten times if werewolves are real. Somehow the answer doesn't seem to satisfy him.

Due to this new perspective, he's sitting in the front passenger seat on my lap, back to the door, fingers wrapped tight around the handle, staring at everyone in the car.

Devil knows what he'll be like when he realizes the black cloud that appeared when he tried to touch me is Stefan, my demon-vampire-husband-master. The realization will probably kill him.

"Okay. Let's think about this." I shift Margaritaman so his boney ass is no longer drilling into my lap. "We can't very well go to The Groove without interrogating Goldenrae. We have to try to figure out why Cletus was after her and what the hell he wants with her so we can come up with a plan to keep her safe on a go-forward basis. Also, we need a strategy for hiding her from Stefan."

"Oh, yes. This is true." Cynthia turns around in the seat and yells into the trunk, "Tell us who sent you. Who sent you? Answer me, vampire! Answer me!"

Slowly, I turn to face Noelle, lips pursed, one eyebrow raised. "It's been a long couple nights for me. This is her first taste of freedom in a couple thousand years."

Noelle shakes her head and slides her sunglasses up her nose. "I'm less interested in the interrogation and more interested in how you plan to keep us from getting killed by the Master."

"They aren't going to possess me are they? I don't want to be possessed. It's bad enough I drank blood, but I don't want to be possessed." Margaritaman makes the sign of the cross.

"Okay, stop that." I pull his hand down to his lap. "They aren't going to possess you. They're trapped in those..." I turn to face Jackson. "Hey, you never told me what she meant when she said—"

"We should question the prisoner. I mean Goldenrae. Come on, Cynthia." Jackson grabs Cynthia's hand and shoves Noelle's seat forward, smashing her into the steering wheel, causing the horn to blare as he leaps from the car, pulling Cynthia behind him.

I jerk Noelle backward, dump Margaritaman onto her lap and climb out the window after my demons.

"What's going on? What are you hiding?" I block their path to the trunk. "What has he done that you're not telling me?"

"Now is not the time, master," Jackson whispers, sending a chill down my spine.

"Stop doing that. You have to know I hate when you whisper. It's so demon-y."

He pushes me aside, gently, without knocking me down.

"That was very good," I say, proud of his accomplishment and thoroughly pleased for not landing on the ground.

"Thank you. I've been thinking about this and learning to control the amount of force exerted by each limb. It's not that difficult. Though, it does take concentration." He stretches his arms in front of him and then circles them around and up overhead. "You know, humans are stronger than they realize. They just don't push the boundaries. Laziness."

"Complacency," Cynthia adds, tugging at the waistband of her Dickies.

"Yes, I've always thought that to be the case myself," I say. "Do you know I once saw a man—"

Margaritaman smashes into my back, arms wrapped tight around my waist. "Don't leave me with her again."

Noelle appears behind Jackson, grinning.

I growl. "You didn't."

"Of course not. I know better. It was just fun to play with him a bit." She cocks her head to the side and lets her fangs slide down.

"Teasing him is not very nice." I try to release Margaritaman's grip. "She won't hurt you."

Cynthia pulls him off, only to have him snap back to me like a magnet drawn to a refrigerator door.

"Just leave him. We'll be here all night at this rate," I say.

"So, did I hear you call her master, demon?" Noelle sidles between Jackson and me, her chin dipping forward, sunglasses sliding down her nose to expose narrowed eyes.

"No." Jackson fumbles with his button fly, never looking directly at Noelle.

"Yes. She's our master," Cynthia blurts. Long strands of blonde hair twine around her fingers as she clumsily attempts to remove a leaf stuck in the dirty yellow mess on her head.

"A demon master." Noelle leans against the Javelin and pushes her sunglasses back into place. "You've learned the forbidden art of demon calling?" Even with her sunglasses again covering her eyes, I can see her cold stare aimed directly at me.

"Ow." Cynthia winces. Jackson intervenes, bending her over to help dislodge the leaf and her fingers without pulling out another clump of hair. She already has two bald spots on the left side of her head.

I weigh my options. Stefan knows I'm the one who released the demons and therefore, I am their master. So, no worries on that front. However, that one word, *forbidden,* leads me to think he's probably keeping this incident a secret from the Federation and most everyone else.

Unless, Noelle is simply exaggerating.

I focus on Noelle, calling up Poker Face. "I don't know what you're talking about."

A slow grin slides across her lips, exposing her slightly crooked fangs. "Oh, I think you do."

Now, it's not really a far stretch in either direction on the demon master issue. Yes, I am master of a couple demons. We won't mention the other ten I'm hoping to pick up at some point.

But, to say I've "learned the forbidden art of demon calling" is a bit of an untruth. I didn't really learn anything. I just happened to find the right book and read it out loud.

Mind you, I didn't know what I was reading. In fact, I sort of made up the words as I went along. It was in Greek. And though Stefan has spent many hours trying to teach me the language, I really hadn't thought I'd retained any of it.

It's a difficult language.

So much easier to just speak English. If I had my druthers, demons would all speak English so I'd always know what the hell they were saying. This is assuming any of them don't speak English. What the hell do I know?

"Where did you two come from?" Noelle points her finger between Jackson and Cynthia.

"Well," Cynthia begins only to be stopped by Jackson climbing up her body, one hand still trapped in her hair, to engage her mouth in a very deep kiss.

"Cheng gave them to me," I answer. Have you ever heard demons kiss? It's noisy. They're clumsy lovers. Not even sort of, kind of, maybe a little bit sensual. Slurps happen. They moan when they kiss. Moan as if they were almost, you know. I shake my head. "They're…very close." A loud pop follows a suction sound as their lips disengage for one deep breath before slurping back into each other.

Margaritaman moans and rubs against me.

I glance back at him. "Don't you start." His grip tightens.

"What the hell's wrong with him? Knock it off! If Stefan finds us because of you, I *will* bite you." Noelle jerks Margaritaman off my back and sends him sailing over the Javelin.

"He *is* human," I remind. "Breakable." I work my hands between Jackson and Cynthia and pry them apart. "That's enough." Googly eyes. That's what they have. Kissing may actually be a drug for demons. I'll have to check into that.

Goldenrae bangs the trunk.

"What are we going to do with her?" Cynthia asks. She's bent over again with Jackson diligently working to release his fingers from her hair. If I didn't know better, I'd swear her hair was eating him, beginning with his hand. "We can't go to The Groove without getting some answers from her. We can't stay here. Eventually, someone will see us."

"She does have a point." A red Afro peaks over the side of the Javelin and two green eyes blink at us.

I don't know where to go. We certainly can't go to my house or to Stefan's office. And I don't really have another place safe enough to unleash a hungry fledgling.

"I have an idea." Noelle marches around the Javelin, sunglasses on, keys jingling in her hand. "Get in."

CHAPTER TWENTY-TWO

A dozen moths flutter around the porch light, each taking turns dipping toward the warm glow. Not a single lamp illuminates any of the fourteen front windows. I dread having to break in. But, we've come this far. No sense in giving up now.

"I'm not sure this is such a good idea." Jackson shifts the front end of the securely bundled Goldenrae under his arm. "What if we get caught?"

Margaritaman mumbles, "I don't want to die." He stands between Jackson and Cynthia, doing his best to keep an eye on both demons and the fledgling at the same time. The poor guy's head is practically swiveling.

Cynthia inches closer to Jackson, holding her end of the bundle tight against her body. "Oooh, I love this plan." She giggles, raises up onto tiptoes and shivers.

"We won't get caught." Noelle peers in the window.

"I hope you know what you're doing," I say.

This would not have been my first choice for a hideout. We might as well have gone to Stefan's office.

"Charlie can be trusted." Noelle's gaze fixes on my demons for a moment then lands on me.

In spite of what I know from my blog, I find the idea of Charlie being trustworthy hard to believe for several different reasons, the most disconcerting of which being her oldest brother Rob is so closely aligned with Stefan he's practically a seventh captain.

Noelle leans close to me, and glancing around like she's studying the shadows for spies, whispers, "Charlie is Moongirl2nite."

"Yeah. I know." I don't bother whispering. "If you know she's who she is, then why did you bring us here? Kind of puts us right in front of Stefan, don't you think?"

"How'd you know?" Noelle continues to whisper, though now she sounds worried instead of secretive. "Have you told anyone?" She steps back toward the door. "If her brothers find out…"

"I'm Eva, remember?" I let my fangs slide down. "I keep several secrets."

Noelle curls up her lip and flashes her fangs. "She can be trusted." Behind her dark shades her eyes narrow.

"We'll see. But like you said, it won't be me Stefan kills." I let my fangs recede. She flinches and her mouth drops open.

"You gonna knock? Or are we gonna stand on this porch all night?" I ask.

She bangs the brass wolf head doorknocker three times.

"I don't want to die." Margaritaman lets go of Goldenrae and twists around, taking a few shaky steps back toward the car.

He only gets an arm's length away before I jerk him back into place. "You're supposed to be helping."

"We don't really need his help." Cynthia waves her left hand above her head while using her right hand to heft Goldenrae up into the air. "See?"

The movement unbalances Jackson and he tumbles forward into Noelle, who falls against the door. Jackson lands against her and Goldenrae smashes into him. With a loud thud and several groans they fall on the floor in a heap. Margaritaman steps to the right, but Cynthia, trying to keep hold of Goldenrae, trips and knocks him onto the pile before slumping over him.

Noelle rants, actually she yells swear words at the top of her lungs. Jackson grunts. Goldenrae thrashes about like a giant caterpillar trying to break through her silver–bonded cocoon. Margaritaman mumbles, "Why didn't I stay at work? What was so bad about being a burger boy?"

"Sorry. Sorry. Sorry." Cynthia heaves Margaritaman to his feet.

Noelle crawls out from under the pile, sporting a burn mark across her cheek from the silver chain. "I hate these fucking demons." She glares at me.

"They mean well." I shake my head and point at her face. "You're oozing."

"I know that!" She dabs the edge of her T-shirt on her skin. "Thanks to her. I'd like—"

The door finally opens.

"Noelle?" Charlene Soldati holds a bowl of ice cream in one hand, a can of whipped cream tucked under the same arm. "Chryssie?" Dressed in cut-off shorts and a tight pink T-shirt, she looks like she just got home from a hayride. "What are you doing here? Wait. What are you doing together?"

"Hi Charlene." I smile, trying my damnedest to look non-threatening, unassuming, demure, and all those other personas Stefan says a vampire should master. (And I will master them. Someday. Remember, time is on my side.) Even my pleasant face, the one I call "Gentle Innocence" in spite of Vinnie describing it as "the-you're-clearly-trying-to-hide-something-from-Stefan-face," rarely keeps her from...well... from running away.

It's not my fault. She's very sensitive. It's her brothers' fault. With eight overprotective brothers you'd learn to be afraid of everything, too.

"I have a little surprise for you." Noelle tucks her shirt into her jeans and swipes her sunglasses off the porch. For what reason I don't know. The lenses were pulverized in the pig pile. "You like surprises." She pushes the barely intact frames up onto her head, pulling her hair back from her face.

"Noelle, what's going on? What's in there—" She points toward Goldenrae and sniffs deeply. "I smell shifted vampire." Her big brown eyes narrow, and just like any young werewolf, she is way too obvious with her moves. She sniffs audibly, clenches her jaw and hunches a full eight inches as though she's preparing to shift into her canine body. Her high brown ponytail bobs above her head like a squirrel's tail, sending signals out to the rest of the squirrel neighborhood.

"Don't go all wolf on us." I step over Goldenrae, hands in front of my body.

One thing about young werewolves I actually enjoy is their heightened emotions and the accompanying physical reactions. Though, as they get older or stronger they master the ability to control this stuff. But Charlene is neither old, only nineteen years (that's human, not dog), nor is she strong. The sound of her racing heart echoes right out of her open mouth. It beats so fast a hummingbird's would appear still.

"My brothers aren't home and I shouldn't have visitors." She drops the bowl and can and scurries backward, grasping for the door. "I'm not prepared for visitors. Was just going to bed. Come back tomorrow." She swings the door forward, the full force of her body behind it.

But two diving demons block it from closing.

"I want the whipped cream." The can bobbles out of Jackson's grip and rolls across the foyer. And like a streak he chases after it.

Cynthia lands face first into the bowl and doesn't bother to come up for air until she's licked it clean.

Charlene scrambles backward. "My brothers, where are my brothers? I need my brothers."

Noelle rushes to her side. "Charlie, we really need your help. It's a matter of life and death."

"You can't come in. I rescind your invitation." Charlene backs away from Noelle until she's flat against the wall. "Vampires, I rescind your invitation. Please go away, Noelle," she begs, eyes closed, face turned toward her left shoulder. "Don't make me call my brothers."

"You better stop her before she sends some wolf call out to the pack," Cynthia whispers. But of course it's not really a whisper. It's a deep-throated, slithery, breathy, heebie-jeebie order that doesn't help.

"Who is she?" Charlene points at Cynthia. "Why does she sound like that? Who're they, Noelle?" Her voice goes down, deeper. Not a good sign. She's panicking. Alert: werewolf shift right around the corner.

"I told you about whispering!" I snap at Cynthia.

"Sorry," she whispers.

"Aaah. I don't like that." Charlene runs from the room.

"It is quite upsetting," Margaritaman says. He's managed to work his way behind me away from the demons, Goldenrae and Noelle.

"Charlie, I really need your help." Noelle chases after her. "I've never asked for your help before."

I drag Goldenrae into the house and prop her against a wall. Poor Charlene. She's never quite understood she can't rescind our invitation. The whole bond with Stefan thing makes it impossible for her to stop any of his vampires, er, any vampire, really, from entering her home. I've always liked this house, too. The rooms are enormous. They'd have to be to house the Soldatis.

"Jackson, I think you polished off the whipped cream. Stop sucking on that." I tug on the can.

He grins and nods, but holds onto the canister. "Yesss."

With Margaritaman glued to my back, I follow the sounds of Noelle trying to soothe Charlene through three rooms and into the parlor.

"Charlie, calm down. There's nothing to be afraid of." Noelle kneels in the corner of the sectional couch with her butt in the air as she hangs over the back.

"Make her leave." Charlene cowers between the couch and the wall.

"If she apologized, would that help? You know she didn't mean it." Noelle glares over her shoulder at me.

"I'm not apologizing." I shake off Margaritaman and plop into a chair on the opposite side of the room. Like I said, it wasn't my fault.

Noelle's lips tighten over her teeth and she stares at me, clearly believing she can will me into apologizing. "Chryssie?"

"She hasn't changed," Charlene whimpers. "She's the same as she was during the Lamborghini Incident."

I roll my eyes.

"What was that incident?" Margaritaman asks from behind my head.

"Oh, yes. Do enlighten us." Cynthia strolls into the room. And I use "strolls" loosely. From the look of her upper body you'd expect her to go right, but she goes left, trips over a table and lands on the loveseat.

"Soft landing," I say.

"Yes. It was." She slides to the floor in a split before Jackson appears at her side to help her.

Made for each other. That's all I can think.

"My kitten. She tried to kill my kitten." Charlene's big teary brown eyes appear above the sofa.

"I did not. Your idiot brothers tried to kill it."

"Her. Her name is—"

"Kitten. I know her name." I shake my head. "Where you got such an original idea is beyond me."

That damn kitten has been the bane of my relationship with Charlene since 1998. November 12, 1998, to be exact. Charlene's sixth birthday.

Kitten was stuck in the engine of a Lamborghini in the parking lot of The Blue Moon. Her brothers were willing to simply rip the engine out, anything to make their baby sister happy, but Stefan pointed out such an extreme approach would most definitely be noticed. He called Noelle. It was absolutely the most ridiculous situation.

The thought of it makes me grind my teeth.

"You're still mad about that night," Charlene says.

"Stefan and I had to turn around halfway to Boston because of that cat." I cross my arms over my chest. We had plans for the night at a new club, Elegance. The place had just opened, and all the reviews promised a wild night of music and dancing and tasty treats. "We were meeting Roland."

Noelle rests her hand on Charlene's shoulder and grins at me like a damn fool. "If I remember correctly, you weren't just meeting Roland."

"Who's Roland?" Cynthia asks. She and Jackson have finally settled on the loveseat, cuddled up like teenagers.

"Don't start anything over there." I shoot a warning glare at them before the slurping begins.

"Roland is an old acquaintance of Stefan's." Noelle turns sideways on the couch, facing me, one leg dangling over the edge, one folded beneath her, and an arm still wrapped around Charlene. "If I remember correctly, he was bringing his lady-friend, Estelle to your meeting." She laughs. "Was that your first missed interview?"

"What's so funny about that?" Margaritaman's fingers inch up onto my shoulders, and he begins to massage my neck.

"Hey. Don't touch her!" Noelle snarls and stands up so fast I'm sure I'm the only one who realizes she's moved.

Abruptly the massage ends, and Margaritaman drops down behind the chair. "Don't let her hurt me."

"Is that necessary? You don't need to frighten him." I know exactly why she's responding this way. I've been forced to remain completely focused on the black vortex swirling with rage at the very edges of my consciousness ever since the incident in Water Place Park.

"Yes, I think it is. Margaritaman, you know what could happen." Cynthia nods, her fingers laced between Jackson's.

"They were only trying to help me. It wasn't Kitten's fault you had to turn back." Charlene must be kneeling now. Her head and shoulders appear fully above the couch.

"Exactly why did you bring a cat to The Blue Moon for dinner? I've never understood that part," I say. Seriously, who brings a cat to a four star restaurant?

"I didn't bring her. They brought her. That's where they gave me my gift." Charlene stands up, holding Kitten against her chest. She walks around the couch to sit beside Noelle, nuzzling that stupid cat the whole way.

I lean forward in my chair, elbows resting on my knees. "You mean to tell me your brothers thought they should set a cat loose in a restaurant?" The crazy cat freaked out and raced around the dining room like an over-drugged coke fiend, hissing and clawing at anyone who came near it.

The Soldatis took chase. You can imagine what the place looked like after the four brothers demolished the dining room attempting to catch the cat, who shot out the door when an hysterical patron marched out, wearing her dinner.

"They were trying to surprise me."

A loud, wet slurp ends and Cynthia breaks away from Jackson long enough to ask, "Were you surprised?"

I'm fairly certain the slurp-induced wave of nausea washing over me crashes onto the rest of the room, too. Everyone appears to have a slight green tinge.

I pull my demons apart and put Jackson in the chair I vacated, leaving Cynthia to sit with me on the loveseat.

"Their boneheaded move made Vinnie very upset. We lost business that night and for several weeks afterward. And it ruined my evening." I stare at her. I've never been able to discuss this with her. I'm sort of enjoying this opportunity to clear the air.

"If you got along better with your own siblings, you'd be able to understand how brothers and sisters try to do nice things for each other," Charlene shoots back.

"Leave my family out of this. We're discussing the fact that five werewolves and a cat created pandemonium in our restaurant and then brought it out to one of the most expensive cars in existence." I shake my head. "If your older brothers had been there, this never would have happened."

"They were working for Stefan." Charlene cuddles her happily purring cat.

She is right, of course. They were away on some assignment in Vermont. We learned from the Lamborghini Incident that the oldest four brothers could not all leave town at the same time and expect the younger four to handle anything having to do with Charlene in any logical manner. I'm completely certain the last four were made for brawn alone, not a complete brain among the bunch. Though, they're all very nice to look at.

"Well, it all worked out fine." Noelle leans over and rubs Kitten's ears. The cat purrs high and even. "Isn't that right, Kitten?"

When I think back on that night, I vividly remember Charlene's brothers standing around the car like apes trying to open a magic box. Of course, aggravated werewolves did not put Kitten at ease. Their nervous shifter energy buzzed around the parking lot, making everyone's hair stand on end. Poor little Kitten just wound herself deeper into the engine. Charlene cried on Stefan's shoulder, her banana curls draped across his chest. Nothing is more pathetic than watching grown werewolves whining and pacing around a smoking hot car while the region's master vampire, dressed in a silk shirt and leather pants, holds a sobbing little girl as she blows snot all over his collar.

About thirty seconds into the event, *I* was willing to rip the engine out of the Lamborghini to get the cat. And I do not like getting my nails dirty. Also, I have a real appreciation for cool cars.

"You did save her." Charlene smiles at Noelle. It's a pretty smile, warm and meaningful. Noelle really is her hero.

I can't understand that either.

"Did you take the engine block out?" Margaritaman asks. He's crawling from behind the chair, past Jackson and Cynthia to get to me.

"No. Of course not. No need to disturb the car. I just lay beneath it with some cream and tuna, and out she came." Kitten rolls around on the couch between Noelle and Charlene.

Cynthia nods. "So, if Noelle removed Kitten without any issue, why do you want an apology from Chryssie?"

Noelle's eyebrow shoots up. Charlene's back stiffens. Even Kitten stops moving to glare at me.

My lip hitches.

Have I ever told you I'm not proud of everything I've ever done? I still insist the Soldatis provoked me, but that doesn't mean I'm proud of my actions. Remember, we all make mistakes. It's what we take away from those lessons that really counts. I did learn from that night. A lot.

I scratch my head and lick my lips, not making eye contact with Charlene. "It wasn't entirely my fault."

Nobody moves. Everyone simply continues to stare at me. Even my demons maintain a state of complete stillness.

"Fine. I'm sorry. But it wasn't all me. They started it." I tap my foot.

Charlene blinks. Kitten snickers. Noelle glares.

"Fine!" I stand up, one hand jammed onto my hip and the index finger of my right hand pointing in the air. "But for the record. It's never happened again since that night."

It was bad, a very dark point in my life. I was wrong. I admit that. You have to remember, we all make mistakes. I was under a great deal of stress with the New York debacle (we'll discuss that another time), my sisters popping in and tormenting me for three weeks (we'll discuss them when hell freezes over), Stefan's lack of attention to me and the fact that I had once again lost an opportunity to meet a potential friend. Overloaded, that's what I was. Oh, and thirsty. I was thirsty, too. We were supposed to feed at the club. See, if we'd gone to Club Elegance none of it would have happened.

But as it was, Charlene would not stop whining and crying and blubbering. It was a high-pitched wail no normal human child should make, and I just couldn't stand it. Her moron brothers bounced around, barely able to control themselves. They were of absolutely no use.

And snot, there was lots and lots of snot. She produced an inordinate amount of mucus. You'd have snapped, too when she blew boogery goo on you. It was in my hair. Well, I lost it, simply lost it.

I yelled at her. Her brothers yelled at me. I yelled at her brothers. Stefan did not yell. He spoke very softly, causing everyone to focus on him. Everyone except me. I didn't even notice him. I was too busy hurling giant werewolves around the parking lot.

I might have bitten a couple or four. I didn't bite Charlene. But not because I didn't want to. I wanted to bite her like you can't imagine. My wild frenzy caused such a ruckus Stefan handed Charlene off to Noelle and Titus. (Another horrible detail. Titus hasn't let me forget this incident.) They took Kitten and Charlene home, but not before the six year old saw me lose control, shift, and bite her brothers, which forced them to shift in front of human on-lookers. Not that I noticed any audience as I was too busy in a hand-to-hand combat session with Stefan, who by this point had also shifted. In the melee I trashed the fucking Lamborghini, the cost of which came out of my paycheck, which was another fight all together because at the time I was between jobs.

"I certainly hope you wouldn't do that again," Charlene says. Kitten hisses. Noelle shakes her head.

In fact, everyone shakes their heads. As if this bunch has any right to judge me. Two dysfunctional demons, a pothead, a vampire mechanic whose marital status is questionable at best (remember the story of her husband), and a wimpy werewolf. The only one who really has any leg to stand on in the judgment arena is the damn cat.

"I've had enough of the psychoanalysis." I turn on my heel and march toward the foyer, calling over my shoulder, "What's your plan, Noelle? We need to question our captive."

"What captive?" Charlene asks.

I haul the growling, wiggling bundle into the living room and plop it on the loveseat beside Cynthia.

"Who's in there?" Charlene demands. "And why is he shifted?"

"Oh, not he. This is Goldenrae." Cynthia pulls the silver chains and blankets off Goldenrae's head. "We needed a place to interrogate her so we came here."

"Goldenrae? You mean…from the web…how…who…what?" Charlene bolts up from the couch. "What's happening?

CHAPTER TWENTY-THREE

Goldenrae spits out the gag. "Master! Master, help me!"

"Oh, my God. What happened to her? How did you get her? Noelle, what's going on?" Charlene scoops Kitten into her arms and backs toward the dining room.

"Mine. Mine. Mine." With jaws chomping, Goldenrae leans toward Margaritaman. He darts across the room to hide behind the chair.

"Charlie, it turns out we all have a little something else in common." Noelle frowns. "You're never going to believe this." She runs her fingers through her hair, catching her demolished sunglass frames in her hand.

"What happened to her? Why is she shifted?" Charlene covers her mouth and nose. "She smells awful."

"You get used to it." Cynthia presses her nose to the side of Goldenrae's head and inhales. "I've smelled worse."

My cheeks tighten as though I just sucked on a lemon, which I have not done in more than one hundred and seventy years. "Stop smelling her. You're making me sick."

"So it turns out..." Noelle twists the frames in her hands until she snaps them in half, then smiles at Charlene, tossing her destroyed shades onto the coffee table. "Now don't get nervous. I know how sometimes you get nervous about things, but this is nothing to be nervous about."

"Oh, we don't have all night. Quit fumbling. I'm Eva," I blurt out the news.

"You're who?" Charlene drops Kitten, and the calico races from the room as if its tail is on fire.

"I'm—"

"No you're not." Charlene paces back and forth in front of the sliding glass doors. "I like Eva." Her hands rest on top of her head like she's trying to keep it from skyrocketing off her shoulders. "I trust Eva. She's kind. And helpful. And caring. And…and…" She storms out of the room without another word.

Noelle looks at me and shrugs.

"She'll be back." Cynthia pats Goldenrae on the head.

"Master! Master!"

"Stop petting her. You're pissing her off." I walk to the doorway and peek around the corner in the direction of Charlene's footsteps. Her mumbled complaints about being duped and "should have known better" and "now what am I going to do" and "maybe she knows Mac. God I hope she doesn't get him killed" become more and more distant as she disappears into the depths of the giant house. "I did apologize. You'd think she'd at least give me some credit. And, I am all those things—kind and caring."

"And helpful. She did say helpful, and that you are," Cynthia interjects. She's wrapped her arm around Goldenrae who looks like she might have a seizure at any moment.

"Obviously. I mean, I must be, right? I *am* Eva." I tap my foot and glare at Noelle. "Coming here was your stupid idea."

"Stealing someone else's fledgling was yours," she shoots back.

"I had no choice. I couldn't let Cletus have her. How quickly everyone forgets this was not about me. I was trying to save a friend." No one ever gives me credit for the good stuff.

Charlene marches back into the room carrying a laptop computer.

"Charlene—" I step toward her, prepared to convince her I'm a worthy friend or at least make a damn good case for how she really does like me and how we can be friends because we already are on the blog.

Her palm appears in front of my eyes. "Where have you been all night? Do you have any idea what's been happening on the blog? Have you kept in contact with anyone?" She flips open the computer and clicks onto the web page. "No. You haven't or this would not be occurring." She grabs my wrist and yanks me down onto the couch beside her.

-Eva Prim Writes-

Twenty-Eight Comments

Studmufflicker69 says...

WHERE IS SHE? I WANT MY FLEDGLING.

The Chef says...

I'll help you find her. Where are you?

Studmufflicker69 says...

IN YOUR BACKYARD. STAY AWAY FROM HER.

Fangman333 says...

I tend to think you're in our front yard, Cletus. You left the back several days ago.

Studmufflicker69 says...

YOURE SMARTER THAN YOU LOOK IF YOUVE FIGURED THAT OUT. IF SHES HURT YOU WONT LIVE LONG ENOUGH TO KNOW WHAT ITS LIKE TO SERVE A NEW MASTER.

The Chef says...

We have sworn our fealty to one master and will die defending him.

Fangman333 says...

You are no match for the power of our territory.

Studmufflicker69 says...

WHAT POWER? YOU HAVENT STOPPED ME YET. IVE TAKEN MAINE. FRANCOIS IS NO MORE. THE OTHER CAPTAINS ARE LIKE HIM—WEAK. ILL RULE THIS ENTIRE TERRITORY BEFORE THE WEEK IS OUT.

The Chef says...

Maine has not fallen.

Studmufflicker69 says...

*FALLEN AND DEAD. I DID ENJOY MY STAY AT RIVERS EDGE. IT WAS
SHORT BUT ENTERTAINING AND DELICIOUS.*

Polly? River's Edge is one of my favorite places. A colonial bed and breakfast
run by a werewolf-vampire couple. Polly is the were. Christopher is her husband.
Stefan takes me there once a year. We started going some thirty years ago when
Kennebunkport began celebrating Prelude Weekend. Polly's always been so nice to
me even when Christopher told her about the incident with Sheila. I swallow hard
and continue reading.

Mac says...

*What do you mean Maine has fallen? Maine is perfectly fine. There hasn't been
any mention on the news of an attack. Eva, where the hell are you? This guy is
completely delusional.*

The Chef says...

You will pay for the damage you've done to our region.

Studmufflicker69 says...

*FOOL. YOR REGION IS MINE. I CONTROL MORE OF IT THAN YOU
KNOW. CHRIS IS MINE. POLLY IS DEAD.*

My stomach knots. I liked Polly. I was so close to having her as a real friend. We
did girl-things on the weekends when Stefan and I visited, like shop, and she taught
me how to make chocolate Madelines. How could he kill my friend? That fucker. I
snap the end off the coffee table. "Sorry." The apology is more of a growl than not.

"Keep reading and let go of that pillow." Charlene jerks the pillow from my
hand and removes the others from behind me.

Fangman333 says...

Meet us in battle. Then we shall see who is in control.

PenPro58 says…

Cletus, I just spoke to Polly, who is very much alive and she says Christopher will be fine. He's not at all in allegiance with you. She did say you made a terrible mess of her neck and chest and when they see you next, which they plan to do when the Master announces a battle, they're going to kill you. She's going to rip your face off. That was exactly what she said. I did explain she was being somewhat less than ladylike to which she espoused some amazingly unladylike terms. At that point I ended our conversation. She was a bit too upset to continue. And honestly, I was becoming rather offended.

I'd also like to comment to Mac. Eva is indisposed at the moment. I'm sure she'll be back in touch with us all very shortly.

Eva, if you're reading this, I understand the Master is not feeling his best, which never bodes well for anyone in the area. Please be careful.

Stefan's not feeling well? What's wrong with him? I stand up. Sit down. Stand back up. Take a step away from the computer then step back and sit down. Should I call? Do I text? Do I dare contact him? He's not happy with me. He's made that perfectly clear. From the black cloud visit at the park to the constant buzzing in my head, he's made his desire to know what I'm doing very, very evident. But I have to know what's going on. I text. *Are you all right?* Then I continue reading while I wait for a response.

Mac says…

Indisposed? Didn't she start all this? How is she indisposed? Where the hell is everyone else? Margaritaman, are you out there?

Studmufflicker69 says…

RIP MY FACE OFF? YOU IDIOT. THEY ARE BOUND TO ME. THEY CANT KILL ME.

PenPro58 says…

Oh my. You really aren't very bright, are you? I had thought maybe all those things I read on the daily V Mail weren't true. But there's no doubt. You just aren't very smart.

You can't bind someone just by biting them. You must know that. And just because you roar like a rabid lion and can half-shift and walk in early morning light does not make you a master. Nor does it make you unstoppable. Also, it does nothing to make vampires and werewolves want to follow you. We really only think you're acting like a fool and putting our kind in jeopardy. I think you've done more to rally the troops against you rather than gather an army to fight for you.

Studmufflicker69 says…

YOU BITCH! SHUT UP! I AM A MASTER. YOU WILL FOLLOW ME. YOU WILL OBEY ME. YOULL LOVE ME TOO.

PenPro58 says…

Now that settles it. You're a complete idiot. I will certainly not follow you. I will never love you. You are no master. And DON'T CALL ME A BITCH. Your potty mouth needs to be washed out with silver. When my husband hears about this, you are going to be sorry.

The Chef says…

PenPro58 it would be best if you stopped engaging him.

Mac says…

Come on, man. There's no need to talk to her that way.

Studmufflicker69 says…

YOULL LOVE ME. 1 WAY OR ANOTHER.

PenPro58 says…

And I will not shut up. Don't tell me to shut up. Who do you think you are? I'm the wife of the Region's Master. You can't talk to me that way.

My heart stops. All the words vanish except "I'm the wife of the Region's Master." Ho-ly. Shit.

Ding. Ding. A text arrives. *Come home. Now.*

I don't respond. Instead I slide to the floor on my hands and knees, trying desperately to hold him off. My brain literally rattles as I feel him trying to call me back to him. A black void hovers on the edges of my consciousness, ramming against the barricade I've built. To say he's angry doesn't quite describe him.

Flaming hot jabs slam against my mental wall, banging and banging as though he's smashing his entire body against me.

Little cracks begin to form. I squeeze my head and rock back and forth on my knees, focusing on fortifying the wall. I don't breathe. My heart doesn't beat. I just focus on my defenses.

Two cool hands rub my back. Two more wrap over my head. They stop me from rocking, hugging me tight, forming a protective cocoon. The banging subsides. The searing pain in my head dissipates. The black fog that had seeped into my mind gets sucked back out and my vision clears.

My demons protect me.

"I think she's going to be fine," Jackson says.

"Me too. We are a good team," Cynthia says. The sound of a slurp follows, and my stomach does a quick flip.

I open my eyes and realize I'm sprawled on the floor with two demons lying on top of me. "Don't. Don't kiss him again. Don't." I pry them apart and wiggle out from under them.

"We were just celebrating." Cynthia topples to one side.

"There's no time for celebrating." I sit up, grab my phone and text, *What the hell? There's no need to fry my brain!*

"You really should read the rest." Charlene places the computer on my lap.

"What's wrong with her?" I point to Noelle, who is slumped against the wall staring at her feet.

"He's summoned everyone. He wants us to appear at the round." Noelle barely moves her lips. "It wasn't a call to battle. It's an inquisition." Her eyes dart toward me. "Another one."

"Oh for devil's sake!" I grab my phone and text, *Why are you doing this? There's no reason for an inquisition.*

"Read the rest." Charlene shoves my head toward the computer.

"Don't push me!"

"It gets worse. Read it!" Her eyes bulge and hot pink flashes in her cheeks.

Worse? Worse than someone announcing on the Internet she's me? How?

CHAPTER TWENTY-FOUR

Studmufflicker69 says…

YOU REALLY ARE AS CRAZY AS I THOUGHT.

The Chef says…

Stop writing. Stop right now.

Fangman333 says…

Little one? What have you done?

Mastergardener says…

PenPro58, you have a lot of explaining to do.

Mac says…

What? What the hell is going on?

The High Commander says…

All communications on this blog are to cease immediately. Anyone caught continuing to use this blog will be executed without question.

"But I'm Eva, not PenPro58. Even I wouldn't have told anyone I was me. Who the hell is PenPro58?" I look from Charlene to Noelle.

"Who is The High Commander?" Margaritaman sits crouched behind the chair across the room, keeping one eye trained on Goldenrae.

"The High Commander is an egomaniac." Charlene works her ponytail, splitting the long blonde mane down the middle and pulling in either direction until the elastic slides to the top of her head.

"He's also the third highest ranking vampire in the Federation," Noelle adds. "Last year he had eight vampires chained in silver to the eastern wall of the Denver office when he found out they had been thinking about "coming out" to their neighbors, who had already figured out the truth. Then he personally scrubbed the poor family's minds." Her chin drops forward and she sighs.

"Is he going to kill us?" Charlene asks.

"Probably." Noelle slides down the wall and rests her elbows on her bent knees, head cradled in her hands.

"I don't want to die," Charlene says.

"Me neither." Margaritaman crawls out from behind the chair to sit beside Charlene. "And I don't want my mind scrubbed either."

Charlene nods and tears roll down her cheeks.

"No one's going to die. We just have to find Cletus and kill him and stay off the blog for a while." I tuck my phone into my pocket. Is that really all that hard? "Oh, and figure out who PenPro58 is and maybe kill her, too." Though I did like her.

"Master! Help me!" Goldenrae thrashes about, flips off the loveseat and attempts to inch her way across the floor to Margaritaman, who jumps up and dives behind the couch.

"Knock it off. You're not going back to him. But, you are going to help us find him." I catch her by her feet and slide her back, shoving the gag back into her mouth. Cynthia tosses her onto the loveseat. Goldenrae's eyes narrow when the demon grins and wraps an arm around her.

Noelle glares at me. "Your stupid blog is going to get us all killed."

"No one twisted your arm to participate. You chose to do that on your own. So don't go pointing fingers at me. You needed me just as much as I wanted to have a blog." I plop down beside Charlene. "We need a plan."

First, who the hell is PenPro58, who I thought liked me, but apparently is a total nut job? Second, how are we going to feed this starving fledgling so we can get her shifted back into a normal looking vampire? Third, how are we going to catch Cletus? Fourth, how am I going to explain everything to Stefan and get my answers about his demon past before the Federation steps in? Fifth, what if once I've done all these things, I don't want him? What if he doesn't want me? What if…

Cynthia burps, a long, deep, manly, disgusting sort of sound.

"What is wron—" I never finish scolding her.

What appears to be one gigantic cramp takes over Cynthia's body. She stiffens straight as a board, hands contorting so her fingers bend inhumanly, pinning Goldenrae against her chest. Her heels click together, toes pointed in opposite directions. Her head strains backward, neck elongated. I can literally see the blood moving through throbbing veins. Like spinning pinballs her eyes roll in her head and her teeth chatter.

When her eyes stop spinning, they're black as molasses and focused on me. "Chrysanthemum." It's not her voice. But it's a deep voice, a deep heavily accented voice. The next words spoken don't even register with me. They're in Greek. Just who does Stefan think he is calling me Chrysanthemum in front of everyone? And possibly more important, though the verdict is still out on this one, what the hell is he doing *in* Cynthia? "Answer me."

I look around to find I'm the only one left on this side of the furniture. Jackson and Margaritaman cower behind the couch with Noelle and Charlene, who is whimpering like a puppy. Goldenrae silently ogles Cynthia's body while Stefan seems to settle into it, stretching the neck and rolling the head from side to side.

"Are you ordering me around? Who do you think you are? I don't take orders from you." My response may seem a little strange considering he is my master, but I'm still pissed about the demon-vampire thing he's neglected to mention since 1832. "You have a lot of explaining to do, mister." I straddle her—his—*the* feet of the body that is supposed to hold Cynthia but is currently controlled by Stefan, my fists resting on my hips. "Now get out of Cynthia's body right now." I kick the left foot.

A black glare pierces into me like two laser beams. Cynthia's pretty blue eyes are gone, replaced by the blackest, angriest voids I've ever seen. "You are to come home." Greek. I understood it. I've heard that command, oh, about six million times.

"No. I'm not. I have things to do. Now get out of my demon."

"Demon?" Charlene shrieks. "You brought a demon into my house?" What sounds like a bowling ball hitting the floor echoes in the room.

"Her poor head. That had to hurt," Cynthia says, only her lips don't move and it sounds like she's behind the couch.

"There you are," Jackson says. "I was wondering where you went."

Noelle yelps.

"Well, I couldn't just float around out there forever. It was cold." Her sing-song response doesn't match her baritone voice.

"I like you better in a girl," Jackson says.

"Me too, but I couldn't very well take over Charlene. She'd probably drop dead. Then where I would be?" Cynthia's voice cracks.

"Help me! Get out. Get out!" Margaritaman cries, bouncing up from behind the couch, his arms jerking in opposite directions, Afro jiggling above a contorted face. He falls back down, feet flipping up in the air.

"Oh shit." I peek over the couch, keeping the stiff blonde host body now housing Stefan in my vision.

Jackson hugs Margaritaman, who half hugs and half shoves him. Noelle leans against the wall, holding the unconscious Charlene who already has a knot the size of a grapefruit on her forehead.

For the first time in probably two centuries I'm speechless. This is getting complicated.

Stefan roars. It's an angry deep howl.

I spin around to find Goldenrae has bitten through her gag and is latched onto the neck of the blonde body now housing Stefan. She's grunting and feasting in a very sloppy, very disturbing sort of way.

"My body!" Cynthia yells. The left side of Margaritaman's body attempts to crawl over the couch while his right side clings to the windowsill for dear life.

"No! I'm not going over there," Margaritaman says.

"Stop fighting *me*," Cynthia snaps.

"*You* stop fighting," Margaritaman says.

He slaps himself with his left hand.

"Stop hitting *me! I'm human!*" His right hand grabs his left.

I'm confused, but I know one thing. That fledgling needs to stop feeding on my demon-vampire-husband-master. Devil help me. When this is over, I'm going to kill him myself. I leap across the room and try to beat Goldenrae off Stefan. "Let go. She, he is not yours." I plug her nose but this tactic doesn't work.

"Release me, fledgling." The calm words penetrate my very core, and I know everyone else in the room felt the command, too.

And just like that, Goldenrae stops feeding and slumps down off the loveseat onto the floor, blood dribbling down her chin.

"Where did you find the fledgling?" Stefan casts a black glance at Goldenrae and she whimpers.

I attempt Poker Face. It doesn't really feel like the best time to discuss the whole fledgling issue. I mean I want to keep her so I really need to prove I'm capable of managing her before he tries to take her away. So, I do what seems like the smartest thing to do in this situation. I ignore the question. "Get out of there, Stefan." I press my hand over the pulsing gash at his throat.

"She'll die if I leave." His gaze now focuses on me. "You know what you must do."

I can't tell if he's bluffing, but before I can trick it out of him, Cynthia yells, "Don't let her die. I liked my host body. Plus, you know. Please Stefan?" She and Margaritaman are still struggling for dominance.

"What is she talking about?" I bite my wrist and offer it to Stefan, allowing his lips to seal over my skin. I can't let the body die. Cynthia needs a host and clearly Margaritaman doesn't like sharing.

Stefan blinks slowly, controlling the eyes much better than Cynthia ever could. He only drinks a little before the body relaxes and he pulls my wrist from his lips, keeping his gaze locked on mine as his tongue glides across the fang marks. He smiles, but it's not the same smile I've become accustomed to seeing on Cynthia's face. He shows a lot more teeth. "She was allowed to remain outside The Book as long as she conserved the body she was given. She and Jackson swore an oath not to possess any other bodies. If they did, they'd go back to The Book, never to be released again. His grin is so wicked, I barely recognize the face in front of me.

I yank my arm away. "You tricked her."

"She's broken more than one oath. Hasn't she?" He sits up, completely in control of Cynthia's body and focuses on Margaritaman, who continues struggling to stay behind the couch. "Margaritaman, calm. No one will hurt you." Stefan's voice, seductive, sensual, charming beyond all resistance, lingers in the room.

"Don't listen to him, Margaritaman." Cynthia's voice comes out of Margaritaman's body. "Let's go back." Margaritaman attempts to dive behind the couch, but his hands catch the edge and he ends up stuck half on top and half hanging behind.

Jackson grabs his head and tugs.

"Relax." The word hisses from Stefan, winding through the room, touching each one of us.

Margaritaman "aaahs," climbs over the couch, and sits opposite Stefan, looking as though he's lost in another marijuana trance. Jackson rises to his feet and vaults over the couch to sit beside Margaritaman, twining their hands together. Immediately following him, Noelle, carrying Charlene, walks around the opposite side and perches on the arm of the couch. Every one of them focuses on Stefan.

He's always had this power. Vox Potens. It's a skill every vampire dreams of possessing, but only the most powerful ever master. The ability to manipulate your voice so it wraps itself around your target, lulling them into a calm, willing state is more than just charming a meal into offering himself. Stefan need only visualize the person or people he wants to control and speak the words. From across a football field he can control one single person or the entire stadium.

His voice feels like soft velvet flowing over your skin, luxurious and warm. Enticing. Sensual.

At least that's what I hear. "Stefan, knock it off." I stand in front of Margaritaman. Vox Potens doesn't work on me. Not sure why, it just doesn't. I feel it, but it has no impact. We have to be quite intimate for him to be able to do anything like that to me. "You can't punish her, if you force her out of her host body. It's not fair."

"Chrysanthemum, she knows the rules." Stefan rises from the loveseat in one smooth movement. Even in a badly dressed female demon body he's sexy. His dark gaze caresses me like cool silk sliding over my bare skin. Only a thin line of white teeth appears between his lips. It's the same smile he flashes when we're alone. The one that says he's hungry for me. His fingers brush my hair from my shoulder as his other arm wraps around me, pulling me against him.

I close my eyes and lean into his embrace. "Stefan." My voice is merely a whisper. I've missed him all night. I hate running from him. I want to go home.

"Yes, my flower?" He tilts my chin up toward him and his lips hover just above mine.

I inhale, wanting to drown in his scent, the vanilla-y, woodsy-campfire-ish aroma blended with Eternity. But that's not what I smell. Instead, the odor of charred flesh assails me. I cough and open my eyes.

Cynthia's mouth nearly touches mine.

"Eeew!" I shove out of her arms. "You sneaky bastard!" We stumble apart. "Get out of her Stefan, and I mean it." Who does he think he is popping in here and taking over my demon?

His gaze never leaves mine. "Come to me, demon." I know a challenge when I see one.

Both Jackson and Margaritaman stand and step toward him.

"Oh no you don't. Get over here, demons." I wave at my demons.

They pivot and step toward me.

"Come."

Like robots they spin toward Stefan.

"Jackson, Cynthia, *I* am your master. Get your asses over here!" I order.

My demons turn toward me. This time I don't wait. I grab them both, holding onto them for dear life.

Stefan's lips don't even move, but his voice booms around us in Greek. "Come." My demons practically break my arms trying to get away. Stefan speaks in some sort of demon-tongue, a truly hideous sound. It's like a guttural Greek only in a tone so deep and dark it's completely terrifying.

Margaritaman and Jackson inch toward Stefan, shaking like leaves. Noelle stares, mouth agape. Charlene grimaces and curls further into Noelle's embrace.

I do the only thing I can think of. Using the oldest vampire territorial claiming strategy to mark them as my own, I bite Jackson and Margaritaman. Then I do something totally unthinkable. I bite everyone else (except Stefan who, at this moment, I'm tempted to divorce instead of claim for my own).

Noelle, who has a sworn bond with Stefan, Charlene, who will probably need therapy after tonight and whose brothers are definitely not going to be pleased, and Goldenrae, whose master is already so pissed off he'll probably literally feel me bite her, all snap out of their lethargy.

Noelle yells and drops Charlene who wakes up confused. "Why am I bleeding?"

Stefan's chanting grows louder, darker, more warped.

Goldenrae grunts and thrashes about, trying to bite anything she can get her mouth on.

"Noelle, set Goldenrae loose. We need her," I yell and launch myself at Stefan.

CHAPTER TWENTY-FIVE

If there was ever a time when I was grateful for my lack of ability to keep from shifting under duress, it's now. My ears and nose twitch and stretch, my jaw clenches, and I try like all hell not to breathe in the funk coming from my mouth. Noelle's borrowed T-shirt is suddenly so tight I can feel each individual fiber shredding against my hard chest muscles. My clawed feet tear through my boots leaving only my ankles covered. "Damn it!" I'm left with no choice but to stop and rip off my jeans, which for some reason have merely split down the back, and of course, my thong is wedged up my ass.

While I'm trying to get a little more comfortable for battle, Stefan morphs. I hadn't thought about him doing it, but knowing what I know, it makes sense. The conversion makes it very, very clear—he's a fucking demon-vampire. His face transforms, scales appearing where soft skin once was, and eyes, more crimson than my Lollipop Red nail polish, never lose sight of me. He hardly looks like his usual shifted self.

I should have bitten him before he shifted. He's going to be a problem now. If I hadn't been watching, I'd never recognize him. He still has long blond hair. That never happens when he's in his own body. We always lose our hair.

"How did you do that?" I kick off the last of my boot.

He growls, curling back his lips as giant canines grow up and down.

Fangs. He has them on the top *and* the bottom. I might be outmatched here.

He steps forward, and the house rattles. Did I mention he's taller? A lot taller? At least twelve feet tall.

"Chryssie, this is very, very baaaa—" Noelle's voice breaks off as she crashes through the French door out onto the patio.

Goldenrae screeches and charges after her, wings unfurling as she hops.

"Get her!" I yell and turn to follow them. But I don't get far. An invisible force grabs hold of me and squeezes, not too tightly, just enough to make me squirm to free myself.

"Leave them."

It's amazing how even when you don't think something has sunk in, it has.

"My mate, come to me."

I would never have thought I'd be able to understand demon-babble. But, here I stand, totally comprehending everything he says. It really does sound like Greek but it's darker, more demonic, I guess you'd say.

"You will come to me. *Now.*"

Here's the issue. As you'll remember, I'm not so good with orders. Yet typically, there's a part of me that wants to follow them. A very, very small part of me. I call her Ninny. Then there's the rest of me. The part that not only doesn't want to follow orders, but actually has a physical reaction to being given orders. That part makes up, oh, let's say, 99.99987654 percent of me. The other .00013 percent is all that's left for Ninny. You can see where this is going, right?

"Chrysanthemum."

"Oh for fuck's sake. Stop calling me that. You know I hate it." I squirm out of his demon grip and hurtle the couch across the room. "I hate that name! And *you* know it."

Stefan bats the couch away like he's swatting a fly, a fly that ends up pulverized and strewn across the floor. Puffs of stuffing float in the air. He steps toward me. "Come home. The safety—"

"Don't give me any crap about the safety of the region. I've got this under control. The region will be perfectly safe when I'm done. You'll see." I hunch, daring him to step closer, hoping he doesn't do it. "And this is all *your* fault anyway. If *you* had just taken *me* to Boston, I'd have been able to help capture Cletus before he took Goldenrae."

"What?"

Have you ever seen a demon-vampire confused? It's a strange sort of look. Think surprised giant gargoyle. Weird. Not even remotely attractive. Even less so than your average confused shifted vampire, which you can bet, I've also seen.

"Yes, Stefan. It's your fault." I point a curved claw at him. "Again. You never let me do any of the fun stuff." All right, so that might not be entirely true, the part about not doing any of the fun stuff. I do a lot of fun stuff, just none of the battle stuff, which I am quite good at. "If you'd taken me, I could have caught Cletus and saved my friend. But no, you left me home in charge of Command Central: Operation Cletus. Do you realize you left me in charge of CCOC? AKA cock. I'll never hear the end of it when Titus realizes I'm in charge of cock. Just pisses me off." I know better than to rest clawed hands on my hips. Even though we heal quickly, injuries still hurt.

"You have revealed the existence of vampires on the Internet and you think capturing Cletus will make this better?" He roars. Literally. Head back, mouth wide, cheeks vibrating. The remaining stringy hair on my head blows back. In fact, everything left in the room slides back a few feet. My toenails leave scratch marks along the hardwood floor as I try to hold on.

"I most certainly did not!" I stumble back a few steps and bang into a wall. His accusation hurts worse than silver on bare vampire skin. "How can you think so little of me? You know I'd never—"

"The Federation is now involved. You will most certainly be punished." Stefan's voice drops to a demon whisper, and my skin crawls.

I turn around, clenching my teeth, "There is no need—"

"Get her! Margaritaman! Oh no!" Charlene yells and darts past the glass door.

The sound of a metal chair clanging on the concrete patio reverberates off the walls.

"Jackson! Help me." Cynthia cries.

"*Me.* Help *me.* And get out! *Get out.*" Margaritaman continues struggling with Cynthia over who's in charge of the limbs and they end up zigzagging across the pool cover with Goldenrae bouncing along behind them.

"Goldenrae!" Jackson trips at the edge of the pool and falls onto the cover, sending Margaritaman shooting onto the concrete. "Come back here, vampire. Leave her alone."

Goldenrae's claws rip through the cover and she sinks into the water, growling. Jackson scrambles off the sinking cover and races around the pool to catch Margaritaman.

"Get her out of there." I race toward the door. "Noelle, what are you doing?"

"I can't swim," she answers, as she drags Margaritaman to his feet. Half of him clings to her while the other half twists around, flailing at a deck chair.

"Me neither." Charlene backs away from the pool to hide in the shadow of a giant oak tree.

Stefan lunges forward. "You're coming home. Leave them!"

I leap through the only intact French door and feel glass tear through my right bicep. "Ooooww. I can't leave them." There's no time to focus on healing the cut. Instead I dive straight into the water, my sights on Goldenrae.

Vampires who don't make an attempt to swim, sink. We don't breathe, remember? So, no air in the lungs means no floating. The fledgling stands on the bottom of the deep end, eyes wide in complete bewilderment. I really do need to feed her. If she wasn't this hungry she'd have the good sense to get the hell out of the pool. And run like mad. Her wings flap, creating waves, making it damn difficult to get to her. She hops, a slow motion exercise as the waves she's creating rock her back and forth. Then a high-pitched squeal comes out of her, piercing my ears. If I wasn't looking at her, I'd swear a dolphin was swimming in the pool.

Her nose twitches as though she's scenting the water. Then her tongue sticks out and she smacks her lips. Suddenly she moves her arms like she's doing the breast stroke. Her stumpy legs kick out behind her, frog fashion, and her wings flap like propellers.

The next thing I know, she's coming at me like a submarine. Jaws snapping, tongue wagging, gaze locked on…my arm.

Oh shit.

Fledglings will eat anything or anyone. They don't have the wherewithal to know better.

"You don't drink from every vampire!" I howl as my head breaks the water with her jaws locked onto the ripped flesh of my bicep. "Only if it's offered! And it's not!" I pull on her hair and smack her on the nose. "Bad fledgling. Let go! Damn it. Get off." My feet wedge into her abdomen and I try pushing her off, but she won't budge. She sucks and slurps and all I can do is climb out of the pool with her clinging to me, wings hanging down behind her, ears pricked up, eyes at half-mast. Another of my so-called-friends in a blood-induced haze.

"Chrysanthemum." The low hum of my name vibrates up my spine and through my limbs, making my eyeballs jiggle. Goldenrae's bite tightens on my arm like an electric jolt hit her. The next few words are vaguely familiar. Demon-babble.

"Hartoemine, comtoome. Bounbiblou."

I glare at him. "What are you doing?"

He raises his arms to the sky, tilts his head back and prattles on.

"Hartoemine, jointoome. Bounbiblou."

The wind picks up, whipping around us as if a tornado was blowing in.

"Chryssie. You have to stop him. He's going to take us." Jackson pulls on Goldenrae, fingers sliding under her bottom jaw and breaking the suction. He dislodges me from her grip and secures her in a headlock, stepping on both wings.

"Not us. He wants her." Cynthia's voice is higher than usual and squealing out of Margaritaman who is now clinging to Noelle as though she's the last life preserver on the Titanic, the last shifted-vampire-life preserver wearing only a bra and panties. It's not a pretty sight. "He said Hartoemine. That's her." Margaritaman points at me. "He's going to put her in The Book."

"What? Me? How can he put me in The Book? *Why* would he put me in The Book?" I lean around Jackson and Goldenrae to find Stefan bent backward, nearly in half, hands motioning toward the sky as if to summon the clouds down onto him. "What are you doing? Stop it. Whatever you're trying to do, just stop." I march toward him.

"No! You have to counter him." Jackson manages to grab my arm while still holding Goldenrae in a headlock. "Use a blocking incantation. It's the only way to stop him. Then you can use the deflection chant to send him out of Cynthia's body."

I stop walking, but never look away from Stefan. "Okay. Little bit of a problem here. I don't know any incantations or chants or spells or anything else that would possibly render Stefan weakened or useless or whatever." I wave toward my demon-vampire-husband-master who continues chanting and waving, his voice deepening to a barely comprehensible tone.

"Hartoemine. Sworntoome. Bounbiblou."

Clouds swirl about us. Lightning streaks across the sky. Thunder claps overhead.

"You must remember something you said to get us out of The Book," Cynthia pleads. It's crazy but I'd swear Margaritaman's green eyes have darkened to the same ocean blue of Cynthia's. "Anything. Even one or two words?" Margaritaman hangs on Noelle like he's getting a piggyback ride.

I bite my lip. "Oh. Oh. I remember a couple words. Well, I think they're words." And I only remember them because it seemed so peculiar to hear them in one sentence.

"Well?" Jackson coaxes.

"All right." I face Stefan, arms raised, index, pinky and thumb fingers pointing at him, while my middle and ring fingers are bent toward my palms. It's the same gesture I'd seen in the diagram in The Book. "Shoe sing. Dong hole. Toe jam. Hairy poop. Fire game. Take a leak. Fee fie foe fum." I giggle. "I added that last part for fun. I mean, hairy poop? Take a leak?" I can't stop myself from laughing. Poop jokes still make me laugh. "Oh, oh, one other thing. Spring to fall. Return the call. Or something like that." I jab my fingers in Stefan's direction one more time for good measure.

"Close enough." Jackson tosses Goldenrae over his shoulder. "Come on, Charlene." He picks her up by her waistband and shoves her in front of him. "Chryssie. Run!"

I can't. I'm frozen staring at my husband. His onyx black eyes replace the red slits, and deep within them I see pain, a torment I've never seen before. "What have you done?" His voice is barely a whisper. And then he collapses.

"Stefan?" I rush toward him. "Stefan? No!" Did I just kill my husband? Did I send him to The Book? What the hell did I do?

Chapter Twenty-six

Lifeless. The body slumps on the concrete, a tangled mess of yellow hair covering the face, arms bent beneath it and legs crumpled to the side. Only the smell of charred flesh lingers. No vibe of Stefan. No pulse of power. Nothing but a faint heart beating in the body of a tall blonde beauty barely clinging to life.

"Stefan. Stefan? I'm so sorry." As fast as I've ever moved I roll the body over and pull him into my arms. My shaking hands fumble and I forget to bite my wrist before prying open the lips. "Damn it!" My fangs pierce my wrist, and I press the open wound to his mouth. "Drink, Stefan. It will help."

"He's gone." Jackson squeezes my shoulder and kneels beside me. "That won't bring him back."

Tears flood my eyes. My husband. Gone. What have I done this time? "The heart still beats."

"Yes. But not for Stefan." Jackson rubs my shoulder.

A cold head leans against my back, nuzzling me and then giant trembling wings wrap around me and the host body and Jackson.

I sniff. "What is she doing?"

"I believe she feels your sadness, master. I feel it, too."

Goldenrae heaves a loud, wailing cry. Her claws dig into my skin as she squeezes me from behind and wipes her face on my wet back.

In spite of the fact she's just cocooned us into a death-breath cell, her sobbing tugs at my already fragile heartstrings and I weep. Really, it could be defined as blubbering. I bawl my eyes out along with the confused, starving fledgling. Jackson wails and snorts.

"Why are you crying? I didn't think you liked him," I ask, still trying to get the host to drink, not wanting to believe Stefan is gone.

"I always liked him," he manages to say between hiccups. "I'm just afraid of him." He sounds like the Tin Man, and I feel like I should warn him about crying too much and rusting himself.

"Well, nothing to be afraid of now. He's gone." I snivel and whimper. My husband. Gone. Who will love me?

The body suddenly latches onto my wrist and sucks like a Shop-Vac. Its hands reach up, clinging to my arm, eyes snap open, wild and ravaged. Its teeth dig into my skin and it moans, groans and grumbles. "Mmhhbbbfff." Its knees bend, feet pushing off the pavement to wiggle further into my embrace. "Mmmiiimmmbbbaakkkmmm."

"What? What did he say?" I lean my ear closer to my wrist, hugging him tight against my chest.

Goldenrae growls. Her claws reach for the host.

"Oh, oh. She's back. She's back. It's Cynthia. She's back in the body." Jackson catches Goldenrae's claws. "No. Don't touch."

The fledgling snaps at him, and he glares, face morphing to match hers. "Don't touch."

Goldenrae flinches and brings her claws to her chest.

"What do you mean Cynthia's back? Not Stefan? I thought Cynthia was with Margaritaman." I turn the host body so I can see its face. The eyes aren't ebony like Stefan's, but they're not blue like Cynthia's either. There's an amber glow within them. Something's not right. "Let go of my arm." A wrestling match ensues with Cynthia clinging to me while Jackson holds my wrist against her mouth. Goldenrae tries to pry my arm away from both demons, though it's clear from her chomping mouth and repeated "Mine. Mine. Mine," she's not trying to help me.

"Let go of my arm. Bad fledgling." I try to keep my balance while smacking Goldenrae's nose.

Her wings unfold and we end up rolling around on the ground arguing over my damn blood.

"She needs more. The body needs to be strong." Jackson presses my arm to Cynthia's mouth so the teeth embed in my flesh.

"Ooowww!" I yank on my arm, shoving my free hand against Cynthia's forehead.

"Mmmmluuuvvvmmmmiiittt," Cynthia mumbles, her legs encircling Jackson.

Goldenrae howls, "Mine. Mine. Mine." And her claws cling to Jackson and me, pinning us against Cynthia.

"Get off me. All of you." I land on top of all three of them, Goldenrae on the bottom, wings crushed below her, Cynthia lying face down on top of her, mouth still suctioned to my arm, and Jackson lying beneath me, securing my arm against Cynthia's lips.

Hushed whispering catches my attention, and I glance to my right. Noelle, Charlene and Margaritaman sit on a lounge chair together. They look like they've just seen demons and vampires wrestling. Noelle and Charlene shake their heads. Margaritaman's mouth hangs open.

"Jackson, that's not me." Cynthia's voice comes out of Margaritaman.

I look down. When the demon sucking on my arm grins, blood runs down her cheeks.

"What? Who is it? Who's in there?" Jackson demands.

"Stefan?" I roll to the side and jerk Jackson out of the way. "Stefan, is that you?"

"Mine. Mine. Mine. Mine." Goldenrae clings to me.

"Knock it off." I slap at her hands.

"It's not Stefan," Cynthia says. Margaritaman kneels at our heads. "I don't want to share with him. You know what he's like." She's clearly speaking to Jackson, who rolls his eyes and kneels beside her.

"I know. But you have to. You heard Stefan. He'll send you back." Jackson pats Margaritaman's hand.

"You should share with him. I'm sure it's not that bad. You don't want to go back, do you? How much closer should I get? Do you think you can make the leap now?" Margaritaman's voice is just a touch hysterical. His Afro brushes the top of Cynthia's head as though he's trying to dump his brain into her forehead.

"Ooooohhhhh nooooooooo," she wails.

And with that Margaritaman kisses Cynthia. A full-on, open mouth, tongues-involved kiss.

Even Goldenrae shudders as we watch. Something comes up my throat and hovers at the top before I'm able to swallow it back down. Charlene vomits.

"Jackson, make them stop." I turn away.

Jackson pries Margaritaman's face off Cynthia's, jerks her to her feet and shakes her. "Cynthia, I'm sorry, but this is for your own good. If you ever do that again, I'll…" The rest of the threat turns into demon babble and leaves Cynthia's head bobbling worse than ever. Big tears pool in her eyes as they flicker from amber to blue. I don't realize Jackson's speaking English again until I hear, "And as soon as we get to the city she's picking a host for you. Now bow to your master, pig."

Cynthia drops to her knees. And as if I wasn't confused enough by the body hopping, it just gets worse. A higher-pitched-than-Cynthia-could-ever-be-capable-of voice comes out of her. "Madame, s'il vous plait, I'm sorry. Merci for releasing me from The dreaded Book. I am forever grateful and forever your eager and willing servant, you tasty master, you." A sinister grin appears on her face and Jackson whacks the back of Cynthia's head. She snarls at him.

"Master, this is Pierre." Jackson massages Cynthia's head and she smiles a Cynthia smile. "One down. Nine more to go," he whispers.

"Let me understand this. Cynthia is now sharing her body with another demon. Pierre?" I could use a drink. I'm tempted to bite Margaritaman. I recall feeling very good after feeding from him. "Where the hell is Stefan?"

"Oh." Pierre-Cynthia looks up at me. "The demon-vam-peer-ay is not here. It is only me." He sweeps his hands in front of himself in a wide circle. "And me." A much deeper, less confidant voice adds. "Oui. And her." The nose snickers.

"But where is Stefan?" I watch the eye color float between amber and blue, and I'm pretty sure the demons inside the body are fighting for control.

"The vam-peer-ay has gone back to his own body. I never understood why he would hop around when he has one of his own that does not decompose. He was always a strange demon. No? Oui, c'est vrai." Pierre rises to his feet in a much more graceful movement than Cynthia has ever managed. "Of course, he was never this bizarre before."

A sigh of relief escapes me and I realize I've been holding my breath. Pierre covers his nose. Stefan's still alive and not in The Book. I fall into a chair. Back to his own body.

"Before what?" I watch Pierre prance, literally prance around the pool side. He studies Noelle and Charlene, drops his hand and smiles like a shark.

"Vous. That's what." Pierre points to me. "He was never this strange before you, master." His attention stays focused on the pretty little werewolf.

Charlene growls. For once she's decided to play it tough. Of course, this might not be the most opportune time. Demons do love werewolves.

"Demon, leave her," I order, not bothering to take any chances.

"Tsk. A simple remedy to my unfortunate state." Pierre bats his amber eyes and works his hands from his breasts to his hips.

"No. Charlene and Margaritaman are both off limits."

"Margaritaman? Qui?" He turns to face Margaritaman, blond hair swinging about his face. "Lui?" He points at Margaritaman. "No! Absolument pas! No! I would not even consider such nonsense. No."

"Hey. Knock it off. There's nothing wrong with him." Other than the blood crusted clothes. The red Afro, million freckles and seaweed green eyes sort of grow on you after a while.

"I would rather keep this body." He smells the hair. "It needs to be washed, but otherwise, it will do."

"You're not keeping that one. It's Cynthia's body." Jackson snarls and his face takes on the appearance of a lizard.

Pierre grins. "You were always so cute when you were angry, mon cher."

A low humming growl erupts from Jackson. Hands morph to claws.

Charlene whimpers. "I cannot believe you brought demons to my house." She cowers behind Noelle.

"All right. Stop." I stand between Pierre and Jackson, realizing Jackson has shown outstanding self-restraint to this point and it's my turn to take control. "We have work to do. We need to get some info out of Goldenrae and go capture Cletus, get another host body for Pierre, who will behave until he has his own body. No teasing Cynthia or Jackson or Margaritaman or Charlene."

"Tres bien. But before I assist with anything, I must change. I stink. By the way, so do you." Pierre turns on his heel and heads toward the house.

"Without Stefan I can't shift back," I mumble. A point I had not considered when I was so pleased to be able to shift in the first place.

Cynthia comes running back. "I can help you, master. Remember? I can help! Let me. Let me." She tackles me, and we land on top of Goldenrae, who's been watching the entire situation unfold without trying to bite anyone.

My eyeballs vibrate like an out of control movie reel. I hear Jackson say, "Charlene, they'll need some clothes." Then everything goes black.

CHAPTER TWENTY-SEVEN

"Really?" Cynthia asks.

"Absolument. Jamais," Pierre says.

My head bounces against the floor and I open my eyes to find Cynthia's face only inches from mine.

"Hello, master. Did you sleep well?" She's wearing her "I did it" smile.

"What happened?" I sit up and find myself on the floor of a speeding van. The aching knot on the back of my head makes it very difficult for me to focus, but not impossible for me to figure out we're in Chris Soldati's work van. There's a moon roof above me, way above me and behind the metal shelving unit on the passenger side posters of half-naked women cover the walls.

"Your demons knocked you out with some black magic voodoo and shifted you back," Noelle answers from the driver's seat. The condescending tone in her voice makes it very clear she's still not enthralled with Cynthia or Jackson and probably not Pierre, either.

I glance down to find not only am I back to my feminine state, but I'm also clean and dressed. And I'm not looking too bad, though I'm not wearing a bra and I am wearing a see-through blouse. "Who dressed me?"

"Oh, I did." Cynthia tucks my shirt into the front of my jeans before adjusting the leather belt slanting at my waist. "Charlene doesn't own bras in your size," she demon whispers, and a chill shimmies down my spine.

"No whispering," I say, and in a flash Cynthia's blue eyes fade to amber.

"Tres bien. Your tits are much bigger than zee little girl's. So…no bra," Pierre announces with a flourish and pat on my left breast.

"Don't touch her." Jackson growls and shoves Pierre backward then gently rubs his hand.

Pierre frowns just before the familiar deep ocean blue color returns to his irises.

"Master, please get him his own host. Please," Cynthia begs.

"Enough." I pull my knees under me while rubbing my aching head and lean back against the bench seat running the length of the driver's side wall. It wraps around the back of the van straight across the doors. I happen to know for a fact the backseat props forward for backdoor access or converts to a double bed. Chris has been known to use this van as a love mobile. "Where are we going?"

"The Groove, so you're actually dressed just fine," Noelle answers. She's dressed in jeans and a mechanic T-shirt, one that reads, "Let me jack you up."

Charlene sits in the passenger seat, back to the door, watching us. She's dressed in khakis and a pink cardigan sweater over a button-down white top. Her wavy, brown hair is swept up into a high ponytail. She is not dressed well for the evening. In fact, she'll probably be the only person in the club who looks like she stepped out of a 1950s teeny-bopper movie.

The demons aren't much better. Jackson is still wearing Stefan's jeans, though he's changed his shirt, and it obviously belongs to one of the Soldatis. It drapes across his legs, the hemline hanging below his knees. Cynthia and Pierre have clearly been fighting over their wardrobe. They have on a black dress shirt, knotted at the waist and unbuttoned nearly to their belly button, men's dress pants, one sneaker and one cowboy boot and half their face is made up like a French hooker while the other half doesn't have a drop of makeup.

Margaritaman has on an oxford tucked into jeans that are at least five sizes too big, cinched with a jute belt and work boots, laced all the way up his calves. He looks like the Ronald McDonald of the underworld.

"Where's Goldenrae?"

"I'm here, master," a soft voice calls from the very back of the van. She's sitting in the corner hidden behind the metal shelves. Her giant blue eyes watch everyone. Correction to one of my previous statements—there will be two young girls from a 1950s teenybopper movie in attendance at a vampire bar tonight. She's wearing a pale blue sweater, polka-dotted silk shell, jeans and loafers.

Devil help us. We'll never sneak in with this crew.

"Noelle, you couldn't help them pick out clothes?" I climb onto the seat beside Goldenrae.

"We don't have a lot of time. It's already one. Maybe we can work the fashion review in around 3 A.M." Noelle glares into the mirror. "This is all your idea and you go passing out. What vampire passes out? And in a crisis no less."

"I would like to know myself." Pierre unbuttons another button. Cynthia whines. Jackson re-buttons the button. Pierre complains and pounds the bench with his right fist while the left one bangs his right leg, "Mon demon!"

"To quote you, Noelle, 'we don't have a lot of time' so I'm going to hold off on the explanation until after the fashion review." I turn to Goldenrae. "I'm so sorry I couldn't find you sooner." I reach for her hand.

"Why did you do this to me?" Her eyes bat as though she's trying to hold back tears. But she hasn't fed enough to create any.

"Well, I couldn't leave you for Cletus to have. I had to rescue you. Stefan will help get you established after we kill Cletus which you're going to have to help us do."

"Cletus? Who's Cletus? I can't kill anyone." Her fingers ring the corner of her sweater into a tight wad and she nibbles her bottom lip.

"Oh, yeah," Noelle calls from the driver's seat. She leans up and watches us in the mirror, a grin plastered across her face. "Our little friend there has no recollection of Cletus and she's bonded to you."

"Bonded to me? How?" How the hell does a fledgling bond with anyone other than her maker?

"Oh, well, that sort of thing happens when—" Cynthia turns in the seat to face me but tumbles over sideways and lands face first in Jackson's lap.

"Not now," Jackson snaps and helps her sit up.

"Mon demon!" Pierre huffs and fixes the hair on his side of the head.

Noelle leans up and peers into the mirror at the demons then looks at me. "You bit her. She bit you back. Wham-O. You got yourself the fledgling you thought you'd never have." She pulls the van into a parking space, jams the gearshift into park and turns around. "Good job, genius. I'm sure Stefan is going to love this." Her index finger wags between Goldenrae and me.

My eyebrows knit together and I bite my own lip, mimicking Goldenrae. "But…"

"Don't tell me this is actually complicated for you," Noelle says. The amusement in her steel blue eyes hurts. "How do you think she got back into her current state? She couldn't shift back herself. Instead, her master did it for her." She stretches her arms out in front of her like she's displaying a game show prize.

"Well. Yes, it is complicated. I thought, well, everyone knows fledglings bond with their makers, not someone else." I purse my lips.

"You know, you really aren't ready for your own fledgling, if you don't know how it works." She fixes the lace on her boot. "The Bond begins with the first bite and continues with the first feeding, but it's not sealed until after the fledgling awakens. The master vampire marks her fledgling and then feeds her." She grins. "Stefan is going to be so pissed."

"Well, she first fed from Stefan, not me," I say, realizing, of course, this could be a slight problem. What if she's bonded to him and me and Cletus?

"You marked her, and then she fed from you. I don't think the Stefan bite has anything to do with it," Noelle says.

Jackson's eyes bulge and he shakes his head so fast his face becomes a blur.

"Stop her!" Pierre's right hand flies to his mouth. His left hand follows, working its way between the fingers as Cynthia tries to pull the hand away.

"No, Cynthia. It's best to keep some things to yourself." Jackson flings himself onto her and they crash to the floor.

"Oh, they are so subtle," Noelle complains. "Tell us, demons. What's the situation with Stefan?"

Cynthia manages to shake off Jackson. "He can sense the fledgling, follow her every move. Possess her, if he wants. A demon-bond." She rattles the words so fast Pierre doesn't have a chance to gain any control of their mouth.

"A demon-bond," Noelle, Charlene and I echo.

"Uh-huh. Sort of like the one you have with him." Cynthia points at me and her head bobbles. Then her eyes fade to amber and she grimaces.

"Stefan's a demon!" Charlene drags in a shallow breath and gasps.

"Calm down. Breathe. Take a deep breath," Noelle coaches and shoves Charlene's head between her legs.

"Well, what the fuck did you think was happening back in your house?" I'll admit I'm losing patience.

"Stop yelling at her," Noelle says.

"Oh, come on. Even I knew he was a demon," Margaritaman says.

Noelle snarls and leans toward him, fangs descended.

I hiss and jump in front of Margaritaman, ready to meet Noelle's challenge.

"There really is no time for this macho behavior," Pierre says, appearing between us. His French accent makes all the TH's sound like Z's. "We must find and kill this Cletus and then procure a host for me. These conditions are not acceptable." His left hand slaps his face. "That was your side so it did not bother me," he says.

Jackson jerks him backward. "You be quiet. Your needs are of no concern."

I face the demons. "There are logistics that don't make sense. For example, Stefan and Goldenrae have not sealed…" and I use air quotes when I say "sealed" "…their bond. And he was in your body, Cynthia, not his own when Goldenrae bit him. So I'm not buying The Bond thing, though it is best we assume he might have some sort of weird link to her." I glance at Goldenrae. She couldn't look more worried if Van Helsing opened the door and jumped in. Her brows are pulled together, eyes wider than billiard balls, mouth agape. "You don't remember Cletus at all?"

She shakes her head. "My throat burns."

"I know." I remember the feeling from all those years ago. The thirst. You're insatiable in the beginning, only able to control the need to feed by staying closely aligned with your master. It's a pain in the ass. The older you get the easier it is to ignore, plus you learn to feed at appropriate intervals so you don't feel it. "We'll get a drink later."

"I don't want to be a vampire or a demon." Her gaze leaves my face, wanders across Cynthia-Pierre and Jackson and lands on Noelle.

"Too late for that now, honey." Noelle pulls a comb from her jacket pocket and rakes it through her black hair. "Not that it's going to matter. You're bait anyway and not long for this life." She checks her hair in the rearview mirror.

"Bait?" Goldenrae leans forward and Pierre skitters to the side. "What do you mean, bait?" In true fledgling fashion she again loses control.

"It's all right, Goldenrae. Nothing's going to happen to you." I sit beside her and rub her back, hoping I'm wearing my most sincere and gentle expression, before turning on Noelle, lips curled back. "I'll thank you not to make this situation worse."

"What did she mean, bait?" Goldenrae demands.

And here's the thing. I've never had a fledgling. I mean…I didn't even create this one so I'm not entirely sure how to keep her from shifting. Also, I'm not particularly adept at controlling my own shifting so I'm probably not the best person for this job. I hate to admit it, but Stefan might have been right about the whole fledgling issue.

"Cynthia, if you wouldn't mind keeping Goldenrae in this state, it would be very helpful." I slide out of the way so she can sit beside my panicking fledgling.

Cynthia kneels beside me and whispers, "Master, I can only help you. Not your subjects."

My skin crawls.

"Sorry," she whispers.

Goldenrae's fingers elongate, talons growing where nails had once been. She screams. "What's happening?"

"You'd better stop her. We didn't bring her another change of clothes." Noelle slides back into the driver's seat and clicks on the radio, spinning the dial until she finds some head-banging rock.

"Don't panic. Everything's going to be fine," I say. No, it's not. I know it's not. "Don't shift. Focus on happy thoughts. Happy, happy, happy thoughts. Bubble baths." Her eyes redden and sort of turn beady. "Um…the beach…" Her ears begin to wiggle. "Ah…chocolate…ah…wine…er…beer?" Her nose twitches. I'm running out of things. I don't know what she likes. "How do I stop her?"

"I don't know," Charlene squeaks. "But this doesn't look good. I'm getting out." She wrenches open the door and jumps out, slamming the door behind her.

"Me too," Margaritaman says. "She likes me way too much for me to witness this." He climbs over Jackson, steps on Cynthia's hand, and smashes into the door, unable to stay calm enough to find the handle.

"Help him!" He's right. He shouldn't stay in here. She'll eat him. I'm not sure she'll realize just a few sips would suffice, and that she doesn't need to eat him. She hunches forward, panting. Nope. I'm pretty sure she'd devour the whole of him.

Noelle leans over, opens the passenger door, and foot on his ass kicks him out before jerking the door shut. I really do need to teach this group some manners. But that will need to happen later. Another item for the Fix-It List.

I fumble around in the pockets of my jeans. "Where's my phone?" I need Stefan. He'll know what to do.

"In your fanny pack." Cynthia spins the leather belt around my waist and unzips the pack.

Let me just say this. Even in the 80s I did not own a fanny pack. I have never worn a fanny pack. No fashion conscious woman would be caught dead in a fanny pack. "Your lipstick and phone are in there. Also, some breath mints." She points toward Goldenrae and giggles as if she's just done the world a favor.

I try not to bite off my own tongue. Two deep breaths. One high-pitched snort from Goldenrae followed by a whimper and then a cry as her nails scratch her skin when her hands fly to her face to cover her mouth. I recall the need to remain calm, keep my fledgling calm, continue with my goal of getting Stefan on the phone.

I retrieve the phone and press number one on my speed dial.

Not even a full ring later Stefan answers. "Where are you?" It's not really a question. It's more of a demand.

"Hi."

Silence is never good. Yet, that's what I hear.

"So, obviously you made it back to your body. That's great to know. I was worried. I thought maybe, you know, you might have been sent somewhere or maybe something worse might have happened. But clearly you're fine." I pause, sort of hopeful his razor sharp edge will dull a tad.

"Come to me."

I feel it, The Summons, the nearly impossible-to-resist command. It begins deep in my core, spiraling and burrowing into my very being, searching for the piece of him residing somewhere in my depths, the piece of him that will have no choice but to respond, no choice but to return to him.

"Let me just ask you, how do I stop a fledgling from shifting? Is there some sort of chant or some sort of hex or something I can use?" That little part of him, the one typically existing silently inside me rises from the pit in my stomach, eager to join him.

In the middle of my chest a slow burn begins, and I feel like I've got indigestion. That probably sounds funny. A vampire with indigestion. But it happens. Well, to those of us who insist on trying new foods. You know I like to live on the edge.

I burp. "Excuse me. That was your fault. Could you just answer the question and stop with all the vampire dominance crap?"

Goldenrae's hair has thinned, leaving her head sparsely covered. Blonde curls have sprung from her rather large nostrils. She's hideous.

"Stefan, the safety of the region depends on you telling me this information." My body inches toward the van door. That son of a bitch is really turning up the heat. "I'm going to hang up if you don't just tell me. Then what will you do?"

"You must feed your fledgling." Have you ever heard someone say something that sounded as though it had been coerced from his lips, ripped out of his brain and forced into spoken word? That's what this advice sounded like.

"Is that the only way? You know how I feel about letting anyone but you drink from me." I glance at Goldenrae. Her clawed hands still cover her mouth, nose and ear hair shoot out in every direction, and her beady, red eyes bulge. On the plus side, she has shrunken. Of course, if her wings sprout, she'll rip through her clothes. "And, I never said anything about it being my fledgling."

He sighs. "You will not come to me tonight, will you?" His call for me dwindles. "You've grown too strong for your own good. You resist me."

"It's not that I don't want to see you. But I'm a little busy at the moment. I've got this fledgling situation, Cletus, the safety of the region, and some other stuff I need to sort out. I'm hoping to wrap it all up in the next couple hours and be home by sunrise." If he's not still pissed off.

"You disappoint me."

The words pierce my heart. He's never said something so hurtful, not in all the years we've been together, not through the fires, battles, deaths, scandals. Never. "Stefan."

"Tonight you have gone beyond a boundary where even I cannot protect you. You are my love. My entire heart resides with you, but you have broken the most supreme vampire law."

"No I didn't," I counter, rolling up my sleeve, cringing at the thought of Goldenrae biting me. I stick my arm in front of her and turn my face, unable to watch.

She wastes no time and latches on, teeth breaking through my skin like a ravenous boar's. I shudder and force myself not to jerk my arm away and club her over the head.

"Chrysanthemum, you announced on the Internet you were the Region Master's wife. It is clear you knew about this Eva Prim's website even before I did. You had been participating, putting our world at risk."

So, now what? Yes, I did know about Eva. Obviously. But no, I didn't out our world. In fact, it was completely anonymous and untraceable until that stupid PenPro58 announced she was me. Which she is not! Some things just can't be explained over the phone, possibly not face-to-face either.

"Wait a minute. I am not PenPro58. I don't know who that nut job is, but believe me, finding out is high on my Fix-It List. Right after killing Cletus."

"Cletus is not your responsibility. You are supposed to be—"

"I know! At the CCOC. I remember. I'm heading up cock. I'm still pissed off about the CCOC thing. And Cletus is my problem. He's threatened my master and my region. I have to kill him or he'll steal back his fledgling from me. And she's my friend now. I'm keeping her." I wrench my arm away from Goldenrae's mouth and wipe her pretty face. She's full sized again. Her eyes are still red and her nose is obscenely large. But I love her.

"Am I to understand you and the demons are the ones who stole Cletus's mate?"

"Mate? I'm…I…well…did she know she was his mate?" I stare at Goldenrae, swallow hard and realize I don't have enough troops to battle a love-crazed vampire fighting to get his mate back.

Chapter Twenty-eight

"Where are you?"

It would probably make the most sense to tell him we're only four blocks from The Groove. Then he'd come and so would Martin and Cheng and the five captains and the Soldatis. With all of them I could probably defeat Cletus. The problem is, well, you must be able to see the multitude of problems in this situation. Do I really need to rehash them? I don't think so.

"Let me call you back." I hang up. "Okay. So we don't exactly have the most powerful force here. Two vampires, a fledgling, a wimpy werewolf, one human and three demons sharing two bodies does not make for a highly skilled task force."

"Did you really just hang up on the Master?" Noelle shakes her head, then rubs her hands over her face. "How did you resist his call? How has he not destroyed you in all these years?" One eyebrow creeps upward as she studies me. "Why does he keep you around?"

"How has Tom not thrown your ass into the street?" Okay, so maybe now is not the time to pick a fight with her, but I don't think I should have to explain my marriage to a woman who forced her husband into an eternal bond because she wasn't exactly truthful about her state of being from the beginning. It makes me wonder if she did put the whammy on him when she wanted him to court her. That's the rumor. That he never really loved her but was charmed into the nuptials.

She scowls.

"Maybe you could check the website to see if anyone else will help us," Cynthia suggests. "I know PenPro58 is an oddball, but she might still be of use."

An oddball is an understatement. Would it be cruel or unfriendly to allow her to assist in the eradication of Cletus and then kill her? Her death would be for the greater good. Let me know what you think about that idea.

"What about Fangman333? Why haven't we heard from him?" Jackson asks.

"Oh, Fangman333 would be very helpful. The problem is, he would also be deadly and he's angry right now and he's got a slightly different agenda than ours."

I'm still not sure I should tell anyone who he is. I don't want him caught up in my *situation,* you know with Stefan so angry and The High Commander offering to execute everyone involved with the blog. Martin is my blog-friend. Now that I think about it, I guess I'd say he's my friend off the blog, too. He must be, right? Who else remembers your birthday and sends text messages that make you laugh and calls to inquire about how you're feeling and what you're doing?

I can't let anything happen to him.

The demons are terrible with secrets. They'd end up telling Stefan. Charlene would have no choice but to tell her brothers, if they ask. Noelle might crack, if interrogated. Margaritaman would blurt out the info without realizing he wasn't supposed to, and Goldenrae is too new to vampirism to realize she shouldn't say anything. Nope. I can't risk Martin's life on this group. Not yet.

I log onto my blog and begin reading the comments. Apparently, while I've been busy with this crew everyone else has been busy arguing. And the number of participants just keeps growing. This is exactly what I'd hoped for—more friends.

"Read them out loud. We're not mind readers." Noelle clicks off the radio. I snort because really some of us sort of are mind readers, when we need to be with the right people, that is.

-Eva Prim Writes-
Forty Comments
Studmufflicker69 says...

WHERE IS SHE? WHAT DID YOU DO TO HER? WHY CAN'T I FEEL MY GOLDENRAE?

Mac says…

Executed? What is wrong with you, man?

Shadowman says…

Okay, I've been watching this blog for the last few nights and I've finally decided to stop lurking. There's definitely something weird about this group. I think some of you think you're real vampires. I'm down with that. But mainly I'm just looking for a good time. My blood type is A positive. Let me know if you're interested.

Fangman333 says…

Where are you, Cletus? I'm happy to help you find what you seem to have lost.

The High Commander says…

Yes. Executed. Make no mistake. I will find each of you and you will meet the true death. Now cease and desist!

PenPro58 says…

I just want to say I think what I said earlier, about being the Region Master's wife may have been misinterpreted.

Mac says…

I think we should report this guy to the police. I'm fairly certain it's illegal to threaten to kill people.

The Chef says…

What's to misinterpret? It was a pretty clear statement.

Alpha 1 says…

Yeah, it was a very precise admission. No confusion here.

Fangman333 says…

I understood it.

Mastergardener says…

As did I.

Britman says…

Me too.

Greek Warrior says…

I've said it before and I'll say it again, she's a loose cannon. Qualified to be in charge? Not on her own life.

PenPro58 says…

No. I'm quite certain there is a level of confusion.

Studmufflicker69 says…

IF ANYTHING HAS HAPPENED TO HER YOULL PAY. YOU AND YOUR MASTER. THE SUN WILL SEEM LIKE YOUR FRIEND. NOW WHERE IS SHE?

Mac says…

I have to agree with everyone else here. You were pretty clear. You said, "I'm the wife of the Region's Master." There's really nothing difficult in understanding that statement. Of course, you'd have to know who the Region Master was or what he was or really if he was. Honestly, some of these conversation threads are bizarre. I liked it better when we discussed drinks and cologne.

Shadowman says…

I'm not really into the BDSM stuff, but if it doesn't go too far, I could be persuaded.

Chinchilla Lover says…

Hi ya'll. Loved the Bleeding Vlad recipe. I'm looking for something with pink grapefruit. Any suggestions?

PenPro58 says…

Well, yes. I did say I was the Region Master's wife. And it is true.

Greek Warrior says…

Bleeding? No. It's Bloody.

Fangman333 says…

Bloody.

Studmufflicker69 says…

WHAT THE FUCK IS WRONG WITH YOU ASSHOLES? IVE TOLD YOU ITS BLOODY. WHERE DO YOU LIVE CHINCHILLA? IM COMING FOR YOU.

Britman says…

Bloody.

Alpha 1 says...

Wow. Bloody.

Mac says...

It's definitely bloody. Trust me on this.

The High Commander says...

Bloody. And it never should have been shared in the first place. This conversation will stop now.

Chinchilla Lover says...

Don't get so hot. God.

PenPro58 says...

Oh dear. I hit send before I was ready. It is true. I am the Region Master's wife, but that doesn't mean what you think it means. And it's bloody. I've explained the difference before. Please check the other posts.

Fangman333 says...

You have to stop. Just turn off the computer.

Alpha 1 says...

Walk away now before it gets worse.

The Chef says...

For the sake of the entire region please stop.

Greek Warrior says...

Even I can't believe you've said it again.

Mastergardener says...

PenPro58 you must go home to your master. Let him protect you.

Mac says...

I think you could actually substitute lemonade for the tomato juice and leave out the Tabasco sauce. Add a bit of Grenadine and some lemon for garnish or maybe a cherry and you'd have a nice girly drink.

Shadowman says...

Blood type A going once. Going twice. Anyone?

The Chef says...

Yes. Go home. It's the only way to be safe.

PenPro58 says…

Going home is not an option.

Mastergardener says…

It is your only option.

The High Commander says…

Going home will not save her. I know exactly where she lives. And the true death awaits her and her master.

Studmufflicker69 says…

I KNOW WHERE SHE LIVES, TOO. IM COMING FOR HER AND HER MASTER. I KNOW THEY HAVE MY GOLDENRAE. SOON ILL HAVE HER AND THE REGION. I CANT WAIT TO TASTE PENPRO58. MY FLEDGLING WILL FEED WELL.

PenPro58 says…

I'm so nervous I keep hitting the send button before I'm finished. And he does know where I live. He just doesn't know who I am. You all think I'm someone I'm not. I'm not that horrible little vampire. I've never caused those types of things to happen. I'm a very nice girl.

Mastergardener says…

Eva, please check your email.

"I'm really starting to hate PenPro58. I'm not dreadful or horrible." I open another page on my smart phone and log into my email.

I can't wait to find her and live up to her image of me. No. No. I won't do that. I won't give her the satisfaction. Instead, I'll get someone else to do it. Yes, that's it. Someone else can take care of her. Martin? Would he do it? He would. He'll want to protect Stefan and me. I'll just talk—

Eva—Your blog is putting several lives in jeopardy. You must encourage PenPro58 to stay off the blog. She is in great danger, if she does not go home to her master. The

Federation has issued an Execution Order. The High Commander has assigned himself to the task. She must go home and she must stop commenting on the blog. Please. I beg you, shut down your blog for the sake of her life. Damien.

Oh shit. If I shut down the blog, how will I know what's going on?

"Master? What are you thinking about?" Cynthia's big head appears in front of me.

"Why aren't you focused on the situation at hand?" Noelle huffs. She's sitting sideways in the seat again. "You must be able to understand why anyone would think you're rotten. You can't possibly be that dense."

My mouth drops open. "What? No."

"No, you're not that dense or no, you don't understand?" Pierre asks. His tone is so snotty. French and snotty. I just want to punch him dead in the mouth. "Because everyone knows. It is the reason we demons like you."

"I am not... What?" I sort of want to cry, scream, bite someone, smash the van into the ground and run away to hide. I'm so confused by how I feel I can't move.

Noelle rests her elbows on her knees and leans toward me. "Chryssie—"

"Eva," I correct.

Her eyebrows dart up. "Fine. It's not as though your past has been one of thoughtfulness and selfless acts of generosity. Not that I expect you to be... who was that nun, the one from Calcutta? What was her name?" She snaps her fingers.

"Oh, oh! I know." Cynthia's hand shoots in the air. "Lydia." She nods.

Noelle rolls her eyes. "Shut up, demon."

"Mother Teresa," Goldenrae offers. Her voice is soft, matching her pretty face. She's completely shifted back into a teenybopper. Though, now that I look more closely she doesn't appear that young.

"Right. No one expects a vampire to be Mother Teresa." Noelle smiles. It's not her usual "you're a dumbass" smile. It's actually much gentler.

"I am thoughtful and I'm not self…" I might be a little selfish. And since I don't want her to add liar to the list I stop there. I glance at Goldenrae again. Something around her eyes takes away from the youthfulness.

"Okay." Noelle inhales and closes her eyes. "Milk toast."

My nose crinkles, and I scowl. I'd forgotten about the milk toast incident.

"What's milk toast?" Goldenrae asks, slowly blinking. The demons all look up at the ceiling like they're trying to avoid me.

The short and easy answer, "A delicious little cracker. I happen to like them with wine."

"Mon demon," Pierre mumbles and picks his nails, both hands working without incident.

"That situation was not my fault. I had nothing to do with setting that fire." I push Goldenrae's long honey-brown ponytail off her shoulder. "How old are you?"

"When one starts a war by arguing with a master's mate over the dinner menu at a vampire gala, thus getting the mate so worked up he loses all common sense, enslaves more than fifty humans and then sets them loose on the city, the only acceptable thing to do is admit you've done wrong and apologize." I'm almost able to ignore Noelle's incorrect summary of the events from that evening.

"I still think a little milk toast would have made Illianna feel better." She had complained about indigestion the entire night before. I was trying to help. "I'm telling you a little milk toast would have done the trick." Illianna was the chambermaid to Jacquelyn, The West Coast Master, and her husband Darius. "And I was not arguing over the dinner menu."

"Yes you were." Noelle's deadpan expression annoys me.

"No. I. Wasn't." I open up my fanny pack and grab my lipstick. "Though, I do think vampires should be a little bit more daring in their meal choices. At least add dessert. Chocolate is a wonderful thing." I stretch my lips and smooth on the Cherries Jubilee, then pucker to ensure full application. "And he was unstable to begin with. There was no reason for him to react in such a harsh manner." I offer my lipstick to Goldenrae.

"Twenty-eight. Do I look ridiculous? I never dress like this." Goldenrae swipes the lipstick from my hand and smears the bright red color across her lips, then puckers and rubs them together to end in a loud pop. I love her.

"Well, I think once the forty-foot chocolate fountain with human dipping elements arrived he thought he'd lost control of the his own house." Noelle's top lip sneers below her squinting left eye.

"Actually, according to Stefan, Darius managed to hold it together for that part," Cynthia says.

"I would like to attend a party with that kind of menu. Sounds wonderful," Pierre purrs.

"And it was. I had a fantastic idea. Everyone could pick her own human for dipping. What's better than that? Chocolate and blood." I grin. It was a brilliant idea. "I've never quite understood why Darius hated it."

"It was the added condiments. The kiddie pools filled with coconut, chopped nuts, rainbow sprinkles, those are the things that sent Darius over the edge," Jackson explains.

"Rainbow sprinkles." Cynthia giggles.

"I thought it would be fun. They'd dip and roll." I still don't understand why the evening turned out so badly and why I've never been allowed to attend any of the west coast events. I love a good party and I'm a lot of fun. I miss the Seattle Sleeper Fest, the Academy Awards, the Pancho Rio Festival.

"That doesn't really sound bad to me," Goldenrae says. I wouldn't have expected my little fledgling to be so interested, but her eyes are lit up like she's dreaming of dipping a human.

I smooth a couple wild locks of Goldenrae's hair back into place. "It's not. We've done it at home."

"According to Stefan it wasn't so much the dipping fest that was the problem. It was your response to Darius thanking you for your idea and asking you to leave the meeting. The less than demure exit is what caused the incident," Cynthia says.

"How do you know? When did he… Why do you… Has he been telling you things?" I lean toward her. Damn it! Why has he been confiding in my demons?

Pierre's eyes widen and he shakes his head, hands flying to his mouth. Jackson tackles him.

"They really are the dumbest demons on the planet," Noelle says. "No wonder they're yours."

"Oh, shut up." I pry Jackson off Pierre and watch as Cynthia tries to take control of the host, her blue eyes flashing for only a few brief seconds before Pierre's amber ones reappear. "Pierre, let her speak. Cynthia, tell me how you know all of this."

The sparkling blue eyes open wide and her hand comes away from her mouth. "Well, you're a bit of a handful so Stefan writes all about it in the books. We read it. You know, being trapped in The Book can get boring so we read Stefan's journals."

"You mean all the books downstairs written in *demon* babble are his personal journals?" How the hell much can one man…vampire…damn it demon have to say?

"Well, not Ta Biblia Daimon. That one he just commands. But the others are his journals."

"How can you read the journals, if you're stuck in The Demon Book?" I look to Jackson for the answer, knowing full well Cynthia won't be able to explain it before the sun comes up or in any coherent manner.

"He's linked them all in an effort to keep his work safe, hidden. No one until you has ever been able to open The Book, never mind read it or release the demons."

Noelle kicks Jackson's boot. "Demon, do you know why Chry—"

"Eva," I correct.

She pauses, closes her eyes and her front teeth clamp down on her tongue, keeping her silent for a second. "Fine. Do you know why *Eva* was able to read it?"

This time even Cynthia shakes her head. Half her words come out in French. The other half are a low and deep whine about not wanting to be banished to the glossary.

Noelle and I look at each other, confused again.

"What is she talking about? Tell us, demon." Noelle kneels on the floor and spins Jackson to face her.

"Ta Biblia Daimon can only be commanded by the rightful and true leader of the demons," Jackson explains.

"Isn't that supposed to be a demon?" Noelle asks.

All three demons nod.

"Then how am I able to do it? I'm not a demon," I blurt.

"That's debatable," Noelle says.

"You know, I've had about all I'm going to take of you." I slide forward on my seat. But just as I'm about to launch myself at Noelle the door opens and Charlene and Margaritaman stumble over each other to get into the van.

"We should go. We should go. We should go." Margaritaman jumps into the driver's seat, turns the ignition and floors the pedal, sending everyone rolling backward.

"What the hell?" Noelle and I yell at the same time.

Goldenrae sniffs the air and smacks her lips. I catch her foot before she's able to vault from the backseat onto Margaritaman. I pull her down to the floor with me, Noelle, Jackson, Cynthia and Pierre.

"Um, Chryssie—" Charlene begins.

"Eva. Her name is Eva!" Goldenrae growls as she tries to bite me. "Feed me."

"This is a real problem. You have got to learn to control yourself around humans!" I smack her nose.

"Ow!"

"Well, stop it!"

"Eva! Martin has been assigned to hunt us and my brothers are a little bit pissed off and Cheng said to tell you he wants the demons back and Stefan said to get your ass to The Blue Moon in the next twenty minutes because The High Commander is going to find you and then you'll be staked." Charlene has the nerve to buckle her seatbelt for safety as she spews her list of shit designed to make me crazy.

"What? Who does he think he is?" I sit on Goldenrae, her hands pinned to her back, her face against the floor. If Martin catches us, can he possibly "dispose" of us? I don't see how he could in good conscience. I mean he is participating in the blog.

It's not like he's a completely innocent onlooker. He's Fangman333, thus—guilty by association of any crime of which they're accusing me. Hopefully, he realizes this and finds some way to occupy himself other than hunting for us.

"Oh, The High Commander also said to tell you when you are captured and staked, all your friends are going to die for being accomplices." Her voice squeaks.

"I don't want to die," Margaritaman says. "Nope. Not today or tomorrow or any other day in the next less than fifty years." Tires squeal as the van takes a corner on two wheels and everyone tumbles to the right. Tools locked in the metal shelving clang against each other.

"When did you talk to The High Commander?" Noelle asks, shoving the demons off her.

"Rob told me," Charlene answers. "We made a couple calls when we were outside the van waiting for you, and he was one of them."

"Actually, we only made one call and the guy who was on the phone in the car when the cops surrounded us, the same black cloud guy, he…he…he called us back." Margaritaman sounds like he might cry. "Where's The Blue Moon?" His hands grip the wheel, making white knuckles appear as he steers the car around a much slower moving vehicle and up onto the sidewalk, running three pedestrians into the street.

The van sideswipes a parked Prius, flipping the little box onto its side. Then, when Margaritaman tries to make a left turn up a wrong way and has to swerve around an on-coming SUV he takes the bumper off a Camry.

"Not a good night to own a Toyota," Noelle says as the bumper spins into traffic. "Good night to be a mechanic, though."

"Noelle, take the wheel. He's going to get them killed." I'd do it myself, but then Goldenrae would eat Margaritaman and he'd end up dead, which clearly I'm trying to avoid. "Pull over Margaritaman."

"Can't. We don't have time. He's out there. Coming for us. Gotta keep moving." His eyes dart from one side mirror to the other and then onto the rearview. His heart races, beating erratically, blood pumping faster and faster. The wonderful aroma of fear fills the van. "Keep moving. Keep moving. Keep moving."

My mouth waters as the scent wafts in the air. I can't help it. The peppery fragrance of adrenaline is utterly intoxicating to vampires. Goldenrae makes a pathetic attempt to toss me off her but there's no way I'm letting her have him when I already know how addictive he can be. Noelle's gaze meets mine in the mirror. Her fangs descend, and a wicked twinkle glitters in her left eye.

CHAPTER TWENTY-NINE

You thought we were going to bite him, didn't you? You actually thought I'd slip over the edge and nibble my friend? How could you? I can't believe you think so little of me.

Oh, he was quite tempting. His racing heart echoed in my ears. I still hear it beating like a drummer on crack. And the demons continue to struggle with Goldenrae to keep her in check. But he *is* my friend. I love him. I would never bite him again. Plus, as we all know, I don't eat fast food. He is fast food and not healthy for me. You remember, the pot situation. I need to keep my wits about me.

Right now I'm dealing with issues. There's no time to goof off. Though, when this is over I'm having a Chianti—with or without Stefan.

So, Noelle is driving. Cynthia, Pierre and Jackson are huddled around Goldenrae, poised for the next time they'll need to restrain her. At the moment she's holding my phone and studying the pictures of Cletus on my website. She's sort of stuck between her pretty self and her not-so-pretty self with a nose and ears that just look ridiculous. But I don't want her to feel bad so I'm trying not to stare. If I'm going to keep her, I really need to figure out how to stop her from shifting.

"Are you kidding me? I'm not mating with him. And why is it called mating. Don't you just marry? Animals mate." She shoves the phone back at me.

"Well, on the mating thing I think that's from years ago. I mean I call it married. Stefan calls it mating. I'm fairly certain it's the same thing. And you have to admit, he does look a bit like an animal so mating is probably appropriate for him." I study his picture.

"I'm not doing anything with that!" She points at the phone. "Is he even human?"

"No, but neither are you," Cynthia answers

Can't say as I blame Goldenrae. Cletus is disgusting.

Margaritaman snorts. He's sleeping in the passenger seat. We had to put him out of his misery. He was panicking. Between Goldenrae's groaning and wails to have him, the impression Stefan left and The High Commander's warning, the poor kid was bound to experience heart failure.

Charlene is sitting on the floor beside Margaritaman, watery wide eyes staring at her phone. She thumbs up and down only a couple times, then her thumbs bounce across the screen like jumping beans.

"You're not texting anyone are you?" I ask, a little worried she's talking with her brothers.

She shakes her head. "You better check the blog."

"Cletus didn't always look like that. In fact, he only morphed into that in the past few weeks. He was quite handsome up until about Labor Day," Noelle explains as she takes the on-ramp to 95 South. We decided to head toward The Blue Moon. I have to get to Stefan and try to convince him to let me keep Goldenrae. That's the only way. I can't hide her anywhere else. I need him to help control her.

I plop down on the bench and log back onto the blog to see what's happening now.

-Eva Prim Writes-

Thirty-six Comments

PenPro58 says…

Taste me! You're not tasting me. My husband will see you dead first. Eva, you were supposed to block him from this blog. Where the hell are you?

Studmufflicker69 says…

YEAH. WHERE ARE YOU? IF YOU BRING GOLDENRAE TO ME NOW I WON'T HURT YOU.

The High Commander says…

It's very clear we have a region completely out of control due to weak leadership. It's hard to believe PenPro58's master was capable of taking over this region from its previous master. One who cannot control his fledgling, especially if she is his wife, most certainly cannot control a region. I believe New England may need a new master and won't be surprised if any attempts are made to unseat the current master.

The Chef says…

The region is under control. There is no need to consider a new master for New England.

Fangman333 says…

That is correct. New England is strong. The Master is still in charge.

Britman says…

Nothing out of the ordinary going on here. We're fine in the east.

Alpha 1 says…

All systems running as per usual.

The Greek Warrior says…

All clear. No need for an intervention.

Studmufflicker69 says…

ID LIKE SOME HELP FROM THE FEDERATION. WHERES MY MATE? COMMANDER—ITS A HIGH CRIME TO STEAL ANOTHERS MATE. I WANT EVERYONE INVOLVED EXECUTED. GOLDENRAE WHERE ARE YOU?

Mac says…

I don't know what you're talking about but New England is doing just fine. There's nothing unusual occurring. The region has governors, not masters and there's one for every state. Honestly, this blog is getting weirder by the second.

BoSoFan says…

The only weird thing happening now is the Sox aren't in the play offs.

Chinchilla Lover says…

Mac, are you in New England? I'm in Massachusetts. We should meet up sometime.

YankMe says…

That's not weird. Think Babe Ruth.

The High Commander says…

You are correct Studmufflicker69. This is an offense punishable by death. I am en route to the region to handle this situation myself. I shall dispose of PenPro58 and Eva with a swift and sure hand.

Mastergardener says…

I assure you your mate will be returned to you, unharmed. I understand your worries and give you my word. Your mate is safe.

Mac says…

Do you think you're a vampire or werewolf? Because I'm not into that scene.

Fangman333 says…

We will find her and bring her back to you. Eva has the best of intentions. She's just somewhat misguided.

Shadowman says…

Chinchilla Lover, I'll be your vampire.

Studmufflicker69 says….

NO ONE CAN UNDERSTAND. GOLDENRAE IS MY WORLD. THE ONLY LIGHT I KNOW. YOUR WORD IS WORTH NOTHING TO ME.

Moongirl2nite says…

Goldenrae is perfectly safe. There's no need to worry about her. And what's so bad about werewolves?

Chinchilla Lover says…

I'm not a vampire or werewolf. Just a girl.

Daywalker says…

I'm pretty sure you'd be better as a victim than a vampire. You're a definite bottom, Shadowman.

Mastergardener says…

Every mate understands The Bond. We will bring Goldenrae back to you before dawn.

Mac says…

Hmm. I'll think about it.

Moongirl2nite says…

Werewolves are girls, too.

Eva says…

Hello everyone. So nice to see some newbies on the blog, even you, High Commander. Moongirl2nite is correct. Goldenrae is perfectly safe. I'm not in agreement on having her return to someone she doesn't know or love by dawn. It's not fair to force her into a relationship she doesn't want. I thought we'd moved past that point in vampire history, at least I thought New England had. I'll thank you very much Mastergardener not to make promises you can't keep and have no business getting involved in. Cletus, you will need to move on. She does not love you and will not return to you. High Commander, all is well in New England. There's no need to visit. In fact, PenPro58 is busy with some issue on the border of her own territory so she's not even around. Also, I believe I am entitled to a trial before an execution. And would my assistance in the hunt for PenPro58 change the charges against me?

Alpha 1 says…

That's enough Moongirl2nite. Stand down. Know your place.

YankMe says…

That's what she said.

The High Commander says….

You will return this missing mate tonight! Participation in this blog is to cease and desist AT ONCE.

Cletus says…

SHE DID CONSENT. SHE DOES LOVE ME. I DIDN'T FORCE HER. BRING HER TO ME. IM GOING TO SEE THE MASTER AND GOLDENRAE HAD BETTER BE WITH HIM.

Shadowman says…

That's what she said? What are you talking about?

Fangman333 says…

Cletus, we will present your mate tonight.

Starfishlover says…

Um, maybe this isn't the best time to ask. But, Eva, how can you tell if someone is being overeaten? That sounds so odd to ask, but I think that's what's happening to my brother. His new girlfriend only comes around at night and he's totally obsessed with her and when they're done with their "date" he's pale and clammy and goofy and crabby all at once. I'm afraid she might be a real vampire who's taking liberties she shouldn't.

YankMe says…

I meant that's what she said about The High Commander disposing of PenPro and Eva with a swift hand. Just not fast enough on the response.

The High Commander says…

Starfishlover, where are you and what's the name of your brother's lover?

PenPro58 says…

Eva! I can't believe you're giving away secrets and turning on me. I thought we were friends. You're a terrible friend!

Moongirl2nite says…

Don't tell me to stand down. I'm tired of standing down. I'm always the one who's stuck at home or in the car or with a babysitter. I'm not 6!

I glance at Charlene. "I'm not so sure you should yell at anyone on the blog. I mean we don't even know who all these people are." It's not like she's the world's greatest fighter. I don't need one more problem because she pisses off someone else.

"Are you kidding? That's Rob. 'Stand down. Know your place.' Do you have any idea how many times he's said that…not just to me, but to my other brothers? He's such a dictator. I'm sick of it." She continues tapping away at her phone. She might actually crack the screen, if she keeps going. "Just because he was born first does not mean he can boss me around."

"No, but the fact he's your pack's alpha does." I crinkle my nose and squint like it will help her see the obvious. She just keeps pounding away at her keypad.

The ringtone on my phone chants with Blue Swede and everyone's attention focuses on my hand.

"I'll bet he can't stop how he's feeling." Noelle's gaze in the rearview mirror meets mine. "You must realize what you do to him, right?" She nods and scowls.

I don't even get a chance to say hello.

"Where are you? Why have you left the region?" Stefan doesn't bother with a greeting.

"Well, hello and I haven't left the region."

"The blog indicates you have left."

"I keep telling you I'm not PenPro58. Why don't you believe me?"

"You must return Goldenrae to Cletus."

"Stefan, I really wish you'd see this from my perspective."

"Chrysanthemum, your life depends on Cletus getting his mate."

"She doesn't even remember him. He took her against her will. That's a crime, too. And since it happened before I took her, which was done in her best interest, he should be executed." I nod. And so do Jackson and Cynthia. Or is that Pierre?

"She consented." He growls.

"No, she didn't."

"I'm not arguing with you. Bring her to me."

"Stefan, she does not have any recollection of Cletus and she doesn't like the term mating. Just so you know." I pat her arm. "And there is absolutely no need to yell at me. I hear you perfectly fine."

The next words are a low, low whisper, and if I wasn't a vampire, I actually wouldn't hear them. "She doesn't recall because you interrupted the sealing of The Bond." He pauses and again I hear sizzling or maybe I feel it. But either way, there's sizzling. "If you recall, you stole her and then bit her."

My lips twitch to the left.

I pull the phone away from my ear and stick a finger in it. The sizzling is giving me shivers.

"Then she bit you. Thus The Bond was not completed. Had you left her where Cletus hid her, she'd be happily bound to him and he'd be in control of himself instead of letting slip vampire secrets, challenging me, threatening you, and calling for a Federation investigation into my leadership and abilities to control my own progeny! Not to mention publically accusing me of not being a good husband!"

"I think you might be reading a little more into those blog comments than was there," I say. I didn't notice that last business on the blog.

"I think when a man openly questions his master's ability to sexually please his wife, it's pretty clear what he's saying."

"What are you talking about?" I can't figure out how to search the Internet and keep the phone connected so I accidentally hang up on Stefan when I flip back to the blog.

~Eva Prim Writes~
Three Comments
Moongirl2nite says…
And no one, I mean no one likes it when you walk around acting like you're better than us. You're not! Mom and Dad even said it.
BoSoFan says…
The Yankees Suck.
Studmufflicker69 says…
WOMAN IS SO OFTEN THE DOWNFALL OF MAN. A DISSATISFIED WOMAN LOOKS FOR WAYS TO PLEASE HERSELF. IF PENPRO58 AND EVA WERE FULFILLED THEYD PROBABLY BE HOME IN BED INSTEAD OF STEALING ANOTHERS MATE. WEAK LEADERSHIP AND INADEQUATE IN THE BEDROOM. NEW ENGLAND DOES NEED A NEW MASTER.

Well, Stefan might have read that one correctly. His text arrives in caps. BRING HER TO ME! NOW!!!

Wait a minute. Did he just tell me she did consent? Why didn't I know?

CHAPTER THIRTY

"Goldenrae, you're sure you don't remember Cletus?" I ask.

"Positive. I'd absolutely remember someone who looked like that." She swallows as though she's struggling not to vomit.

"Hold on. I know there's a picture of him somewhere when he looked normal." I log onto my vmail and scroll through the old news briefings. "Here it is. Does this look familiar?"

I find a picture of him from last summer before he went around the bend. It's from opening night of Francois's new bar in Augusta. In the picture Cletus stands beside Francois. Tell me they're not polar opposites. Cletus has short blond hair, hazel eyes and is tall and thin, like a runner. Francois is tall and that's about where the similarities end. His long brown hair hangs to his shoulders, and he always wears it down so it frames his face. Even in pictures his crystal-gray eyes are piercing. And he's broad and muscular, broader even than Stefan. If I didn't think he was such an ass, I'd say he was quite handsome. Instead, I think he's an ass.

Goldenrae studies the picture. "Is that what he usually looks like? That's not so bad."

"Yeah, that's what he always looked like before, but since last summer he's spiraled downhill into his current state." I pop a piece of gum into my mouth and offer one to her.

"Wasn't he also considered one of Stefan's best spies?" Noelle pulls the van into a parking space at the far end of the building.

"Yeah. He was part of the team that helped to overthrow Aaron." I study the parking lot. Rose bushes grow along the front. A couple pumpkins and ugly chrysanthemums sit on the steps. Have I ever mentioned how I don't like the chrysanthemum? For whatever reason in the past ten years the world has fallen in love with that damn flower. I see it everywhere from September to November. It's awful.

"Hunh. That makes you wonder," Jackson says.

"What does? The alternating chrysanthemums or odd shaped pumpkins?" Seriously? Why has the harvest theme become so damn popular? And why has Vinnie chosen it to decorate the damn building? It's a nightmare.

"No. The connection between Cletus and Francois. If memory serves me, Cletus and Francois fought alongside Stefan when he killed Aaron and claimed Maine. They were supporters of Stefan." Jackson turns to Cynthia. "I'm sorry, Cynthia, but I need to speak to Pierre. Would you mind?"

She pouts, but consents and her blue eyes fade to amber.

"Oui. That is correct. And this happened only four months ago. Stefan was very pleased with the alliance and believed Cletus to be a good ally, possibly someone who could take a command." His TH's all sound like Z's again and he's waving his hands around in the most flamboyant way. "Then Cletus returned from Maine to spend a few weeks training the wolves—"

"Oh, that's right. I forgot he'd come over several times with my brothers to discuss the situation in Maine. They weren't sure if they could trust Francois, but Stefan kept saying he had no concerns of his allegiance," Charlene pipes up.

"Then in August something changed. Cletus became distracted, constantly worried," Pierre continues.

"Yes. Yes." Charlene lurches forward and sits on her knees. "He kept talking about missing the sun or sunshine or something. We thought he was going nuts. What vampire misses the sun?"

Noelle and I look at each other. Um, every vampire misses the sun. We're just not crazy enough to go see it. Well, not usually.

"He kept saying something about feeling the rays on his skin or standing in its light. It was weird because he'd been completely focused on securing Maine and then it was like a switch flipped and all he ever talked about were the golden rays of the sun. He kept getting weirder and weirder." Charlene is more animated than I've seen her all night. Her eyes are wide as though she's cracking open a case she's been working on for months. "When they went off to battle in Maine, he could barely keep his wits and Stefan assigned four of my brothers to monitor him. But somehow in the melee, he escaped."

I'm not saying I wasn't paying attention. I did hear everything she said. But I pretty much stopped focusing when she said, "…golden rays of the sun." Honestly, it's no wonder Rob is so protective of her.

"Let me just make sure I heard you correctly. Cletus talked about golden rays of sun? That doesn't ring a bell?" I lean close to her.

"Oh." Charlene blinks. "Maybe, now…" She glances toward Goldenrae.

"Yes!" Cynthia announces, but is quickly subdued by Jackson.

"No. I didn't know you'd read that much. No. No. Don't say it." He lands on top of her and they crush Goldenrae between them. "Remember the promise. We're not supposed to…"

Every indication leads me to believe demons are idiots. I've yet to see one that isn't, not that I've met any others. But these three are just killing me.

"Spill it," I say.

"Cletus loves her." Cynthia holds Goldenrae in front of her, proudly displaying the gargoyle-y vampire. "He asked and Stefan granted the mating, but not before first meeting Goldenrae and ensuring she was willing and not just seduced into making the decision."

Jackson lets go of Cynthia and sits back. He shakes his head and stares at his feet, listening with the rest of us.

"Stefan met Goldenrae for lunch because he knew Cletus would have little to no power over her. He had to be sure. He's really not a bad guy. Just scary, but not bad. He was looking out for Goldenrae's best interests. Wanting to be sure she did love Cletus and understood what she'd be getting into becoming a vampire and mating and—"

"You mean to say Goldenrae is part of an approved mating?" Noelle interrupts.

"Yes. And she was very willing. She told Stefan she was fully aware and since her family lived so far away and she wasn't particularly close to them she wasn't worried about them noticing something strange. She loves Cletus and has never felt this way about anyone else. It was quite romantic, according to Stefan's note." Cynthia hugs Goldenrae. "You're in love. Isn't it wonderful?"

"Eva?"

My vision fades to red. My fangs slide down.

How could he? How could he keep such a secret from me? Another one. That bastard.

My ears and nose and hands twitch.

"Master. Remain calm." It's Jackson.

Hands slide over my skin. Arms wrap around me. My demons help me to stay in control.

I call to Stefan. *Why? Why didn't you tell me about Cletus and Goldenrae?*

My flower, come to me. Let me explain.

So many lies. How could you?

My heart hurts. It feels like a lead weight trying to beat in my chest, only it's solid and hard and doesn't move. Tears build behind my eyes. He doesn't trust me. And he probably never has.

CHAPTER THIRTY-ONE

Chrysanthemum, you must come to me. We must reunite Cletus with his mate. The separation is driving him mad. Soon I will have no choice but to accept his challenge and kill him. What will become of Goldenrae then?

Goldenrae is back in the corner, looking forlorn and utterly distressed. Tears stream down her cheeks.

Cynthia and Jackson sit beside Goldenrae, weeping.

Charlene whimpers and wipes her face on her sleeve.

Noelle sniffles.

Margaritaman jolts awake and starts bawling his eyes out.

"Why are you all crying?"

This whole situation is a mess. Goldenrae's mated to someone she doesn't remember and if he dies, she'll live a miserable existence. Stefan doesn't trust me and he lies. A lot. I've accidentally made a lovesick vampire go crazy. And now demons, vampires and a werewolf are crying.

Everyone answers at once and then the crying ramps up to extreme sobbing.

"I think I miss Cletus."

"Why won't my brothers let me make my own decisions?"

"I really do love Tom."

"I love working at Burger Boy. I don't want to be an accountant."

"I want my own body."

"Why doesn't Stefan like me?"

"I want turkey."

What the devil? This is my army. Sobbing in the back of Chris Soldati's love vehicle. And with sobbing comes mouth breathing.

Everyone gets a mint. I literally toss one in every open mouth.

"Okay. Stop crying. We're going to fix this. All of it." I motion to the entire group. "Goldenrae, if you want to go back to Cletus, fine. I'll give you back. Margaritaman, you can go back to work tomorrow."

"I walked off my job tonight. I'm sure they fired me." He wails and wipes his nose on his shirt.

"I'll take care of that. I'll get you a job in another restaurant." That's an easy one.

"Pierre, you're getting your own body sometime soon. Stop crying. You don't have to share with Cynthia forever. Cynthia, you'll get turkey in a little while. Jackson, I don't think Stefan hates you. I don't think he'd have let you stay out of The Book if he did, so stop crying."

I turn to Charlene and Noelle. "We'll need to work on your issues a little more, but we'll figure something out." I squeeze Noelle's hand.

"He's still angry," she says without looking up at me.

"I know. But he can't be that angry. He lets you stay in the house with him, and he hasn't had you killed."

She nods. "That's what I keep telling myself, but nothing seems to change. I love him so much. I was afraid to tell him. That's why I never mentioned it. I purposely left hints to make him figure it out on his own. I never even marked him until the night he tried to..." Her voice cracks and she drags in a ragged breath. "...the night he tried to stake me. I should have let him kill me, but I couldn't. I couldn't just lie down and die. That was when I bit him. That's the only time."

My eyes flood with tears. Damn it! I hate crying. I hate when I do it and when anyone else does it. And her pathetic story reminds me of Stefan. "He just needs some help seeing what's directly in front of him."

She glances up at me and nods. "Don't tell anyone." Tears stream down her cheeks.

"Never." I know what it's like to be in love and there's no way I'd ever let my friend down. I'll help her win back her husband.

Charlene hugs Noelle. "He does love you. He has to. Otherwise he wouldn't stay with you."

She's right, of course. Why else would Tom allow Noelle to live with him? Maybe he's just embarrassed by the whole incident. You know how men are. They can't stand to be fooled. Then to have no say in the matter, that must have driven him insane.

"At least it's only the one man. My brothers are never going to give me a chance." Charlene sighs. "I hate being the youngest and the only girl."

"Stefan can help with this." Of course, I'm not sure how I'm going to ask him for any help when I can't even trust him to tell me the truth about himself or to keep promises he's made to me. Devil only knows what else I don't know and what possibly waits for me inside that building.

With Cletus's public challenge to both Stefan and me, not to mention PenPro58, who says her husband's a master, which means Cletus has openly challenged two masters, plus the revelation about the existence of vampires, the theft of an approved mate, sharing of classified vampire information, the forbidden art of demon calling, not telling Stefan about the blog, oh, the little fact that I'm Eva, the suspected kidnapping of a werewolf, and the new marital problems I'm having, I feel like it's best if I go this one alone. I'm fairly certain there could be some amount of casualties during this meeting.

"Here's what we're going to do. I'm going in alone. I'll call Noelle when the coast is clear for you all to come in." I reapply my lipstick, pop another mint and zip my fanny pack.

"No way. You can't go in there alone. What if The High Commander is in there?" Jackson asks. "He might try to kill you."

"He said he was en route. I don't think he's here yet. Besides, Stefan won't let anything happen to me." I spin the fanny pack around.

"Stefan may deal with you on his own," Cynthia offers.

"I'm going in alone. That's final. I started this whole mess with my blog. I'm not letting anyone else take the fall for it. Well, if PenPro58 shows up while I'm gone, call me. I'd definitely let her take the fall."

Before anyone has a chance to argue every door on the van opens at once. Martin and Cheng stand outside the slider and passenger side door. Rob, Chris and Tommy Soldati stand at the back of the van blocking any potential attempts to exit through the rear. Jack and Troy Soldati stand at the driver's side while Neil, Max and Luke Soldati appear in front of the van.

The wolves are all in human form, but the way they're growling makes it clear—anyone could shift at any moment. And Martin and Cheng don't look all too happy with descended fangs and swords drawn.

This might be the angriest welcome reception I've received in about sixty-eight years.

CHAPTER THIRTY-TWO

"She wouldn't make that face, if she actually wanted him." I feel compelled to point out what seems tragically obvious. Come on. Goldenrae has that look you get when you've just realized the thing in your mouth is rotten. Don't act like you've never put something bad in your mouth, like old milk or a chunk of apple containing the missing half of a worm.

"Sunshine?" Cletus's voice is much smoother than I would have ever imagined possible. On all the news briefings he's always growling or howling. I never anticipated a smooth, comprehensible voice, never mind one so soft and pleasant.

"You? How could you do this to me?" Goldenrae growls. Her fangs descend, eyes fade to red, nose hair lengthens, and her breath... "You asked me for sugar." That statement is punctuated by two sharp tips shooting up from her ears.

"What the fuck? Do you have to upset her? Stay calm, Goldenrae. It's okay." I move toward her.

"Stop. She is my mate. I will soothe her." Cletus blocks my path.

"You're not touching her." This time I snarl. Who does he think he is? She clearly doesn't want to be his mate and we all know she doesn't want to be a vampire. I dart to the left, but he follows. "It would be quite helpful if my demons would do something right now. Do I have to do everything around here?"

But they don't move. "Master, we feel it. The Bond. He loves her. We cannot interfere with that," Jackson explains. "They are mated, whether she remembers or not. And we can't interfere."

"You cannot mate someone who does not consent. Just taking someone for your own is not mating. It's rape, right Noelle?" I glare at yet another of my band of unhelpful, suddenly paralyzed, and utterly useless friends.

"I did not rape him," she argues. Cheng's hand comes down on the sofa beside her. The furniture groans under his iron grip, and Noelle squeaks at his silent warning.

"That's not what I said. I'm just asking you to agree with the definition." I lean to the right and speak to Goldenrae. "Take a deep breath in and try to hold it for as long as you can before releasing it."

"She would not react this way, if you had not interfered!" Cletus barks. He paces back and forth behind Goldenrae, who still refuses to look at him. She's literally facing the wall.

"Master, maybe if he didn't continue to look so…" Cynthia snickers toward Cletus. She and Jackson are cuddled together on the couch in Stefan's office, where we were promptly delivered after being apprehended, as Titus put it. Thankfully, we're here and not in the round where I suspect hundreds of vampires and werewolves have gathered for the inquisition, which I'm still hopeful will not occur.

"Yeah, maybe if you shift back to your old self. Maybe then she'll…like you." Though, how she could is beyond me. His extra long nose hair takes the award for grossest vampire standing.

"I'd love to, but I CANT!"

"Yelling at me does not make her like you better." I point to Goldenrae, who is now hiding behind the bar. "And it seems awfully odd you can half-shift, fully-shift, but not shift back! What's wrong with you?"

I move Cynthia to the chair across the room. Thankfully Stefan's office is large enough for this type of meeting. I helped decorate. The stone walls are lined with dark velvet curtains, and silk drapes hang down from the ceiling, gathering above the four chandeliers.

Cletus leans over the bar watching Goldenrae.

"Leave her alone." I rush to the bar.

A giant leather sofa and three chairs sit to the left arranged nicely around a glass coffee table (though we never drink coffee there). Stefan's desk is positioned along the back wall and a giant bar complete with stools, wine rack, and fridge take up the right wall. Behind the door on the left side of the room is a bedroom with a bathroom including a Jacuzzi.

In spite of the accommodations, this is not how I envisioned my arrival to go. I had intended to slip in and have a conversation with Stefan without mentioning my entourage (his name for them, not mine) was in the van in the parking lot, get him to agree to terms that granted everyone their freedom, including Goldenrae, and then send the signal out to the van that they could all go.

But, that's not how it went down. As he said, I should be happy no one is in silver chains. And I am, in spite of everyone looking miserable.

Charlene looks like she might start screaming at any one of or maybe all her brothers. Rob keeps staring her down. Funny thing, she's actually staring back at him, only glancing away when Neal elbows her. The rest of her brothers buzz with nervous werewolf energy.

Margaritaman is hiding from everyone, especially Stefan. He's on the floor behind the couch trying to keep his eyes on the entire group. Cynthia keeps inching closer to Jackson. Jackson can't take his eyes off Stefan. Pierre tries to keep Stefan in view, but every time Stefan looks at him, Pierre turns away in the most obviously paranoid way. Noelle is clearly keeping her senses tuned to Stefan, Martin and Cheng. I think if anyone tapped her on the shoulder she'd cry and shift and possibly shit all at once.

Martin and Cheng are perfectly silent as always or at least as always when on duty. Cheng is dressed in his usual relaxed slacks and shirt, though he's wearing a scabbard for his sword, which means he has some other knife neatly concealed in his braid. Martin towers behind Noelle. At six feet eight inches he's a giant. He has the blackest skin I've ever seen and long, I mean all the way down his back, thick dreads. He's dressed in a black suit, black shirt and black shoes. He literally blends into shadows. If he stood against the wall, you'd never know he was here.

He glances at me, and I would swear he was trying to tell me something. I've seen that look before. It's a cross between watch yourself and shut your mouth.

"What?" I mouth.

He barely moves his head in a negative response then glances at Cynthia-Pierre, who flinches under his gaze.

There's so much to watch. I can't decide who to focus on.

Stefan swirls wine in a crystal glass before taking a sip. "Perhaps strengthening The Bond will help," he suggests and draws my attention from my nervous friends back to Cletus and Goldenrae.

"Master, what does that mean?" Keeping her back to him, Goldenrae walks around Cletus and makes a beeline for me.

Well, that was all it took. Cletus explodes into full-on-shifted Cletus. Goldenrae yelps and dives into my open arms. Margaritaman passes out. Noelle shifts. Charlene begins yelling at Rob and pounding on his chest. Cynthia lunges into Jackson's arms and cries about not wanting to go back to The Book, and the seven other Soldatis all become wolves.

The place is pandemonium. There's more crying, screaming and growling going on than if we were actually in a war.

"Give me my mate!" Cletus storms toward us.

"No! She doesn't want you." I pick up Goldenrae and run around the room, dodging wolves and Cletus. "Stefan! She's mine. She doesn't remember him." I tip over one of the chairs and Cletus lurches over it to land in front of me. When I spin to the right I come face-to-face with my husband.

"Darling, you have no idea what it's like to be lovelorn. Look at him." He turns me toward Cletus, which lands Goldenrae staring at him.

She covers her eyes and shakes her head. "I don't love him. I don't want him," she whispers, but of course, with vampire hearing (and even wolf hearing) we all hear what she says.

Cletus groans. "You did consent. In June. Don't you remember? We took a gondola ride in Providence during WaterFire. You told me you loved me and wanted to spend the rest of your nights with me. Sunny, do you remember that night? We danced in the moonlight while the orchestra played. Your hair smelled of sunshine and lavender." He raises his wrist bringing a turquoise blue ribbon to his nose. "You took this from your hair and tied it to my wrist so I could take it with me into battle. Don't you remember?"

His eyes brim with tears. And my heart aches to think he has a romantic bone in his disgusting body.

"Moonbeam? Is that you?" Goldenrae croaks, and a single bloody tear trickles down her cheek.

Cletus nods, keeping his gaze locked on hers.

She studies him, dropping out of my arms to stand in front of the fully-shifted, totally gross Cletus.

"Where have you been?" She reaches up to touch his cheek. "What happened? I thought…I thought you'd died?"

Cletus brushes the tear from Goldenrae's face, kissing her cheeks and hugging her so tight he might crack her in half. "I went to battle but my separation from you was more than I could bear. I should have bound us before I left, but I didn't want to leave you as a young fledgling without being here to care for you. The first years are the hardest. The first few months are the most torturous. I wanted to wait until I could ensure your safe transition." He nuzzles his face into her hair.

"Wait a minute." I grab them each by a shoulder and jerk them apart. "You expect us to believe you love her and she knew what she was getting into and agreed to this? You buried her in a basement. We had to dig her out to save her."

"Oh, Chryssie—" Goldenrae begins.

But I'm not finished. "Oh, and you killed her friends. What kind of psycho are you?"

He sighs. "Have you never seen a lovelorn vampire?"

"Uh, yeah." Who hasn't? Vampires get their hearts broken quite often, especially the ones who have limited control. You know, the whole accidental overeating thing.

"And she was blogging about you scaring the shit out of her with your nose hair and breath and the constant nightly visits for who-knows-what."

"But, Chryssie," Goldenrae interrupts.

I put a hand up. "Just give me a minute here." I turn to Cletus. "And you were a perverted fucknut on the blog." I jam my finger into his chest. "You rude, disgusting, pig-jerk-asshole. What is wrong with you?"

"Chryssie, he loves me." Goldenrae doesn't bother to look at me. She just continues to gaze at dirty Cletus as though she's looking at the most handsome man in the world.

"So? He still shouldn't have made those threats. I've never seen a vampire type those things." I know. When have vampires ever had an opportunity to blog? "You challenged everyone on the blog. You threatened to bite us."

Cletus has the decency to look ashamed. "I apologize." He turns to Stefan. "Sire, I never meant any disrespect. Certainly, I have no ambition to rule any part of your territory. Please forgive my indiscretion. Without my mate—"

"There is no need to explain. I am fully aware of what happens when the mating process is interrupted." Stefan rests his hand on my shoulder.

"Wait a minute. Goldenrae, does any of this sound familiar? Do you remember the boat ride and the ribbon?" I hold up Cletus's hand for all to see the stained and torn ribbon still tied around his wrist.

She clasps his hand, bringing it to her chest. "I do. I do. I love you, Cletus."

"Even after he buried you in a basement and killed your friends and said those disgusting things on the blog?"

"I didn't kill your friends. They were alive and sleeping when I left you, hidden where I'd be able to find you the next evening to help you rise." He brushes stray hairs from Goldenrae's face before turning to me. "How did you get her out of the house? You shouldn't have been able to enter the domain." His eyes are now a lovely hazel, though still tinged with red tears. "I did write those things on the blog and for that I'm sorry. I have only my inexperience at love to blame."

"Don't change the subject." I tap my foot, hands on my hips. "And how do you do that partially shifted thing?" I nod at his eyes.

He opens his mouth.

"Never mind. Don't change the subject." I wave him off.

"It was us. We went in. We saved Goldenrae," Cynthia offers, head bobbling like the idiot demon she is.

Cletus's face is a deadpan stare. I purse my lips. You'd think for once my demons could keep quiet.

He sighs.

"Moony. I've missed you." Goldenrae's hands come up to Cletus's cheeks and he turns to face her.

You've probably never seen shifted vampires kiss. I've seen it, done it, wished it away more times than I'd like to remember. She's not even fully shifted, but that nose is something else.

"You think maybe you could shift her back so she's a little less gross?" I swallow hard. Between the site and sounds of it, I'm feeling a bit queasy.

"I'd love to, but she's bonded with you." Let's just say there's more than a slight note of irritation in his voice and those lovely hazel eyes are like laser beams.

"Well, who knew that could happen? It's not like it's a common every evening sort of occurrence."

"I knew," Noelle says and shakes her head.

"Me, too," Charlene says.

"Oui. We knew as well. All three of us," Pierre adds, motioning to Jackson and Cynthia.

"Oh shut up." I shove my arm at Goldenrae. It's pointless to argue with this group over anything.

Cletus catches my hand and lowers it from Goldenrae's mouth. "If you don't mind…" His voice is soft and gentle and his gaze is focused on Goldenrae. "…I'd like to finish bonding with my mate."

Stefan nods, and Cletus carries Goldenrae from the room.

"Well, that seems to have turned out well." I turn to face the room. "Though I didn't expect—"

"I am not going back with you! I'm moving out! I want my own place without you eight! I'm not a baby anymore." Charlene stomps to the door, throws it open and storms out behind Cletus and Goldenrae. Eight agitated wolves follow her, grumbling, growling and snarling at each other.

I look at Stefan. "Maybe I should—"

No. That has nothing to do with you. His voice booms in my head. *You have done enough. Now let Charlene deal with her brothers on her own.* His eyebrow arches.

I would, except let's face it. They aren't going to let her—

She must deal with the ramifications of her own actions and words. Just as you will.

Uuullllll. My lip curls up.

"Take the rest of them to the dungeon. We'll deal with them later." Stefan walks to his desk and sits down without so much as a glance at anyone. He begins working at his computer as though he's alone in the room.

Amongst whimpers from Margaritaman, whines from Cynthia, shaky encouragement from Jackson and Pierre and absolute silence from Noelle, Martin and Cheng march the captives toward the door. I trail behind them, miserable and more than slightly annoyed that we're being relegated to the dungeon.

"Really? The dungeon? Ridiculous." I snatch a handful of mints from the bowl by the door.

A firm hand comes down on my shoulder. "Not you."

Chapter Thirty-three

It's annoying. It's always been annoying. I'd swear he does it just to be annoying.

The repetitive drumming of his fingers on the desk makes me want to break Stefan's wrist. Tap, tap, tap, tap.

You must've been in a relationship with someone long enough to be annoyed by some ridiculous habit, one that might have seemed adorable or endearing when you first met, one that made you sort of giggle in the beginning because it gave away exactly what he was thinking. But then, as time passed the cuteness wore away and that damn habit became nothing but annoying.

Finger-tapping is the one habit of Stefan's that drives me crazy. When he's aggravated, irritated, or altogether angry he finger-taps. It's a rapid-fire succession from index finger to pinky. Tap, tap, tap, tap. Tap, tap, tap, tap. Over and over and over.

And, as you may know, or maybe you don't know, vampires have strong nails. It's wonderful in terms of manicures, but terribly destructive as it relates to finger-tapping and furniture. We have more divots in our furniture than a country club golf course following an afternoon of drunken fundraising.

Tap, tap, tap, tap. Tap, tap, tap, tap.

And how he manages to keep the same pace for such a long time is utterly beyond me.

"How can you possibly continue to be angry with me?" I pace back and forth in front of Stefan's desk, arms crossed over my chest.

I'm well aware he's annoyed I left the house. I mean, wouldn't you be annoyed if you'd hexed the house to keep me in but I escaped anyway? However, I'm not the only one at fault here.

"You didn't tell me. We had an agreement about the approved matings and you didn't follow it. I should be mad at you! In fact, I'm really angry." I pause in front of him and jam my hands onto my hips.

He doesn't respond, just continues to stare at the computer screen, not even glancing in my direction, fingers hammering at the wood.

I flick woodchips off my jeans. "You're ruining the desk." He's skipped past the slow drumming indicative of long, thoughtful moments of planning and strategizing and staccatoed right into pounding thuds with barely a millisecond of separation.

Tap, tap, tap, tap. Tap, tap, tap, tap.

I sigh and step out of the shower of tiny wooden pellets. "Honestly, there was no reason to send my entourage to the southern quadrant." The dungeon. The group is in the dungeon. Under lock and key with Martin and Cheng guarding the demons and the Soldatis guarding everyone else. As if any of them could escape anyway. They'd never be able to find the exit from the labyrinth.

I have to hand it to Stefan. He was brilliant in his design of the lower level. It's the size of six football fields, housing the dungeon, the round, which is an auditorium with a coliseum-like feel, our emergency housing, a ballroom, a private hotel, three vampire bars, and The Den, which was supposed to be a wolf bar, but I managed to get vampires admitted, mainly because I wanted to know what wolves did in their free time. Of course, I only ever get to go with Stefan or a wolf escort. Anyway, if you don't know the place well, you're not leaving. And not one of his captives, other than me, knows the way out.

And I should not have to consider myself a captive, but it's clear I am.

The activity on the computer screen is nearly as fast as his nail tapping. Comments pop up left and right, and he sits reading each one. I lean across the desk to follow along.

Mac says…

I find it hard to believe you could locate every single participant in this blog and "deal" with us. You're crazier than Studmufflicker69. Maybe you're him.

Sharkstooth says…

This is unreal. I've been looking for a support group. I want to be a vampire. Can you help me?

The High Commander says…

Obviously, Mac, you do not know what you're talking about or with whom you are dealing. You're in great danger and not from me. Pray I find you before Cletus as your encounter with me will be much less painful.

Well, that is true from one perspective. Though I think permanent amnesia could be worse than a few hours of excruciating pain. That's just my personal opinion.

Leprakhan says…

I'm becoming a vampire too! So nice to meet you all. I'm a little behind in this conversation. Who is she? Which master are we talking about? There are so many. It can't be mine because he'd never allow all of this to occur. Mac and Margaritaman, try doubling the Tabasco sauce in the Bloody Vlad.

"I hate leprechauns. They eat your toes you know." I glance at Stefan.

Tap, tap, tap, tap. He glares at me.

I slide off the desk. "This is the thanks I get for bringing Goldenrae to you?" I stomp past him, pivot at the end of the couch, turn and stomp back across the room.

Tap. Tap. Tap. Tap.

"I have done nothing but try to secure our territory. You put me in charge of the CCOC. How can you possibly be angry?"

"Your job was to learn all you could about this blog." Tap, tap, tap, tap.

Oooh. That again.

"And your job…" I point at him. "…was to tell me about Cletus and Goldenrae.

But you didn't. I had to find out on my own. And now I've returned Goldenrae, in spite of trying to keep her safe from a vampire attack, which I thought was happening because you didn't tell me about an approved mating."

"Is that so?" Tap, tap, tap, tap.

"Yes. And stop that!" I swat at his fingers.

He drums them over the wood again before reaching for his drink.

"I am a demon," he whispers and tilts his wine glass, watching the deep red liquid roll along the crystal. "But you already know this. Cynthia told you, didn't she?" He sips his cabernet.

It may seem like an inappropriate thing to do, but I am going to take this opportunity and capitalize on it. I think it only fair to warn you so you're not completely offended by my behavior.

"You have a lot of explaining to do." I step back and straighten my shirt, tucking it into the belt of my damn fanny pack. "You might have mentioned the whole demon thing sooner. I probably would have learned to be fine with it even from the beginning." I walk around the bar. I could use a glass of wine myself. "But now, it's like I have no choice. You know I hate having no say in matters as important as this."

I jam my hands on my hips and spin to face him. "It's as though I've been living a lie all these years." I smash right into his chest. "And do you have to sneak up on me, too? Lying and sneaking. What's next?"

He growls.

"Do I even know you? Who are you really? I don't even know my own husband!" I jab my finger into his chest.

That low growl rises from somewhere near his belly button and travels up his chest until his entire body rumbles.

I softly pat his chest. "Maybe we should discuss that part later."

I try to step back, but end up dangling in the air because his hands have gripped my biceps like two metal clamps, and he is lifting me up, holding me so we're face-to-face, and I'm forced to stare straight into his blazing red eyeballs.

"You have revealed our existence to the world and you're reprimanding me for *keeping* a secret." Remember when I explained Vox Potens back at Charlene's house? Well, he's using it in a very, very, very powerful way. The words pulse along my skin like a hot poker being dragged over my body. If I were human, I'd have peed just now. Involuntarily, of course.

"No. No, I didn't." I didn't. You know that's the truth. I know it. And that damn PenPro58 knows it. "I've done some other stuff, but I did not do that." I shake my head.

His grip tightens and his lip curls up in the most wretched of snarls.

I swallow. "I did steal Goldenrae, but I did it to save her. If you'd told me she was an approved mate, I'd have never touched her." I blink. A lot.

The veins in his neck bulge, and I worry about the one that appears in the middle of his forehead.

"Okay, I probably would have tried to find her, but I wouldn't have taken her."

His bottom lip sneers downward, and I can see every one of his front teeth and most of the side ones.

"I did leave the house, too. But that was because I had to find Goldenrae." I nod, hoping he'll try to follow my logic. "I was…I was trying to save her from Cletus, who was scaring her and she didn't want to be with him because he was scaring her." I nod some more. "I was saving her." I try to smile and end up sort of mimicking his face in a contorted grin.

"I charged you with remaining in the house. And you disobeyed me."

"Yes, well, let's talk about that. I should not be locked in a house. It's not very nice. If you had just taken me with you, this never would have happened." Let's face it. That's a fair statement.

"Chrysanthemum, why were you dallying with the enemy?"

Dallying? Dallying? I have never dallied. I am not a dallier. I'm a full-throttle sort of chick.

"What are you talking about?" I frown.

"You knew about this Eva Prim, had participated on that blog for more than a week, talking with that Eva, sharing secrets. The Bloody Vlad?" His eyes narrow. "A vampire tip page! You requested she create a tip page. What sort of tips do you need that I do not provide?"

Oh shit. So do I tell him now or deny, deny, deny? I look up at the ceiling and bite my lips, holding them together in an effort to keep control of my own mouth. As you well know, I am not PenPro58. I could argue that point and never be proven wrong. Of course, I can't deny knowing about the blog. In that argument I'd never be able to lie. I've just never been that good at lying. I always seem to give myself away with an obvious nervous tic or some other stupid telltale sign.

"Are you even listening?" He roars the question into my face blowing my hair back from my head.

Uh, no! I'm totally trying to figure out how to get out of this situation without getting caught in this situation. "Yes. I heard you." What the hell did he say?

"You will have to throw yourself on the mercy of the Federation and hope your history does not come into play at your trial."

"What?" Mercy? There's no mercy with the Federation. I'd have better luck dodging sunbeams in a house made of glass.

"The charge is treason." He finally sets me down. "Death is the punishment." He returns to the desk to lean against it, his shoulders slump and he stares down at his feet. "I've tried to think of every possible strategy to save you, but none comes to mind. I plan to offer your…" The next word he spits at the floor. "…entourage in your place. Though, I'm well aware the wolves will revolt at the thought of it. A risk I'll take. Then I'll beg for your life, but…"

Beg for my life? What? "I'm not PenPro58. Stefan, you have to believe me. I didn't out us." I race to his side and hold his hands. "I'm not her. I would never say something as stupid as that. I know better. I don't want to die. And you can't offer my friends in my place. That's a horrible idea. I don't want them to die either. "

His hand cups my chin. "There is no point in denying your involvement. You're only making this worse for both of us, and you're a terrible liar." His thumb caresses my chin. "You've never been able to hide the truth from me." He kisses my lips. "Even in the end you continue in your own way to hold onto your own perceived innocence."

"But I am innocent. I'm not PenPro58. I didn't announce our secret." I grab his shoulders and shake. "Are you crazy? I'm not her. I want to kill her. I wanted to use her to find Cletus and then kill her. I'm not her."

"It is no surprise to me you became wrapped up in this blog. I should have known when I gave you the computer, should have seen that you'd fall victim to the seduction of the Internet with its easy access to such unsavory places populated with lowlife participants just waiting to take advantage of my poor unsuspecting mate." He kisses my forehead. "The Internet with all its hidden traps. That website is like a den of iniquity. Only a poorly managed vampire, one whose master does not control her, would create such an inappropriate website where she'd lure unsuspecting victims into her death trap." He strokes my hair. "I have not protected you. I'll never forgive myself." He pulls me between his legs, one hand on my waist and one on my shoulder, massaging and squeezing.

"Wait. It's not that bad of a website. I mean there were some helpful hints on the pages." I fall against his chest.

"I knew you wanted friends. That's why I acquiesced when Cheng and Martin suggested the demons. You've had such bad luck with friends. I never suspected you'd learn to command them in a way that would defeat my power." He wraps his arms around me and holds me in an almost crushing embrace.

"I didn't defeat you." I mumble into his chest.

"I don't know if they should go back to The Book before or after the inquisition." He squeezes me.

"Never. They should never go back," I squeak and try to wiggle free.

"I should have tried harder, should have gone against my instincts and simply forced my subjects to be your friends. If only…" His sob muffles against my neck.

"Wait. I didn't want you to force people to be my friends. I wanted real friends. I mean I want real friends. I have real friends on the blog." I push back from his chest.

"My flower, those are not your friends. Don't you see? That Eva Prim is a vile creature. She tricked you into revealing our secret. She is using you as her scapegoat. You will be punished for her crimes." Tears glisten in his dark eyes. "But I will find her. I will make her pay." That menacing snarl returns to his face. "Until my last breath I will hunt her. I will find her. I will kill her."

I swallow hard. My throat is kind of dry so it's a really hard swallow that sort of gets stuck mid gulp. I lick my lips, but that feels like I just rubbed a cotton ball over sandpaper. I try the swallow once more but end up choking and hacking.

"My flower, do not worry." He still won't let go of me. I shove against his chest and fall backward onto the floor. "If my efforts to win your life are not successful, I promise you, your death will come quickly." He sighs, his voice breaking as he swoops down and pulls me back into his arms. "At my hand. I won't let anyone else do it. I made you. I'll be the one to…" He sobs and buries his face in my hair.

Oh shit.

You know damn full well I am not good with the fucking tears. And that "not good" is made a thousand times worse when it's a man who's crying. Then, that's amplified by a bazillion when that man is Stefan. I'd rather stake myself than deal with this. I look for a weapon. Anything to jam into my own heart. And of course, nothing is within reach.

He's only cried once before. That was when he had to admit he lied to me or really not lied, just omitted a huge, gigantic secret, one that could rightfully be considered equally as big as being a demon. "I am a vampire. I did not tell you, my flower, because I love you. I can't bear to lose you. Chrysanthemum, you are my only reason for existing," he blubbered.

That was two days into our marriage. Two days of me wondering where the hell he went every day. Finally, after two nights of my nonstop badgering he told me he'd been hiding beneath the bedroom in the cellar (a place I never went because it was dark and dirty and scary). It was like trying to get a leprechaun to tell you where he'd hidden his gold. But he broke. And I loved him. So I agreed to be a vampire, too, which meant I got used to dark, dirty, scary places pretty damn fast.

But this, this is slightly different because as we both know (that's you and me, not him) I have quite a bit to do with this whole Eva Prim situation. Though, let's acknowledge everything is Stefan's fault. If he had not been a vampire (or a demon, which may be why he's so sneaky) and just been a normal man, we'd both have died more than a hundred years ago, thus we would not be in this predicament.

His fault.

"This is all your fault." I know you're thinking I'm being childish, but I'm not. I'm working my way around to owning part of this. There's plenty of blame to go around and I like to share. "If you'd never changed me, this would not have happened."

"My love, if I'd never changed you, I'd have died when you died. My very heart would have crumbled to dust." He rubs his cheek against my hair. "You are my world. Everything I do, I do for you."

"Right." I brace my hands against his chest and push. "If you'd been honest… honesty being the best policy…about who you were from the beginning, we would not be in this situation. So, it really is all your fault." Again his firm embrace is unyielding even when I manage to brace both my knees against his chest and push backward.

He shoves my knees down. "You're right, my flower." He yanks me back against his chest. "I had planned to tell you that same night in Bristol, the night I explained my vampire state. Our third night of wedded bliss. I wanted our marriage to be based on honesty." He rubs my back and kisses my head. "But you so quickly replied, 'A vampire. Well, at least you're not a demon. That would be an atrocity.' I feared you'd leave me. I couldn't risk losing you. Not when you'd accepted the vampirism so well. I loved you, Chrysanthemum. I needed you."

"Uuulllll." I slump against him.

"Then, you went on to explain how you believed demons to be body snatchers, thoughtless, heinous creatures possessing unsuspecting humans. I just couldn't bear for you to think of me in such a way." He sighs and his body shakes with more sobs.

I check one more time for any possible weapon to end my own life. Nothing. Not even a table leg.

"Can you ever forgive me? Please don't go to your death hating the man who loves you more than life itself. Forgive me, my flower, for all my wrongdoings."

So I see an obvious escape route. You're going to hate me for it, but I'm taking it. Remember, he's lied since the start of our marriage. I'm entitled to one—never mind how many—to the occasional indiscretion.

"You want me to forgive you for the vampire lie? I mean omission."

"Well, more the demon issue. I thought you had forgiven me for the vampire situation." He presses kisses to my head.

"Well, yes, I have, but let's not forget it. And that I became a vampire for you."

"How could I forget that? It's been the joy of my existence even with all your escapades and other moments." He squeezes me.

"And now you want me to forgive you for the demon problem."

"Well, it's not so much a problem as it has not impacted you in any way."

"Oh, yes it has. I think it's what makes you able to lock me in the house, which I don't like." I wiggle around in his arms so my back is to his chest.

"Yes. Yes, you're correct. It is where that power comes from. And I won't do that again. But you must know I only did it to keep you safe." He snuggles against me. "The thought of losing you led me to be extremely protective."

"Naturally. You were well-meaning, yet misguided."

"Yes. Well-meaning." He kisses my cheek, then trails soft kisses to my ear.

"And misguided."

"Mmm. Yes, misguided." His kisses wander down my neck. He smells so damn good. That smoky aroma. His demon scent. I've always loved it. And it combines wonderfully with the scent of Eternity cologne. My mouth waters.

"Sometimes I'm well-meaning and misguided, too." I lean my head back against his chest so he can keep kissing my neck. "You see that, don't you?"

"Yes. Sometimes you are," he says between kisses.

"And that's okay," I whisper breathily.

"Mmm-hmm." His tongue swirls over the spot on my neck just below my jaw causing my knees to buckle, and he pulls me back against him, rubbing his hard cock against my backside.

"Stefan?"

"Yes, my flower?" He grinds his cock against me. His quick breath on my neck, his hands, one on my left breast and one sliding down past my belly button all make it nearly impossible to make my admission, but I do.

"I'm Eva Prim."

CHAPTER THIRTY-FOUR

You'd think I'd just offered Stefan a double shot of holy water. He heaves deep, loud breaths. Then leans over, gripping the desk like it's the only thing keeping him grounded to earth. Oh, and of course, he's no longer sexy Stefan. He's now angry-shifted-vampire-demon-Stefan. At least he doesn't have scales and that lizard-y look he had at Charlene's. So maybe he's less demon-y at the moment.

I clear my throat and pat him on the back. "You okay?"

His head snaps up, and that strange grimace is back, the one that shows nearly every tooth in his mouth. His eyes are practically crossed. He makes noise. Doesn't form words, but makes a sort of grunting, howling, growling—hhhhh-huuuuuuuuuuuunnnnnnnrrrrrrr—sort of noise. Repeatedly.

I bite my lip. If he was human, I'd offer him a drink to try to calm his nerves. Maybe some absinthe. But seeing as he's a vampire, I'm not offering. Offering an upset vampire a drink is like saying, "Would you like me to pour myself into a glass, or will you drain me dry straight from my neck?" Nope. Not offering. I learned that lesson by accident. Firsthand. Only, you can imagine, I was the upset one. Let's not discuss the finality of that relationship.

"Do you want to sit down?" I pull out the chair from behind the desk.

"HHHHHHGGGGGGGRRRRRRRRRRRRR." He lifts the end of the desk and bangs it down against the floor three times.

"It's really not that bad. I told you I wasn't PenPro58. She's the one who—"

He walks around the desk, coming straight toward me.

I step backward. "At least I didn't…"

He stalks forward.

I walk backwards, moving at just the same pace as he. "…reveal who I am."

The muscles in his cheeks, neck, chest, and arms flex and drops of blood drip from his palms where his claws have cut into his skin. As you know that happens if you make a tight fist when you're in his current condition. He should know better.

I push a chair between us, and he bats it across the room without taking his attention from me.

"We should find her. If we can present PenPro58 to The High Commander, this will all go away." I scamper backward trying to put as much distance between us as possible.

He leaps the last few feet separating us and backs me against the wall.

"I think this might not be quite as bad as you're making it out to be." Gulp.

He slams his fists into the wall on either side of my head. Cracks form in the stone, creating a spider web pattern all the way up to the ceiling.

"I mean I didn't really do anything *that* bad. In the grand scheme of things, this is just a minor hiccup." Once again I try to smile, but my mouth does this sympathy thing and forms a weird grin I suspect is exactly the same as his.

He doesn't move, just stares at me. Have you ever been stared at by a master vampire? I have. But I'm going to assume you have not. To be completely truthful, I have to admit I have been stared at by almost every vampire I've ever met, even the ones who are clearly less powerful than I, which is somewhat insulting, but I'll get to that on the blog at some point. Your mother must have told you it's not polite to stare. Well, it's not. Plus it's really stupid to stare at a vampire who's clearly more powerful than you. Idiots.

But back to the situation at hand. It's most certainly not nice to be stared at by a master vampire. In fact it is not at all an understatement to say it's terribly uncomfortable. I mean, they have x-ray vision. At least that's how it feels. It's like having someone stare into your brain and then take a little trip around your body just checking things out.

Well, maybe that's not how it feels for everyone or maybe not every master vampire has that ability. But Stefan does. Or maybe he just has it with me. Whatever. The point is he's giving me the heebie-jeebies again.

"Stop that!" I bat at my arms and legs and rub my hands over my hair, down my neck to my chest and across my belly. "Do you have to be so skeevy? You know I hate that." I shove him backward, nearly knocking him over.

I really don't like the feeling of someone wandering around inside me. "This is why I can't stand fighting with you. You cheat." I march over to the bar and grab the corkscrew and a bottle of wine from the rack. "If you want to know something, just ask. I'll tell you." Maybe.

I struggle with the cork. I'm usually quite adept at removing these things. I can use the cool corkscrew, the one you just twist and pull, you know, the one without the wings. I huff and yank, but the cork breaks off. Damn it. I am picky about my wine. I prefer to drink it without bits of floating cork.

Stefan removes the bottle and corkscrew from my hand, and I'm overjoyed. On two accounts. One, he's shifted back into his much better looking self, not to mention he smells a lot more appealing. And two, he will uncork the wine for me.

He places the unopened bottle of wine on the bar and removes an iced tea from the fridge. "We are not celebrating. No wine." Before I can argue I was just thirsty, he fills a glass with ice and pours the tea. "What was your point to the website?"

Hmm. So we're still on that, are we?

"I was trying to make friends, if you must know." I take my glass of tea and the half-full bottle and sit on the couch.

"Why didn't you tell me?" He boots up the laptop on the coffee table and sits in the chair next to the couch.

"I wanted to surprise you."

"Well, that you have." The computer blinks to life and he brings up my website. After reviewing the Tips, Myths and Advice pages without so much as a nod, he clicks on the blog. "Your friends seem to be quite busy."

I lean toward him.

~Eva Prim Writes~
One hundred and two Comments.

I squeal. I can't help it. One hundred and two? Yes! I put down my tea, move to the chair and pull the computer onto my lap.

"Darling, I'm sitting in this chair," Stefan says.

We jockey around and I end up sitting between his legs, still holding the computer. I manage to read through the first thirty or so comments before he reclaims the laptop. Let me just tell you I counted about fifteen new screen names. That's fifteen more friends. Isn't it awesome?

"Wow. Look at all the people participating. They're talking about The Shift and The Bloody Vlad and Bonding and they want to know about The Change and what it's like to have a master and whether the whole sunlight thing is true and if vampires really can consume anything other than blood. Wow. Wow. Wow. " I giggle and try to pull the computer back from him.

"This is a problem, not a joyous occasion." He leans around me and ends up only an inch from my face. I back up. "Not only has PenPro58 outed us, you shared details of vampirism. You have made it possible for all these people to discuss us, our ways, the secrets of our existence. People who did not believe we were real are now seriously considering vampires walking among them. This is a catastrophe." He points toward the screen.

"I suspect some of your other minions have been participating." That's very clear and I know for damn sure about Fangman333, but I'm not giving up any names, especially since he's thinking of offering up my friends in my place.

And in spite of the whole "beg for your life" problem I can't let anyone be sacrificed for me. They're my friends, not my body doubles.

"Why are you calling them minions?" he asks, then rakes his fingers through his hair and stretches his neck from one side to the other. "My captains have been on the blog in an attempt to stop you from…" His voice trails off and he rubs his temples.

"Well, it makes no sense to execute them."

"Of course not. Why would I do that?" He's moved on to rubbing his eyes.

"If you're going to kill everyone who had anything to do with the blog, that includes them."

"I am not executing anyone who attempted to save you." He massages his neck.

"Yeah, but THC is. You saw his comment about personally executing anyone who participated on the blog." I pour the rest of the tea into my glass and take a sip.

He sighs. "I can understand his point, and it is well within his authority as The High Commander to deliver such a punishment."

"But that doesn't mean we should let him do it. They are my friends, even if you don't think they're real friends." I sit sideways, lifting the laptop to hang my legs over the arm of the chair.

"You don't know them, darling. You must realize that friends have a connection, care about you. These are strangers."

"Using your logic, I wouldn't really define Tarek as a friend. You haven't seen him in fifty years, yet you call him a friend. I personally think friends should keep up on each other's goings-on and all that jazz."

"Tarek and I are well aware of each other's situations. We simply have not had opportunity to see each other." He watches the comments pop up on the computer screen.

"You mean to tell me in fifty years you couldn't find a few days to get together?" That doesn't sound like friendship to me.

"Darling, I've seen him at Federation events. He's been quite busy. Not to mention I've had a lot going on here in the past several years, what with taking over the region state by state, laying down the law, setting expectations and making my own desires known. Let's not forget gaining control of demons set loose by my own mate. I have been quite busy. And you've been incredibly particular about your vacation plans."

"Speaking of the demons, you're not sending my demons back to The Book, are you? You can't. I won't let you." I look him dead in the eyes. "I love them."

"I know you do." He brushes my hair from my shoulder. "If you're not…" His cheek twitches. "…executed, they will remain free with conditions, of course."

"What kind of conditions? I don't plan to be executed so we might as well discuss these conditions now. I have to agree to them, and I'm not agreeing to anything barbaric or cruel or anything I'm not able to control."

He doesn't respond. Instead he simply stares at me with as blank an expression as he's ever worn.

"I am their master. I should make the deci—"

"And I am your master. If anyone should have any control in this situation, it should be me. Yet, that seems to be a concept you are incapable of comprehending."

"All the more reason for me to have a say in the 'conditions.' You want me to support them, don't you? It's important we appear to be masters in a partnership, don't you think?" I blink a few times.

He sighs again. "Fine. We will come to an accord on the conditions. But, if there's even one indiscretion—"

I kiss him on the lips. "Good. The demons will be fine. I can handle them. We should plan a vacation. I've been working very hard, you know." I reposition the laptop. I'm dying to read through the rest of the comments. There are so many new names, new people to meet.

He rubs his neck and shrugs his shoulders. "If we survive this, I will need a vacation, too."

"I don't mind vacationing in Canada. We could go visit Tarek." When I glance at him, he flinches. "What? What was that?"

"Nothing, my flower. I'll think about a vacation in Canada." He nods toward the screen. "What's going on there?"

He's hiding something. I know it. But the activity on the computer screen is so exciting I can't help but let the subject drop.

I scroll through the last several comments.

MyManSteve says…

I still don't understand The Bond. Is it something that happens involuntarily or do you sign up for it? Are humans completely unaware or do they have any idea it's happening?

Mac says…

As I understand it MyManSteve The Bond can occur without the human's awareness of it. So right now it could be happening to you or me. I don't want to be bound to a vampire or bitten by a werewolf. How did I ever get caught up on this damn blog? They're not real. NOT REAL!!!

Moongirl2nite says…

Oh Mac nothing would happen if you were bitten by a werewolf. You don't just become one by getting bitten. It's genetic.

Shelly521 says…

So Eva, I love someone and he loves me and he knows about me and what I am and he's not upset by that. We want to be together. I'm not sure how to go about getting permission to do this and then how to prepare him for what's to come. Can you help?

Harvey says…

Is there no way to keep the ear and nose hair from growing so long? I'm new to this and struggling to keep from shifting. How do I do it without my master? He's not the nicest guy. I end up in that state more times than I like.

The High Commander says…

First, to whomever asked—All vampires are not evil, similar to the notion that all humans are not simply vessels carrying nourishment.

Second, to Bluegrassgirl— I was unaware of these issues in Kentucky. You can rest assured that I will take action. I'm notifying my Clean Up Crew now.

Third—Use of this blog must cease and desist at once! I cannot be any clearer about this. Continued participation in this blog will lead to severe punishment. Every last one of you will be punished.

Fourth— All interested and willing bounty hunters are hereby notified of an Executive Order for Retrieval and Removal of one Eva Prim and PenPro58. The reward is negotiable, but up to and including a Territorial Challenge of either masters.

SandyLikesManCandy says...

Is it true when you become a vampire all your physical problems get fixed? Like acne goes away and if your back is broken does it fuse back together? Are there any vampires who limp?

MyManSteve says...

So if my girlfriend seems a little psycho and only comes over at night and leaves me completely drained after getting it on several times in one visit I shouldn't worry about her being a vampire?

I start typing with plans to answer everyone's questions, but the computer vanishes from my lap, and I end up sitting on the couch six feet away.

"What the hell? Give me that back!" I jump up to grab the laptop and miss as Stefan bolts to the other side of the desk.

"This is a nightmare. You have to stop. There is a bounty on your head. And mine." He drops the laptop onto the desk. I'm certain he's fighting the desire to smash it to the floor. His white-knuckle grip on the desk sort of cues me into that.

"But don't you see? They need answers, advice, help. That's what I'm here for. I can help them all." I zip to the desk and reach for the laptop.

My fingers barely brush the white edge as Stefan whisks it out of my reach. "That is not what you're here for. You're my mate. Not the Dear Abby of the vampire world! Have you lost your mind? Do you have any idea how serious this is? You've outed us! OUTED US! The Federation wants you dead. Bounty hunters are swarming our region. You're not going to last the night. Why don't you understand this?"

He hugs the laptop to his chest and paces the floor, mumbling about how his whole world is ending because he wasn't a good husband and master and he didn't fulfill my needs or make my world perfect, and he deserves to die in my place but he knows if he offers himself it would leave me with no one to understand me, no one to keep me from opening my mouth five seconds later and getting killed, too. His voice cracks and he spins to face me, tears streaming.

"Why? Why, my flower? Why have you chosen such a wrong and strange way to make friends? How are you not able to see the dangers in this?" He tosses the laptop onto the desk, which by the way cracks when it slides off and hits the floor. Damn it!

"We must fight to the death." He grabs my hands and brings them to his lips, repeatedly kissing them. "Side by side, my love, we will fight. We shall die together. If only I'd allowed you to learn the sword, but I did not." He clutches me against his chest. "It's better this way. We shall die quickly. Overtaken by those bastards, hungry for your blood and my seat." He squeezes me, kisses my head and sobs. "That you should die such an awful death overwhelms me. How could I let this happen?" His body shakes as he's overtaken with grief or something. I don't know. I hate when men cry.

Oh, for the love of chocolate and vampires and all things unholy and holy and everything else that's ever existed he has got to stop with the crying. "What is wrong with you? THC can't be serious. I mean he is blogging, too." I try to break out of his embrace. "Stefan, let go. You're crushing me."

He freezes. The tears stop. The sobs. The shaking. He becomes perfectly still. "Yes. We shall use his decision to comment on your blog to our benefit. We shall turn this around." He pulls me to the door. "Come. We will prepare for your execution."

"What?" I run after him, yet again confused by his behavior. When will it ever stop?

CHAPTER THIRTY-FIVE

Have you ever been to a vampire inquisition? Probably not. So, let me explain what we've got happening here.

We're in the round, which is a gigantic underground auditorium. It's dark, except for the strategically placed torches, which were my idea. Thank you very much. Vampire décor is so vampy, I guess you'd say. Dark silk and velvet drapes fall from the ceiling to be gathered at alternating intervals against the wall, held back by leather straps and chains. It's sort of romantic in a gothic way.

You wouldn't be able to see the crowd with human vision. But being a vampire I have superb night vision. The place is packed. Well, who doesn't love a good execution?

Centered in the round is…me. Where else did you think I'd be? Stefan is seated on the dais on his giant throne, which by the way is quite gauche. It's sort of a Louis the XIV chair, and I've never really been fond of that style. The High Commander is seated to the right of Stefan in what should be my chair. That's annoying and funny. My chair is more like something you'd expect to see Queen Elizabeth sitting in. Gold and red and smaller than Stefan's chair.

The captains, including that traitor Francois along with the Alpha Wolf, Rob, are seated at a long table to Stefan's left. Liam is acting as scribe to record the evening's events. Martin and Cheng stand behind me, guarding this evil prisoner.

Have I mentioned how many times I've sat in this particular seat? Three. I've been brought to inquisition three times. The first time was for a situation that occurred due to a reaction I had to something I thought Stefan did or was doing or meant to do. You should know I've never forgiven myself for that incident, er rather my reaction that caused the incident.

Seated across from me and shaking like leaves are Jackson, Pierre and Cynthia, who can't stop grinning and head bobbling, which signals that all three demons are nervous. Pierre must be hiding somewhere inside the host because he is clearly letting Cynthia control the body. Her eyelids are blinking, though not at all in unison, but at a rate of six hundred blinks a minute or something like it. Noelle is seated on one side of Charlene and Margaritaman is on the other, clinging to her and mumbling about not wanting to be scrubbed. Standing behind them are the rest of the Soldatis, not one of whom looks even slightly amused.

Goldenrae and Cletus must be back in their room, bonding, if you know what I mean.

"Let the inquisition commence," The High Commander announces. His voice echoes around us, though he barely moves his lips. Vox Potens. It is a neat trick. Man I hope I learn how to do it someday.

With a very slight nod of his head Stefan signals to Titus to read the charges.

Titus does not possess the power of Vox Potens so he has to stand and yell. If he'd just use the microphone, he'd look a lot cooler. Instead he looks and sounds like an idiot, not at all like the town crier.

"The first offense is revealing our existence to the world. The punishment—death.

"The second offense is stealing a vampire's approved mate. The punishment—death.

"The third offense is kidnapping a werewolf, a vampire, and a human. The punishment—death."

I roll my eyes. What did I tell you? Death is the punishment for everything. It's so predictable. I tap my foot and stare at Titus.

"Chrysanthemum Mildred Stevens Papadopoulos, how do you answer to these charges?"

My vision fades to red. I hate that name. Chrysanthemum Mildred? Who does that to a kid? Who in their right mind names a baby Chrysanthemum Mildred?

What do you think my parents were smoking in 1812? Do you think by the time they got to daughter number thirteen they'd run out of decent names?

You should know they were hippies from the 1800s. All thirteen of us had flower names. Apparently, I was an ugly baby because they named me after a flower that's really not very pretty and is impossible for a child to spell.

Oh, and Mildred? That was my grandmother's name. If I had to choose between the two, I'd pick Mildred because you can shorten it to Millie, which is sort of cute in a 1920s kind of way.

I actually hear the crowd whispering about my name. And giggling. They're laughing at me.

I growl.

Darling, pay attention. How do you answer to the charges? Stefan's calm voice whispers in my mind. *Remember, you must control yourself during these proceedings.*

"Not guilty, though I'd like an opportunity to respond more fully to the charges."

"The evidence is overwhelming, Mrs. Papadopoulos," The High Commander says.

"Not really." I remind myself of my goal and the fact that I don't want Stefan to offer any of my friends in my place or to throw himself on the stake for me. "First, I did not kidnap a werewolf, vampire or human. Those three…" I glance at my friends. "…all came willingly, of their own accord, without any coercion. They were willing accomplices."

"Accomplices? Than we have more than one criminal on our hands?" The High Commander slides to the edge of his seat.

"Well, maybe accomplices isn't the right word. Maybe they were more like—"

"Friends. We're her friends." Charlene turns to face The High Commander. "We all went willingly on this adventure."

"Am I to understand you assisted Mrs. Papadopoulos in the kidnapping of an approved mate?" The High Commander's voice snakes in the space between us.

"No. They didn't help me. I did that part on my own," I answer before Charlene makes it worse.

"We helped." Cynthia raises her hand. "It was me and Jackson."

"Two demons assisted in the abduction of Goldenrae also known as Sunny Giorno?" The High Commander turns to Stefan. "This seems rather simple. Your men shall dispose of the demons." He motions for Cheng and Martin to move toward the demons.

"No!" I jump up from my seat, and Martin guides me back to the chair. He and Cheng remain behind me, waiting for Stefan's signal. "Stefan, do something."

He nods, and Cheng draws his sword.

Cynthia throws her arms around Jackson and cries. "I don't want to go back. I don't want to go."

I leap out of my chair, but Martin pulls me back. "Leave them Chryssie. You'll only make it worse, if you don't." His voice is so low I barely hear him.

"No. I love them."

Cheng swings his sword back with his eyes focused on Cynthia.

"Stop! I do not want to press charges. I withdraw my claims and beg the court to pardon Chrysanthemum." Cletus descends the steps into the round with Goldenrae at his side. "My mate was returned to me with no harm done and having made friends with Chrysanthemum. For this I am grateful."

Cletus is clean. Bathed. Shaved. Dressed. Hazel eyes clear. Short dark hair combed. Wearing a suit. He's tall and lean, like a runner. And not one strand of nose hair sticks out of either nostril.

Goldenrae is no longer dressed like a teenybopper. She looks like the perfect little vampire in an electric blue suede mini skirt, a sleeveless white lace top with lots and lots of ruffles down the front and stacked black shoe boots over floral patterned pantyhose. Her hair is pinned up in a French twist. She looks stunning.

"Mr. Shiftbottom, your mate was kidnapped. You mentioned it several times on this blog." The High Commander holds out his hand and a thick file is placed in it by a scrawny looking vampire. He quickly thumbs through the stack of forms. "I count twenty-six specific mentions of the missing fledgling." He looks at Cletus.

"I was a vampire in the throes of Bonding Fever. I could barely control myself. I was arrested, broke free, killed a couple guards. I turned my mate and buried her in a basement. Then I left the area. Chryssie and her demons saved Sunny. If they hadn't retrieved her, she'd have died in that basement. She'd have never been able to survive without feeding. I was in no state to care for Sunny during her first couple nights. I owe my gratitude to Chryssie." He wraps his arm around Goldenrae and they both smile at me. "Thank you."

The crowd whispers and hisses.

"I count Ev..." Goldenrae's eyes widen for a split second and then return to their lovely almond shape. "...Chryssie among my close friends. And I'm pretty sure I owe her a car."

I'd even forgotten, but she's right. She does owe me a car.

"High Commander, if Cletus and Goldenrae no longer wish to press charges, then the charge must be dropped," Stefan says.

The whispers escalate to yelling and the crowd stomps its feet and chants, "Drop! Drop! Drop! Drop! Drop!"

The High Commander surveys the group surrounding me and then the crowd. "Very well." He scribbles something on his paper. "That still leaves us to the kidnapping of the wolf, vampire and human. Mrs. Harper, what say you in this matter?"

Noelle stares at me, her steel blue eyes are ice cold. Her jaw is set. Her fangs descend and she snarls at me.

Now what did I do?

She opens her mouth, closes it, swallows hard, glances up at the darkened ceiling and begins to speak. "I was not kidnapped. I participated willingly, just as Charlene did. And I count Chryssie among my friends, too."

"Me, too," Margaritaman offers, though he never looks toward Stefan or The High Commander and he slouches behind Charlene.

"Very well. If no one wants to press charges, we shall drop the kidnapping charges as well." The High Commander motions to his scrawny flunkey and a scroll appears. He rapidly scribbles, his feather pen bobbing away.

My friends cheer and jump up, but the first one to take a step gets returned to the couch by Neil, and the others quickly take their seats.

"We still have the little matter of the blog." The High Commander's voice booms.

CHAPTER THIRTY-SIX

"Mrs. Papadopoulos, please explain your connection to the blog."

I glance at Stefan.

Go ahead, darling.

I inhale, bite my lip, blink at THC and then launch into my explanation. Of course, it's not quite the way Stefan and I rehearsed, but I can't remember everything. "Well, really I was just looking for friends. You see, I received the computer a few weeks back and found blogs posted everywhere on all sorts of topics—books, food, politics, pets, candy, genetics, electricity, nail polish, travel, health, exercise, painting—"

"I get the point. So you found this blog and began participating as a way to make friends. Is that correct?"

He stares at me, and the expression on his face is a mix of irritation, boredom, and desire for vengeance. I happen to know what all three look like because the first and the third I've somehow caused to appear on a number of faces. The middle one I've experienced several times myself. I'm proud to say not once in all my years, both human and vampire, have I ever been the cause of boredom.

His left eyebrow arches, while his right turns into a pulsing caterpillar. He really should consider trimming. His eyes slowly blink as though he's just about to drift off to sleep. His top lip crooks up and toward his left eyebrow. Actually his lip and eyebrow are pretty much doing the exact same thing.

My lip pulses and I pucker to stop it.

Darling, your connection.

I'm getting to it.

"Shall I repeat myself, Mrs. Papadopoulos?" THC asks and slams his fist on the table.

I clear my throat. "No, I remember what you were asking. Thanks for offering."

Every muscle in THC's face constricts.

Stefan leans forward in his seat and sighs so loudly I'm surprised THC doesn't accuse him of contempt or some other ridiculous charge.

"Mrs. Papadopoulos, did you participate in this blog to make friends? Yes or no?" The High Commander demands.

"Sort of. Originally I began participating on candy and perfume and cosmetic blogs. I was a regular commenter on several where the topics turned from cologne to what does a vampire really smell like. So, of course, I could answer that. And when I did—"

"Exactly what did you say?"

"Well, I explained that vampires generally try to fit in with everyone else. We bathe and wear cologne, not deodorant because who's sweating? I explained how we smell far worse when we're in that other state."

"Shifted?"

"Yes."

"Did you explain The Shift on this blog?"

"No. I just mentioned it. It wasn't until the Eva Prim blog that I explained The Shift, which I really didn't explain in full, just gave an overview. There's more to it than we discussed."

"Let me understand. You have discussed The Shift on multiple blogs." The High Commander stands at the table, shuffling pages between three files while his flunkey, whose name is Carl, I heard THC say it, rushes back and forth between THC and a box of information at the end of the table.

"Not exactly. I merely mentioned it on the other blog. And on the Eva Prim blog I didn't give a thorough explanation." I nod. "Though, the information that was discussed seemed quite helpful and has generated a number of other questions. In fact, much of the information on that site is helpful to new vampires and masters and to those thinking of joining us. Really, the entire site is having a positive impact on so many people."

My supporters all nod.

"I'm confused, Mrs. Papadopoulos." The High Commander carries several pages around the table to stand only a few feet from me. Carl organizes the files on the table and runs over to THC with the quill. "I have here, on page 603, the explanation of The Shift. Along with it I have all the ensuing commentary. It appears to me that you did not explain The Shift. Instead you commented on it. I quote, *"Oh, it's not that long for most. If it is long, you really don't care because you're one of those who likes it. The hair remains shorter, if you try to look normal."* Further in the conversation you said, *"Oh, it's terrible. The breath is quite distressing but the nose hair. Oh…"*

I suck my cheeks in and bite down.

So, here it is. The moment of truth.

"You needn't take the entire blame for the discussion of The Shift. Though, I will say you should not have engaged in any conversation involving this topic." He glances up at me as he shuffles through a few more pages.

The corners of my lips involuntarily tug themselves in opposite directions. Everyone around me leans closer and complete silence falls in the round. I scratch my head and briefly regain control of my lips but they betray me and pull back into that dumbass grin.

He turns back to the table and his long black robe flaps, sending a quick whiff my way. He smells like Santal Blush by Tom Ford, the perfect cologne for him. Very manly and commanding.

"I'm Eva Prim."

The High Commander looks up from the table and drops his papers. Carl drops a stack of files on the floor and stares at me, mouth open.

Vampires with gaping mouths always look ridiculous. I'm not sure if it's the descended fangs or the slightly paler than human skin or what, but they look like idiots.

The High Commander turns and walks toward me. Stefan rises from his seat and accompanies him. They stop only a few feet from me, The High Commander looming over me. His eyes are as red as hot tamales, only a lot rounder.

"What did you say?"

I lick my lips and know better than to lock gazes with him. I imagine having him stare into my eyes would be like looking directly into the sun.

"Well…you see…" I peak at him. His eyes flare, and I quickly look at Stefan, who doesn't move.

Cynthia whimpers, hiccups and then wails. Jackson pats her back. "It'll be fine, Cynthia. Shush."

"Oh my God. What's he going to do?" Margaritaman's teeth chatter.

"I don't know," Charlene answers. "Noelle?"

Noelle is frozen, staring into the crowd. I steal a glance into the darkened arena and see her husband, Tom, standing up. The horrified look on his face is very sweet. Now that I see him watching her, it's easy to tell he loves her.

The High Commander's index finger touches my chin, and he tilts my head back to face him.

As quick as I can I close my eyes.

"What did you say?"

I clear my throat. "I'm Eva Prim." No sense in whispering or cowering at this point. I mean, I am her. I might as well admit it, even if the meanest vampire I know has his razor-blade fingernail pointed at my jugular.

His fingers close around my chin. "Not PenPro58? Instead you are the root of this entire problem?"

Now that's a little harsh.

"Well, I am Eva but I wouldn't call me the root of the entire problem. Really, wouldn't the root of the entire problem be the first vampire to exist? He would ultimately be the root of all our problems. Lack of sunlight. Blood diets. The whole shifting issue. Really, how can you possibly believe I'm the root of the entire problem?" Then, like a moron I open my eyes.

Let me just say I was right. Being stared at by any master vampire feels like having someone invade your body. He is burning a hole into my head.

My eyes flutter and tear. My breath hitches and my heart beats out of control, faster and faster until I can no longer tell if it's beating or not.

Then the strangest thing happens. When I stop noticing what my body's doing—like feeling each individual hair stand straight up, which is really weird because two or three would go together, but then one might be alone and then like thirty would go all at once, giving me goosebumps, and it all happens in a matter of fourteen seconds—the most overwhelming sense of loneliness hits me.

Way down, deep in my core, a sadness aches within me. All around cold, darkness chills me. I'm alone. Just me.

I hear whimpering coming from somewhere in the shadow, but it's not my voice. It's a low distant moan. I focus on the sound and hear, "So alone."

"Where are you?" I ask.

And a door slams, yanking me back to reality.

The High Commander stares at me, carving a hole into my brain with a stare that would make a laser beam feel like a flashlight powered by old batteries and that's when I realize what's occurring. I am reading his mind. Holy Moly! I can hear all his thoughts and see his worries and know his secret desires.

I delve back into him. The most disturbing thing I notice is his heart only beats once or twice a minute. That freaks me out and I cringe, not that I move very far. He has quite a grip on my chin.

I turn my attention back to his thoughts. So this is what it's like to see inside a vampire's mind. It's just as dark in here as you'd expect. He's not thinking about bunny rabbits, flowers and the circus.

He really does have a distorted sense of what's right. On one side of his mind all the items he is currently considering are tabbed and filed as though in a cabinet. Kentucky. Eva Prim. PenPro58. Three stakings in Anaheim. (I wonder what that's about.) Stefan's replacement.

But on the other side of his mind lies the unexpected.

I giggle.

He growls.

I pucker my lips and try not to laugh, but end up snorting. Bits of information jumble about his left brain.

Did you know, he's afraid of mice and rats? I didn't. Honestly, all rodents of any kind freak him out. He has a bit of a sock fetish. His socks must be at least eighty percent cotton. He loves to drink a hot cocoa made with milk every morning before bed. He sleeps in the nude and usually with multiple women. He likes my blog. He misses his mom.

Me, too.

He pulls back from me, releases my chin and spins away from me. He ends up leaning on the table, panting.

My brain hurts. "High Commander, I—"

"Silence!" His cape rustles as his whole body pulses, sending the strong fragrance of sandalwood toward me. I inhale, smack my lips. That Tom Ford creates some tasty cologne. Very nice.

The demons, Noelle, Charlene and Margaritaman all run from the bench, followed by the Soldatis. They leap up the steps to the crowd and dive into the rows, hiding among the cowering audience. Stefan and I don't move. Cheng and Martin gather beside us and the six captains rise, ready to face The High Commander.

Oh boy. The last thing in the world I want to happen is for my entire region to be annihilated because we pissed off Bob. That's his real name. Who'd have thought The High Commander was named Bob? I'd have expected a much more powerful name like Zeus. That is, if I thought he had a real name, which never occurred to me until I read his mind.

I zip to Bob's side, place my hand on his back and whisper. "Your secrets are safe with me."

He turns his head. His ears and nose are already in an alternate state. His breath, well you know. And his eyes are still hot tamale red.

"I'm afraid of rats, too. And I like hot cocoa and I miss my mom," I whisper in a voice so soft I'm absolutely certain no one but Bob could have heard. "And I love my blog, too."

He has the sharpest fangs. They're like needles at the end. They can't be natural. He must sharpen them each night.

"How did you do that?" His beady red eyes narrow and his lip sneers upward.

"No idea. I hoped you could explain it." I shrug.

"High Commander, as my wife explained her blog has been more of an aid than anything else. Even you have used it to learn of problems in other areas, to help clear up misconceptions about us and to communicate bits of information. Clearly, your own participation on the blog indicates you understand its usefulness." Stefan appears at my side. "Obviously, our community has good need of you."

The High Commander glares down at the table. "Your point?" He shuffles papers about in an absent-minded way, sloppily placing them in piles. He rips the ones that don't stack well, forcing them to fit.

"High Commander, it is important a vampire of your stature and power continue to lead our ranks with thoughtful oversight. Your execution would have drastic results." Stefan's arm wraps around my waist, and he tugs me away.

"My execution?" There's that confused partially shifted vampire look. It's disturbing in a B Movie sort of way.

I wiggle away from Stefan and lean over to help Bob fix a couple sheets of parchment, roll up a scroll and secure one of the leather straps on his satchel.

Stefan nods, one eyebrow creeping up. "You did indicate on the blog several times that anyone caught participating would be executed. That would include you."

Bob snickers.

"You've never been a man to back down in these sorts of matters. Of course, when something has such positive results for the greater good, anyone could understand why you'd change your mind or make an exception." A very sly, very wicked grin slides across Stefan's lips.

I glance at Bob and nod, my eyes as wide as I can make them, a very slight smile on my face.

"Fine. The charges are dropped." He motions to the stack of boxes holding more paperwork, and Carl begins rummaging. "But the blog must be eliminated. The threat to our existence must be terminated."

"At once." Stefan nods.

"What?" I'm not the only one who asks. I'd say at least half the crowd demands an answer.

CHAPTER THIRTY-SEVEN

So, there was no elimination. There was arguing, some whining, quite a bit of foot stomping, and several fingers pointing, not to mention a lot of loud booing and hissing. But in the end my blog continues. It's now secure which means it requires password access and a security clearance to obtain the password. It's a pain in the neck, but I'm still in business and ultimately I get to decide who gets clearance. So all my friends are still blogging with me.

My Fix-It List is filled with more items than usual. Find all my demons. Get Pierre his own host body, though that item sort of freaks me out, but Cynthia's high-pitched whining, which does seem completely bizarre when she typically speaks in a rough baritone, is driving me crazy. Not to mention I think they're going to slap each other senseless. That needs to move to the top of the list, though you know how I feel about body snatchers. Check up on Noelle and Tom who left the inquisition together. A good sign. Drop by The Blue Moon for dinner. Margaritaman is working the salad line and he was allowed to keep all his memories of that night, though I'm sure he wouldn't mind forgetting a few. I want to make sure he still loves his job. Pick up a housewarming gift. Charlene's brothers built an apartment above the garage so she could have her own place. It's not perfect, but it's better than before. Get catnip for Kitten. Buy a party dress. We just received our invitation to Cletus and Goldenrae's wedding. It's a Valentine's Night affair. I can't wait. Oh, wedding gift. Update the Tips, Myths and Advice pages. Shop for a car.

I still have to answer all the questions that popped up while I was busy with Goldenrae so my new misguided friends can be set straight. And I need to find PenPro58. I promised THC (He prefers THC to Bob. Go figure.) I would. And even though he's told me it isn't necessary, I've vowed to find her and deal with her myself. I'm not letting her get away with what she's done.

Stefan, Cheng, and Martin advise me to focus on my new job as an advice columnist and also tell me I don't need to find her. They know something and have lost their minds if they think I won't figure it out. I'm like a dog on a bone, Sherlock Holmes on the case, a bear with the scent of honey in her snout. I'm on it.

My new job managing *Eva Prim Writes* (which has turned out to be a very much needed, appreciated, and utilized advice column and not just for vampires) affords me lots of time. I'll get to the bottom of the PenPro58 issue. Don't you worry about that. She can't help but comment on the blog. I'll find her.

I'm investigating chat rooms, too. I think a chat room would allow for more participation at a faster rate, thus resolving some of the timing issues leading to odd comments.

-Eva Prim Writes-

November 1st

Good Evening, friends, and I mean all of you.

As promised tonight we'll discuss The Change. No, not menopause. I mean the making of a vampire. First, let me say it's painful. You didn't actually think dying was going to be easy, did you? In this case you die and then wake up again, only you're different. Dead and sort of not dead.

Let me warn you. This is not going to be the most technical explanation, but basically, someone drinks a lot of you. As I've said before, one vampire can't drink a human dry. It's impossible. We just can't consume that much. And besides, a human doesn't have to be drained completely to be killed. Plenty of people die with all their blood still in their bodies. It just happens in this case a vampire drinks most of you then gives you a sip of himself, and then you sort of pass out. You're probably thinking you pass out from dehydration, but really I think it's more shock. You can't actually believe you were crazy enough to drink someone's blood straight from his body. And worst of all, you were so thirsty you liked it.

But you did, thus, when you wake up you're not entirely alive, but not altogether dead either, and you have an insatiable craving for blood.

Consider this info for a while. I've got to go to some dumbass meeting with Stefan and the captains, who I know have all been reading my blog. Don't think I don't know which of you keeps commenting and telling me I'm wrong. Don't make me publicly embarrass you. I'm not above that, you know.

Anyway, I'll be back to explain rejuvenation later tonight. But remember what I've already told you. If you're considering becoming a vampire, get your ass into shape, take care of your skin and for devil's sake don't tattoo anything stupid on your body. You'll be stuck with that ridiculous whore tag above your ass for all eternity. Eva

ACKNOWLEDGEMENTS

Publishing my own book has certainly been an experience, one I would never have accomplished without the great support of several people. First, my family who all "friended" Eva on Facebook and set up Twitter accounts to follow her. Most of this occurred before her first book was completed. What's better than having friends? Having a great family to support you and your make-believe friends.

Once again, the most wonderful critique partner a girl could have, Kat Duncan, plugged along this road with me reading every sordid detail of Eva's story and bringing her back to publishable when she had wandered too far onto the crazy side of her world. Thank you Kat for everything.

Thanks so much to CTRWA for connecting me with two fantastic editing professionals--Judy Roth, a very talented and patient editor and Jane Hartel, whose attention to detail is superb.

But what's a book without a title? I needed quite a bit of help in naming Eva's first book, thus, the Name That Book Contest was created and I had the absolute pleasure of using the Eva Prim method of making friends. It's been a great joy to meet and get to know Danielle Martin aka @_MyManekiNeko. She won my contest by enthusiastically tweeting and commenting on my blog. Thank you, Danielle for all your wonderful support.

And, still last, but never least, thank you to my husband, Ken. Your belief in Eva Prim's crazy story gave me the to courage to write it. I love you.

ABOUT THE AUTHOR

Jordan K. Rose

After trying her hand at many, many things- from crafting and art classes to cooking and sewing classes to running her own handbag business, Jordan finally figured out how to channel her creativity. With an active imagination and a little encouragement from her husband she sat down and began to write, each night clicking away at the keys with her black Labrador, Dino curled up under the desk.

A few short years later she's entered the publishing arena with no plans to ever turn back.

Jordan is a member of several RWA Chapters.

Jordan's first book, Perpetual Light is also available at Amazon and Barnes & Noble.

Find Jordan on her website at *www.jordankrose.com.*

Follow her tweets on *https://twitter.com/#!/jordankrose*

Like her on Facebook at *https://www.facebook.com/pages/Jordan-K-Rose/307285709309992*

Find her on Pinterest at: *http://pinterest.com/jordankrose/*

Join Eva's Snack Of The Week Club for updates on coming events and sneak peeks at Book Two of The Eva Prim Series. *http://evaprim.com/AboutSOWClub.html*

CPSIA information can be obtained at www.ICGtesting.com
Printed in the USA
BVOW04s1843030314

346534BV00013B/354/P